IN FIELDS OF FREEDOM

Books in the Sowers Trilogy series:

Where Freedom Grows
In Fields of Freedom
Harvest of Truth (coming January 2000)

The Sowers Trilogy

In Fields of Freedom

BONNIE LEON

BROADMAN
&HOLMAN
PUBLISHERS

Nashville, Tennessee

0-8054-1273-5

Published by Broadman & Holman Publishers, Nashville, Tennessee
Editorial Team: Vicki Crumpton, Janis Whipple, Kim Overcash
Page Design: Anderson Thomas Design, Nashville, Tennessee
Page Composition: Leslie Joslin
Cover Design: Steve Diggs & Friends, Nashville, Tennessee
Cover Illustration: Janice Leotti, Artworks, New York

Dewey Decimal Classification: 813
Subject Heading: FICTION
Library of Congress Card Catalog Number: 98-48985

Library of Congress Cataloging-in-Publication Data
Leon, Bonnie.
    In fields of freedom / Bonnie Leon.
        p. cm. — (The Sowers trilogy ; vol. 2)
    ISBN 0-8054-1273-5 (pbk.)
    I. Title. II. Series: Leon, Bonnie. Sowers trilogy ; vol. 2.
    PS3562.E533I49 1999
    813'.54—dc21
                                                    98-48985
                                                    CIP

1 2 3 4 5 03 02 01 00 99

ACKNOWLEDGMENTS

Without the cooperation of the residents of Black Diamond, Enumclaw, and the surrounding communities, this book couldn't have been written. There were many willing to answer my questions, let me wander through their establishments, take photographs, and listen to the stories and history of the small hamlets nestled against the Cascade Mountains. I thank you all.

There are some special people who, because of their willingness to open up their lives to me, made the writing of this book richer. They allowed me to see more clearly what life was like in a small town of the 1930s. I owe special thanks to Orville and Elsa Trover, Marie Theilken, Herman and Martha Trover, S. E. (Ship) and Laura Shipley, and Carl and Ann Steiert. Many thanks and God's blessings.

GLOSSARY

Balanda: Trash soup with a wretched odor. It was
                made with fish, including the bones, and
                sometimes contained grains. Leaves were
                often found floating in it.

Dochka: Little daughter.

Draniki: Grated potato pancakes.

Isolator: An open dugout used to punish prisoners
                in work camps. During the winter months,
                prisoners often froze there. Death was has-
                tened by guards who poured water onto the

prisoners. During the summer months, lime was sometimes dumped on the enslaved.

Man trip: An open train of cars used to transport miners in and out of mines.

Mamochka: Mama

NKVD: People's Commissariat of Internal Affairs—administered police organizations in Russia from 1917–1946.

Rope rider: A man who brings the cars up and down in the mines.

Stolypin wagon: Prison wagons used to transport prisoners on the railroad.

Trip: Anytime a car went into or out of the mine, it was called a trip. The cars carried coal, tools, and men.

Zek: Prisoners

CHAPTER 1

THE BUS BOUNCED OVER A pothole, jarring Dimitri from sleep. He opened one eye and listened to the driver work through the gears as the bus rounded a tight curve. He'd been sleeping with his face pressed against the window, and his cheek felt cold. Sitting up, he rubbed his face and huddled deeper into his coat.

The same bright autumn sunlight that coursed through the window glistened off distant snow-covered mountains. He stretched his arms over his head and tried to straighten his legs. The seat in front of him made it impossible. He was stiff and needed to get out and walk. *I don't know if I can stand another minute on this bus,* he thought.

Glancing at the man beside him, he tried to remember his name. *Is it Joe? No, John. That doesn't sound right either.* He mulled

1

over the options. *You'd think after sitting beside someone who talks nonstop for five days I'd remember his name,* he thought. He studied the pale, thin man. *Jim!* That was it. He stretched again. "This seat feels like a rock," he complained.

"It gets worse every hour," Jim said. "I'm glad you're awake. I'll have something to do besides stare at the seat in front of me and think about my aching body. I've never been able to sleep well on a bus." He hit the bench seat with his fist, then pressed his hand against the stiff upholstery. "When we started, it almost felt comfortable. Now it's torture. I'm glad we're almost to Seattle."

Dimitri didn't want to get drawn into conversation, so he stared out the window. Open fields of green and yellow grasses gave way to a lush, damp forest that pressed against the roadside. A sign, with the word Seattle written in large black letters and thirty miles printed below, whizzed by.

Since entering Washington, they'd stopped in towns called Centralia, Chehalis, and Tacoma. The names of these places sounded strange. Jim had explained that they were Indian names.

Monstrous trees blocked the sun and shut off his view. Frustrated, Dimitri peered into the forest. It was dense and jammed with unfamiliar foliage. He'd spent most of his years in the city and knew almost nothing about woodlands. Large fan-shaped plants crowded against the trees, and leafy vines covered the floor.

"Those big plants with the broad leaves and spiny undersides are Devil's Clubs," Jim said, pointing at a cluster of large shrubs. "You want to stay away from them. You get too close, they'll bite you."

Dimitri didn't reply but consciously stored the information. Some of the leaves flashing by the window looked similar to the ones found on maple trees back home. He could also make out slender vines with red and green berries among the dense foliage.

"When I was a boy, I used to come out for the summers and visit my grandpa," Jim said. "These woods are real pretty, but you've got to be careful. There's a berry that grows up here called Deadly Nightshade. It's a real pretty, bright red berry— looks good enough to eat. But from what my grandpa used to tell me, just a couple of them can kill a full-grown man."

Shimmering wedges of sunlight cut through the darkness, showing off a patch of earth carpeted with red, gold, and yellow leaves. Dimitri had never seen anything so beautiful. "Tatyana will love this," he said.

"What? Did you say something?"

Dimitri glanced at him, then back at the scenery, reluctant to miss any of it. "No. I was just thinking out loud." Tatyana's lively green eyes and soft smile danced through his mind. The reality of how much distance lay between them hit him, and a tightness settled in his chest. How long would it be before he saw her again? *I miss you,* he thought, wishing he hadn't left her in New York. He'd had no other choice. The timber company had provided only one ticket. He'd have to wait until he got his first paycheck, then he'd send for her.

Loneliness washed over him as the forest retreated and the open fields rolled toward the mountains once more. Thoughts of his family filled his mind. What was his father, Pavel, doing? It was early in the day. He was probably standing in line at the employment office, and his mother, Augusta, was already working at Mrs. Clarno's. His brother, Samuel, and sister, Ella, were certainly at school. He smiled. As soon as school let out, he knew they'd go in search of bottles to turn in for a few cents. They had always done all they could to help the family. Aunt Flora's soup would already be simmering on the stove. He would miss her and her cooking.

Sighing, he whispered, "I miss you all."

Again, Tatyana's lovely face filled his mind. He longed for the spirit that shimmered in her green eyes and yearned to caress her long, blonde hair. He needed to hold her. Closing his eyes, he remembered their last days. Having her beside him as he fell asleep at night and still there in the morning when he awoke had been like a dream. They'd had too little time. His eyes filled with tears as he considered his bride. Embarrassed, he quickly blinked them back. "Soon I will send for you. Soon."

"What?" Jim asked, but Dimitri ignored him.

So often Tatyana had talked to him about her longing for the family and home she'd left in Russia. He tried to understand but hadn't truly grasped the depth of her sorrow. Now, he thought he understood a little better. And still, he knew her pain had to be much greater than his. The stories she'd told about the soldiers' cruelty and how they'd arrested her parents, then destroyed the livestock, were beyond his comprehension. He'd never experienced anything so horrible. Tatyana and her brother, Yuri, had never seen their parents again. She'd explained that arrests were common, and most never knew what became of their loved ones.

When she left Russia, Tatyana knew Yuri faced many dangers. She had no idea if he or any of her family were still living. Although she'd written to Yuri many times, she'd heard nothing and had little hope of ever seeing him again.

Dimitri couldn't wait to tell his wife about his greater understanding and to apologize for his ignorance and lack of compassion. He pictured how he would help comfort her and support her the way a husband should. He would be strong for her. The coolness felt good as he resettled his cheek against the window.

The bus wound its way through a broad valley spotted with small towns and large farms. They stopped in Auburn, then Kent, where the passengers were allowed to disembark. Some puffed on cigarettes; others paced, working out their stiffness.

Dimitri walked, enjoying the sensation of movement and grateful to stretch his legs. He gazed toward the south from where they had come. Wispy clouds parted, exposing an enormous mountain. Like a sentinel, it stood guard over the valley. The sun shimmered off white slopes, turning the ridges and valleys a deep purple and blue. It reminded Dimitri of an immense jewel.

"It sure is something, isn't it," Jim said.

"What is it called?"

"Mount Rainier." He stared at the peak. "Even before I ever came to Washington my grandpa used to tell stories about the great mountain that watched over the Green River Valley. He settled here over sixty years ago, before there were any big cities. He was sorry to leave, and until his dying day, he never stopped talking about how he would come back one day to live. He died before he could." His eyes shimmered with tears. "I thought I'd give it a try." Continuing in a more light-hearted tone he added, "It's a far cry from Chicago."

"Yeah, I've been there," Dimitri said, remembering the Exposition and the confrontation between himself and his former employer, Mr. Meyers. He got angry again just thinking about the man's improper advances toward Tatyana. "I'd just as soon forget it."

Jim looked at Dimitri. "Bad experience, huh?"

"Yeah. You could say that. I lost a job while I was there."

"Chicago's not so bad. It's where I grew up. Most of my family still lives in the area."

"So, you just visiting Seattle or staying?"

"I think I'll stay a while. It's a nice place."

"Bus number 221 will be leaving in five minutes," called the bus driver.

As he headed back to the bus, Jim continued, "My grandpa always did say it was a real special day when the sun is out." He settled into his seat and looked at Dimitri. "So, what did you say you were doing out here?"

Dimitri patted his shirt pocket containing his work orders. "I've got a job at a logging company."

"Too dangerous for me. My uncle said I could work for him at his clothing store while I'm here."

Nodding, Dimitri returned to watching the outside world.

The bus left Kent behind and made its way toward Seattle. As they crested a hill just outside the city, the morning mists swirled around the bay-front city like shreds of gossamer. It glistened in the sunlight. Skyscrapers, their rows of windows reflecting the brightness, stood like tall watchmen, while toadish warehouses, taverns, and cafes huddled against the harbor. The streets were crowded with buses and automobiles.

"It's bigger than I thought," Dimitri said, the maturity of the city taking him by surprise.

The bus slowed as it rumbled across an overpass and edged into the city. Below, a community of shacks was scattered along the shoreline. Huts stood at odd angles; some were made of wood, others metal. A few had tin chimneys poking up through metal rooftops. Smoke rose from tall trash cans and people huddled close to them for warmth. An old woman sat in front of one hovel, a tattered blanket thrown over her shoulders. She seemed to be looking up at the bus as it passed. Dimitri wondered what she was thinking. Not far from the woman, a group of men huddled on the ground. It looked as if they might be shooting craps.

"Sad, isn't it," Jim said. "They say that ever since the depression started, Hoovervilles like this have been sprouting up all over the country."

"Why do people live like this? New York has homeless people, but nothing like this," said Dimitri. He felt sick at the sight, knowing the people must live with despair.

"Where else can they go? What happens to them?"

Jim shrugged. "Some of the lucky ones will find work, others will stay here until they're forced out or die. And some will move on, maybe to another Hooverville."

"I had hoped things would be better here."

"It's the same all over the country."

Dimitri stifled a shudder, thankful he had a job. He knew what it was like to be without work, but even then, he'd had his family.

The bus left the overpass and turned onto a cramped, drab-looking street. The city had looked more colorful from a distance. They lurched and bumped as they made their way through traffic. The driver stopped just inches behind the car in front of him, clearly impatient. Dimitri wondered if he had family waiting.

Gasoline fumes clogged the air. Longing for a breeze, Dimitri thought, *This isn't so different from New York.*

People crowded the sidewalks, and some darted between cars, ignoring the blast of horns. The light changed, and the bus inched forward. Passing a fish-and-chips house, Dimitri was reminded how hungry he was. He'd eaten his last sandwich the night before. Digging into his pants pocket, he pulled out the last of his money. He looked disparagingly at the change. Three quarters, a dime, and two nickels wouldn't get him far. *Thank goodness the lumber company will feed and house me,* he thought.

"Man, that makes me hungry," Jim said. "How much do you think a basket of fish and chips costs?"

"More than I've got," Dimitri said dryly.

The bus rounded a corner and pulled into the terminal.

Jim stood up even before they stopped. "Looks like we're here." He pulled a small suitcase out from under the seat, looked at Dimitri, and held out his hand. "It was nice meeting you. Good luck."

Dimitri took his hand and shook it. "Same to you." He stood up, careful to stoop so he wouldn't hit his head on the ceiling, and followed Jim down the aisle. As he stepped off the bus, the odor of gasoline fumes mingled with the aroma of hot dogs. It was a strange union of smells, but his mouth watered anyway. Knowing how little money he had, he thought, *I have enough for one.*

Jim gave him a quick nod and disappeared into the crowd.

While waiting for his bag, Dimitri looked for the source of the hot dog smell. A man was selling frankfurters from a cart. Keeping an eye on the vendor, Dimitri joined the line at the ticket window and hoped the merchant wouldn't move on before he got something to eat.

Finally standing in front of the window, he leaned on the counter and asked, "Can you tell me when the next bus leaves for Snoqualmie?"

Dimples showing, a pretty, young clerk smiled at the handsome traveler.

Dimitri could feel his face heat up. Self-consciously, he swept his blonde hair off his forehead.

She glanced at the wall clock. "You'll have a two-hour wait, sir. That bus won't be leaving until noon." She tossed her head just enough to unsettle her brown curls. Pointing at a nearby bench, she said, "You can have a seat right over there. I'll let you know when it arrives."

Dimitri nodded. "Thank you."

"I'll be taking a lunch break in an hour . . ." she let the sentence hang, an obvious invitation.

Dimitri cleared his throat. "Oh. Well I . . . I hope you enjoy it." Not knowing what else to say, he turned and walked away. He wondered what Tatyana would think of such boldness and smiled.

After buying a plain hot dog, he sat down and ate it. His stomach still felt empty afterwards, so he dug into his pocket and counted his money again. Looking at the vendor, he knew he shouldn't spend it. *I won't need any more money as soon as I go to work. The company will take care of me,* he reasoned and decided to buy another. He sat on the bench furthest from the ticket window and slowly ate the second hot dog, enjoying its spicy flavor.

He watched travelers as they hurried to catch buses or greeted loved ones and thought of the day Tatyana would join him. As soon as he received his first paycheck, he'd send her enough money for a ticket. He calculated the number of days before he would see her and wondered how he would be able to wait.

In spite of the hard bench, Dimitri's fatigue got the better of him, and he dozed off. When the bus for Snoqualmie was called, he forced himself awake, longing for more sleep. He sat up, his body aching, and rubbed his neck while he studied the landing. There were several buses waiting, but only one was loading passengers. *That must be mine,* he decided, blinking to clear his vision. He grabbed his bag and hurried to join the line. "Is this the bus to Snoqualmie?"

The driver answered, "It sure is. You got your ticket?"

Dimitri dug into his pocket and held the ticket out for the man. "How long does it take to get there?"

Taking the pass, the driver smoothed his mustache and said, "Well, it's not so far, but we got a few stops to make. If we don't have any problems, no more than a couple hours."

A couple hours seemed an eternity to Dimitri. He'd already spent five days on a bus. With a sigh, he climbed the steps and eased his large body onto another hard seat. He folded his arms over his chest and hoped he'd be able to nap.

They left the city behind, and the paved roadway soon became a graveled lane. As the bus climbed into foothills, it bumped and rattled over the rough highway. Peering through the front window, Dimitri could see the roadway stretching ahead of them, the forest crowding the road and shutting out the sunlight. It reminded him of a tunnel.

Exhausted, Dimitri's eyes grew heavy, and soon his head bobbed with the turns and bumps. Occasionally he'd rouse for a moment and gaze at the sporadic fields and the never-ending forests. He forced himself awake at each town, hoping it would be his stop.

When the bus finally pulled into Snoqualmie, Dimitri sat up and tried to clear his mind. He studied the small hamlet as they passed through. It wasn't much of a town, only a couple of stores, a gas station, and a cafe. They stopped in front of the gas station, and Dimitri quickly gathered his things and exited the bus. As it pulled away, he stood alone on the curb, wondering what he should do next.

A scribbled note had been taped to the station window. It read, "Sorry, gone to lunch. Will return at 4:00."

Strange lunch hours, Dimitri thought as he looked around for someone who might give him directions to the lumber camp. The street was empty. A small cafe was open, so Dimitri stepped into the muddy road and gingerly made his way across, avoiding the puddles.

When he stood in front of the cafe, he shivered and pulled his coat closer. It was much colder here than in Seattle. After stomping and scraping his feet clear of mud, he pushed open the door. A bell jingled, and the smell of coffee and baked goods greeted him. Once again, he was reminded of home and a sense of longing welled up.

A tiny, old woman wiped down the counter. She glanced at Dimitri but didn't stop. He waited for her to acknowledge him. When she didn't, he cleared his throat.

Looking a little irritated, she stopped her work, leaned on the tiled surface, and stared at Dimitri. Her eyes looked bright, denying her age. "Can I get you something?"

"I was just wondering if you could tell me where the logging camp is?"

"Well, that depends on which camp you're talkin' about."

Dimitri pulled out his instructions and studied the paper. "It says here, I'm to see Bill Johnson at the Snoqualmie Logging Company."

"Ah, well, you've got yourself a little walk then. It's quite a ways up the mountain."

"Can you tell me which way?"

"Well, you go up this road," she stopped and studied him. "If you don't mind waiting a bit, I'll be going up to make a delivery. You can ride with me."

"Thank you very much. I appreciate your offer." Dimitri couldn't believe his good luck.

The woman did her best not to smile. She held out her hand. "I'm Josephine Simmons."

Dimitri set his bag on the floor and took her hand. "Dimitri Broido. It's nice to meet you."

"Make yourself comfortable." She nodded toward one of the tables. "I've still got a job here."

"Yes, ma'am." Dimitri picked up his bag.

"You want a cup of coffee?"

"Sounds good. Thank you." Dimitri settled at a table by the window and watched the street.

Josephine set a cup of coffee in front of him, then stood with her hands tucked into the front pockets of her slacks and looked at him. "You just get off the bus?"

"Yeah. I'm from New York City."

She smiled knowingly, fine lines creasing the corners of her eyes. "Seems folks like you are always wanderin' through, mostly lookin' for work."

"I already have a job. The company hired me and paid my bus fare here."

The woman averted her eyes. "Oh," she said and disappeared into a back room.

Sipping the strong coffee, Dimitri turned his attention to the small town. There was little to watch. Either everyone who lived in Snoqualmie stayed indoors on Tuesdays or the town had been deserted. Only one car passed while he sat there. An old man gripped the steering wheel and kept his eyes on the road in front of him, unaware of the stranger sitting in the diner. Dimitri watched the car until it reached the outskirts of town. His eyes followed the tree line to a ridge where the wind whipped the tops of the evergreens.

He wondered what Tatyana was doing. *I hope she will like it here,* he thought. His eyes fell upon a large, two-story white house at the end of the street. A small picket fence bordered its tiny yard, and large, nearly naked maple trees grew close to the house, a blanket of colorful leaves beneath them. A large garden stood off to the side of the house.

Tatyana and I will have a big garden one day. We will grow corn, green beans, peas, and tomatoes. I wonder if it's warm enough here to grow tomatoes? He made a mental note to ask someone.

"Well, are you going or not?" Josephine asked, her sharp voice cutting into his dream.

Dimitri looked up. "What? I'm sorry, I . . ."

"I said, you goin' or not? You've been starin' out that window daydreaming and didn't hear a thing I said." She offered him a crooked smile. "I'm on my way with you or without you."

"I'm sorry," Dimitri said, scooting his chair away from the table and picking up his bag. "I'm coming."

Josephine plopped a broad-rimmed straw hat on her gray hair then buttoned up her coat. Taking short, quick steps, she hurried outside and climbed into a rusted, dented, black pickup.

Dimitri followed and threw his bag in the ancient Ford bed. The door creaked in protest when he opened it. He slid onto the torn seat and yanked the door closed.

Without looking at Dimitri, Josephine pulled out the choke, pumped the gas pedal three times, then turned the key. The engine growled, coughed once, then fired. Keeping her foot on the clutch, she pressed the throttle and pushed the choke in a little. The motor backfired, then evened out, finally settling into a low-throated purr.

"She's seen better days but still gets me where I need to go," Josephine said as she shifted into first gear and pulled onto the roadway.

As they headed south of town, neither of them spoke. When they turned onto a narrow, rutted road, Dimitri gripped the door handle. Josephine barely slowed as they bounced through potholes and began the climb up a steep grade. Snoqualmie fell away below them, a small village amidst an endless sea of trees.

"What do people do here?" Dimitri asked, trying to take his mind off her driving.

Josephine eyed the young man.

"I mean for fun."

"Well, we go over to the falls and picnic sometimes."

"The falls?"

"Oh, yeah, there's quite a waterfall north of town." She cranked her head around and pointed north.

Dimitri gripped the door tighter, wishing she'd keep her eyes on the road and her hands on the wheel.

Returning her attention to the road, she said, "You'll have to take a look one of these days. Mostly we work. There's not much time for fun."

A steep slope swept down the mountain on Dimitri's right. His stomach lurched as he looked into the deep ravine. Josephine seemed unaware of any danger. "Is the camp far?"

"Not very."

"You drive this road a lot?"

"Oh, yeah. It's not so bad, just steep as the devil and you've got to watch for log trucks." She glanced at Dimitri. "You've lost your color, son." She chuckled. "You'd better get used to it if you're planning to work in the woods. These roads are the only way to get around. And you'll be traveling some a lot worse than this."

"I'm fine," Dimitri lied, swallowing hard and trying to keep his eyes on the road and away from the chasm below.

Finally, Josephine turned onto an even narrower track, and a few minutes later, they pulled into the logging camp. Directly in front of them stood a long canvas tent with a stovepipe rising from the middle, its smoke drifting into the air. A log truck, its hood up, was parked alongside the tent. On the north end of the compound, an outhouse sat several yards away from two smaller tents. Dimitri guessed them to be sleeping quarters. Double-handled whipsaws, winches, cables, belts, and equipment Dimitri didn't recognize were scattered throughout the camp. He hoped the company didn't expect him to know how to use it all. Sitting by itself on the south end, stood a large, square tent with a sign over the door that read, Office.

"The man you're lookin' for is probably in the office." Josephine held out her hand. "It was a pleasure to meet you. I wish you luck."

"Thank you." Dimitri shook her hand and stepped out of the truck, careful not to slam the door. Feeling confident, he walked toward the office. There was no door to knock on, so he pulled the canvas flap back and peered inside.

A small man with a large mustache sat at a wooden table, writing in a ledger. When he didn't look up, Dimitri stepped in and cleared his throat.

The man looked at Dimitri and set his pen down. "Can I help you?"

Dimitri's confidence wavered a little under the man's scrutiny. "I'm Dimitri Broido. I'm looking for Bill Johnson."

"I'm Bill Johnson."

"I was told to report to work, sir," Dimitri said, taking the telegram from his pocket and giving it to the man.

After studying the slip, Mr. Johnson handed it back. "We wired you . . ." he began, hesitated, then started over. "I guess you didn't get our second wire." Looking at Dimitri, he stood up. "The work order was canceled."

Shock went through Dimitri and a knot of fear gripped his stomach.

The man sighed and, keeping his hands on the desk top, looked at the young man. "There is no job."

"But, I was told . . . I came all the way from New York."

"I know. I'm sorry. One of our government projects fell through. Some kind of hang-up in Congress." He raised his hands, palms up. "I'm sorry."

"But I came all this way."

"There's nothing I can do." Mr. Johnson sat down and returned to his paperwork.

Dimitri slammed his hands on the table, then leaned on them. "It can't be that simple! You can't just send for a man, have him travel across the country, and then tell him he has no job!"

His eyes hard, Mr. Johnson looked at Dimitri. "I told you, there is no work. There's nothing I can do." His tone was cold and detached.

Dimitri stared at him for a long while, his mind whirling with frustration and anger. What more could he say? He turned and walked into the cool afternoon air. Gazing at the ridge above the camp, but not seeing it, he took a deep breath. "Now what do I do?"

CHAPTER 2

FEELING DISCONNECTED FROM the world, as if moving within a dream, Dimitri walked to Josephine's truck. What would he do? Where would he go? He felt the change in his pocket. There wasn't even enough left to buy a cup of coffee.

He could hear Josephine's voice coming from the large tent where she'd parked. Still feeling dazed, Dimitri found the doorway and stepped inside. There was a large cook stove in the center of the tent with stacks of dishes piled on a table beside it. Josephine sat at a long wooden table, one leg casually thrown over the other. She had a cup of coffee in her hand. A man wearing a stained white apron stood with one foot propped on the end of the bench. Both looked at Dimitri.

"You don't look good," Josephine said. "What happened?"

"No job. I came all this way, and there is no job." Dimitri knew he sounded panicked but didn't care. In a matter of a few minutes, his life had fallen apart.

Josephine drained her cup and stood. "I guess I better be going. It'll be dark soon. Thanks for the coffee, Charlie." She looked at Dimitri. "I'll give you a ride down if you like."

"Uh, yeah. I guess so." He looked at Josephine. "Now, how will I bring my wife out?"

"You got a wife?"

"Uh huh."

"Where is she?"

"New York. She's waiting for me to send for her."

Josephine patted his back. "Well, I guess it's a good thing she's not with you. You can thank God for that." She dropped her cup into a large, metal tub of sudsy water. "See you on Thursday, Charlie."

"Sure thing," the cook said. He nodded at Dimitri. "Good luck."

Picking up a bulging gunny sack and throwing it over her shoulder, Josephine stepped outside.

Dimitri followed and climbed into the truck. His arms folded across his chest, he hunched down in the seat. This time, as they made their way down the mountain, he was unaware of the steep ravines and cliffs. The words, "There is no job" echoed through his mind.

The pickup rattled loudly as they rounded a tight curve. Josephine downshifted and pumped the brakes. Momentarily dragged from his brooding, Dimitri gripped the seat and stared at the rocks cascading down the side of the cliff. Josephine seemed unperturbed.

"It's a beautiful day, isn't it," she said. "Why, look at that sunset." She gazed toward the west.

Dimitri wished she would keep her eyes on the road but couldn't ignore the brilliant red and pink glow in the clouds resting over the distant hills. "Yeah. It's nice. Tatyana would love it." *But, will she even have a chance to see this place?* he wondered. Again, panic washed over him. *I have no job!*

"I'm afraid your hand is going to lose circulation if you don't let loose of that seat." Josephine chuckled. "We're nearly down now."

Dimitri set his hands in his lap. He took a deep breath, unwilling to fight the melancholy that had settled over him.

"Hey, perk up. Something will come along." As they approached another steep section, she pumped the brakes.

Dimitri's stomach knotted as she worked them. "Are your brakes all right?"

"Oh, sure. They've always needed a little help, but they've never let me down . . . yet." She grinned.

The grade finally flattened and the road swung sharply to the right. Josephine slowed. After rounding the curve, she stopped at the intersection.

"I've got an errand to run," she said and pulled onto the road. "After that, you're welcome to stay at my place. A good night's sleep is what you need. Then you'll be better able to decide what to do."

Dimitri felt a mixture of shame and gratitude. He hated needing help, but he was thankful for it. He looked at the unusual woman. "You don't need to do that. I'll make out all right."

Josephine glanced at him. "Well, suit yourself. I just wondered what you would do for the night. It's getting dark, and there aren't many places to stay in Snoqualmie." She grinned and winked at him. "And you never know when you might be in the presence of angels."

Dimitri smiled. "It would be rude to turn down an offer of help from an angel," he quipped. "I guess I could stay at your place." Folding his arms across his chest, he settled back against his seat.

Josephine headed toward town. Before she got there, she turned onto a muddy, rutted lane. Tires spinning, the truck lurched and bumped through potholes. Gripping the steering wheel, Josephine kept her foot on the accelerator. She reached over and turned on the lights.

The forest pressed closer along the narrow road, and the last remnants of daylight were shut out by dense greenery. The lights cut into the darkness. Dimitri braced himself against the jarring and wondered how smart he'd been to ride with Josephine. *What on earth could be back here?* he wondered.

Unexpectedly, the timberland fell away, and they broke into a clearing alongside railroad tracks. Immediately, Josephine slammed on her brakes, downshifted, and turned off the ignition.

A smattering of small campfires flickered throughout the field with shabbily dressed men huddled beside them. Some appeared to be cooking. Others seemed to recognize the truck and stood up expectantly.

"What are we doing here?" Dimitri asked.

"Times are hard. I do what I can, where I can," Josephine said and stepped out of the truck, leaving the door open. Reaching into the back, she took out the bag she'd brought from the timber camp.

One grizzled, middle-aged man ignored her as he removed some kind of animal from a spit. Dimitri didn't want to think about what it might be. Hunkering around his meal, the man stripped away the meat and sucked it into his mouth, chewing and swallowing in a hurry. He reminded Dimitri of a hawk he'd once seen as it devoured its prey.

A teenage boy glanced at Josephine but remained seated beside his fire as he spooned food from a can, guarding it as he ate, as if someone might steal it from him at any moment.

Josephine went to the boy first. Reaching into the bag, she brought out a chunk of bread and offered it to him. He snatched the offering and shoved it in his mouth.

Unobtrusively, Josephine moved around the camp. Dimitri watched, dumbfounded, as she went from one man to the next, offering slices of bread and small round loaves. Maybe she was an angel. Soon, men crowded around her.

Afraid she might be in danger, Dimitri opened his door and stepped out, ready to help if needed. But it soon became clear that no one here wished the kind woman harm. He relaxed a little but remained outside the truck.

One emaciated man purposely ignored her. He leaned over a bucket of water and splashed his face. Taking a bar of soap, he made a lather in his hands and spread the suds over his beard. Holding a piece of broken mirror in his left hand, he studied his reflection in the dim light of his fire. Keeping his back rigid, he took a straight razor and carefully scraped off the layer of soap. He glanced at the visitor once but made no move to approach her.

After all the others had received bread, Josephine walked through the camp and stood in front of him. He glanced at her, then returned to his task.

Josephine didn't move. She said something to him, but her voice was too quiet for Dimitri to hear.

The man stopped shaving and gazed at her.

The old woman dug into her bag, took out a small loaf of bread, and held it out.

For a long moment, the hobo stared at the offering. Finally, his shoulders drooped and, without looking into Josephine's face, he took it and shoved it beneath his coat, then returned to shaving.

Dimitri felt sick inside. How could things get so bad that a man must shed his dignity just to eat? What if he couldn't find a job and ended up living in a camp like this? What would happen to his family, to Tatyana?

"May God bless you," he heard Josephine say as she folded the empty sack and made her way back to the truck.

Dimitri climbed in and closed his door.

When Josephine returned, her eyes shimmered. She blinked hard as she grabbed hold of the steering wheel, turned the ignition, and put the truck in gear. She said nothing as the engine came to life and they headed back down the rutted road.

For a long while, neither of them spoke. Dimitri didn't know what to say. He felt he'd witnessed something private and didn't want to intrude.

Finally, Josephine quietly said, "Someone has to help. Each of those men is someone's father or brother or son."

"Do you come here often?"

"Nope. Just when Charlie has leftover bread."

"He gives it away?"

"It's the extra that gets stale. The loggers won't eat it. But all the hobos care about is filling their empty stomachs. They're not picky."

"How long have you been doing this?"

"Since they started showing up—maybe three years." She brushed her short bangs off her forehead. "Most of them have already given up. Some won't make it through the winter." She took a deep breath and sniffled. "They leave home believing things will get better. They think they'll find something for them and their families out in the world. Used to be if a man worked hard, he could take care of his family. No more. Some have left folks, promising to send for them . . ." Her voice trailed off, and she looked at Dimitri. "It's the ones who despair who end up in the camps. You don't have to."

Feeling like he had to defend himself, Dimitri said, "I had a job. I'll find something. I will."

"I pray you do," Josephine said as she returned to the highway.

Dimitri stared at the road as it passed beneath the truck, his mind searching for an answer. Clearly, there weren't a lot of jobs. The depression hadn't skipped the Northwest. How would he find work when so many others couldn't? His family was counting on him, and Tatyana would have to stay in New York until he came up with something. His heart constricted at the thought of a prolonged separation. He'd been foolish to pass up the job for the CCC. It had been a sure thing. *Why did I have to go for the money?*

"Don't give up, Dimitri. Keep believing. Keep trying."

"I won't give up," he said with more confidence than he felt. What choice did he have? He didn't even have enough money for a fare home.

"You have a bed at my place tonight, and I'll feed you, but you'll have to leave in the morning." She kept her eyes straight ahead, her voice steady. "I wish I could do more, but it's not easy to feed myself. And I've got a sister in Black Diamond who depends on me. She's a widow like me, but she doesn't have a job. Her husband died in the mines. Oh, Lord, that was a long time ago—1915."

"What happened?"

Josephine skimmed back her short hair. "He worked at the Ravensdale Mine, and one day it blew up. Thirty-one men died. The whole thing just blew up."

"That's awful."

"Bad things happen. In this part of the country, the men have dangerous jobs. I thought I was one of the lucky ones because my husband worked in the woods. But that kind of work is no better, really. Men die all the time. My Harry," her voice broke, "he got hit by a loose log, and that was it. They said he died instantly."

Dimitri tried to think of something helpful to say but couldn't, so he simply said, "I'm so sorry." His words sounded hollow.

Josephine turned into a driveway, and the truck bounced through a large pothole, splashing water over the hubs. She slowed and stopped, threw the truck into first, and turned off the engine. "This is it. Nothing fancy, but it keeps out the rain."

The house was small, with a steeply pitched roof. A tiny window, wedged beneath the front eave, overlooked a small covered porch. The two windows in front were dark.

Dimitri followed Josephine onto the stoop. As he stepped on the boards, they groaned.

She turned and looked up at him. "You're a big one, all right," she said with a twinkle in her eye. "Try not to break my porch."

Dimitri didn't know how to respond, so he said nothing. He felt like a giant beside the tiny woman.

She turned the knob and stepped inside, leaving the door open for Dimitri. "It's cold in here," she said, throwing on a switch. A single light glowed from the ceiling. She placed her purse on a small table next to the door and, taking quick, small steps, crossed to the wood stove. Glancing into the kindling box, she sighed. "I'm gonna have to cut more in the morning. This is the last of it."

"I'll do it for you," Dimitri offered. "It's the least I can do."

"Thank you. I could use some of the maple and oak cut too." She wadded up newspaper and stuffed it in the pot-bellied heating stove. After that, she carefully laid the last pieces of kindling on top. Taking a match from the shelf, she struck it against the cast iron door. It flared to life, and she held it to the papers. When they lit, she watched until the wood was crackling, then added two pieces of cedar. "That should do it for now," she said, closing the door and opening the vents. She stood there a few moments, rubbing her hands together. "We'll let that get good and hot and then add some maple. The house will be warm in no time." Walking across the front room, she asked, "Would you like a cup of coffee?"

"Sounds good."

"I warn you, I like mine strong."

"That'll be fine."

She disappeared through a door. "Come on in and sit down," she called.

Dimitri followed her into a small, homey kitchen. Windows along two adjoining walls promised warm, bright mornings.

After shoving wood and paper into the firebox and lighting it, Josephine ran water into a pitcher. She poured it into clay pots with healthy green plants growing in them. They sat along the window sill. "You poor things must be awful thirsty by now. I've been so busy the last few days, I'm afraid I've neglected you." She set the pitcher on the drainboard, opened the cupboard above the sink, and took out a bowl and glass. Then she picked up another bowl and glass from the dishdrainer beside the sink. Pulling open a drawer, she scooped up silverware and placed it on the table along with the dishes.

"This is nice," Dimitri said. He sat at the table, which was covered with a white cloth and had a bowl of nuts in the center.

"I've been blessed." Josephine filled the percolator with water and set it on the stove. Dipping several spoonfuls of coffee into the aluminum filter, she placed it in the pot and pressed down the lid. "Now, something to eat. I'm so hungry I could eat a bear. How about you?"

"I'm sure hungry, all right."

"I made a stew yesterday," she said, peering into a small refrigerator. "There's plenty left for the both of us. It will taste good reheated. Stew always tastes better the second day." She took a covered pot out, pushed the refrigerator door closed with her hip, and set the stew on the burner beside the percolator.

"Would you please add some of the heavy pieces of wood to the fire?"

"Sure." Dimitri pushed his chair back and headed for the living room.

"They're in the bin beside the wall. That maple's good wood and will burn a long while."

Dimitri stuffed two chunks of maple into the stove.

"Oh, don't forget to close down the vents some," she called, "but leave the damper open for now. The fire should be good and hot."

Dimitri closed the stove door. It wasn't like the ones back east that he'd used for coal, but the vents were easy to find, and he turned them partially closed. The heat felt good and he stood for a moment warming himself. When he finally turned away from the stove, the darkness beyond the window drew him. He stared outside. Lights from a distant house twinkled through the darkness, and a sense of loneliness welled up inside of him. Home was so far away. Images of the bums living along the tracks filled his mind. What if he ended up like them? *No,* he told himself, pushing the picture aside. *I will find work.*

The smell of coffee drifted from the kitchen and reminded him of home. He wished it was, but this home belonged to a stranger, one he'd been forced to depend upon. In all his fantasies about Washington State, he'd never imagined this. His pride felt bruised. *I should be able to take care of myself and my wife,* he thought.

"Let's eat." Josephine said. She stood in the kitchen doorway.

"I don't know if I'm more hungry or tired. I'm afraid I'll fall asleep with my face in my plate."

"The best thing for you to do is to fill your belly, then sleep." She disappeared into the kitchen.

When Dimitri stepped into the cozy room, Josephine was filling a heavy mug with very black coffee. She handed it to him. "If you need sugar, it's on the table."

"Thank you," Dimitri said and took a sip. He forced himself not to grimace at the bitter flavor. "It is a little strong. I guess I could use some sugar."

"Most people don't like their coffee so strong. I never used to. But my husband always drank his real black, and I got so I liked it that way too." Taking a half loaf of bread out of the cupboard, she sawed off three pieces and set them on a plate, which she placed in the center of the table beside the nuts. "It's a couple days old and a little stale. Takes me a while to eat up a whole loaf."

"It looks good," Dimitri reassured her.

"Well, the stew is hot and ready to eat. Sit down, and I'll dish you up some." Holding the pot by its handle, she filled his bowl and did the same with hers, then sat down.

Dimitri dipped his spoon in and took a bite. He chewed, and the mingled flavors of vegetables and meat tasted good.

Josephine watched him, then folded her hands and bowed her head.

Embarrassed, Dimitri immediately returned his spoon to its bowl and also bowed his head.

"Dear, Lord, we thank you for your wonderful gifts. Especially for the sunny weather you've been givin' us these last few days. Father, you know Dimitri here is lookin' for a job. I ask you to help him find just the right one, so he'll be able to send for his wife. Thank you. Amen." She looked up. "I always believe in thanking God before I eat."

"Me too. I just forgot. My family always prays at meals." He contemplated his food. "I never really did understand the reason for saying prayers every time we ate, though."

"I think God wants to hear from us any time. And if he's the one who provides our food, seems only right to thank him for it don't you think?"

Dimitri nodded, a little embarrassed at being so off-handed over something that was clearly important to Josephine. "When you pray, you act like God is right here in this room. My parents and my wife do the same."

Josephine leveled an even gaze on Dimitri. "He is in this room."

"I guess I just never felt his presence the same as some people."

"I think you need to spend more time reading your Bible, young man."

"I have my Bible. My mother made sure to pack it."

"Well, I'm sure it will help you." She smiled. "The only thing you need to remember right now is that he loves you." Taking a slice of bread, she dipped it in her stew and took a bite. "Pretty good for stale bread and leftovers."

Remembering his hunger, Dimitri took another mouthful. He could feel the heat of it in his stomach and felt warmed.

"This is venison, not beef," Josephine explained. "I shot it myself."

"It's good," Dimitri said, dipping his bread into the broth. "So, you hunt? I never heard of a woman who hunted."

"Well, I do. And I like it too; plus, it helps keep me from starving."

Neither Dimitri nor Josephine spoke for several minutes while they ate. Dimitri quickly finished his food, and Josephine scraped the last of the stew into his bowl. When she finished her meal, she immediately took her dishes and the dirty pot to the sink, put soap and hot water in a pan, and washed them. "Never did see why folks leave their dirty dishes sitting on the table. I believe when you're finished, you clean up after yourself. I'd appreciate it if when you're done you would wash up your things."

She left the room. Dimitri heard the creak of the stove door and the thunk of wood. He smiled. Josephine was certainly an unusual woman. One moment prickly as a sticker bush, the next gentle and compassionate.

CHAPTER 2

He sopped up the last of his broth with his bread and forced down his coffee. He washed the dishes and placed them in the rack to dry. Turning, he found Josephine leaning against the door frame watching him.

"You do good work." She seemed to be thinking, then said, "I heard they might be hiring at the Indian Mine. You ever work a mine?"

"No."

"It's dangerous, but the pay is good."

"What kind of mine is it?"

"Coal. That's the only kind around here."

"Where is it?"

"Highway 169, about six miles outside of Renton."

"Is that far?"

"It's probably more than you want to walk." She grinned. "You could catch a ride in the morning with someone going that way. I'd take you, but I've got to work."

"Are you sure there's work?" Dimitri asked.

"Well, think so. I just heard about it yesterday. Most news comes through the cafe."

"Do you think they'd hire me even if I've never mined before?"

"Are you willing to work hard?"

"Yes. That is one thing I can do."

"Then I figure you've got a chance. They want good strong men who are willing to put in a full day's labor."

Dimitri could feel hope return. *Maybe it won't be so hard to find a job after all,* he thought. "I'll go see them tomorrow."

"This time of year, the mines are putting on workers. Demand for coal always picks up during the winter." She yawned. "My day starts early. There's a blanket and pillow on the couch for you. The bathroom is down the hall and on your right. I'm going to bed. When you're finished, just turn out the lights. I'll see you in the morning."

"Thanks, Josephine," Dimitri said.

After cleaning out the sink, Dimitri washed up, then returned to the front room and stretched out on the couch. All was quiet, the crackling of the fire and an occasional creak of the house, the only sounds. The sofa felt lumpy and his pillow had lost most of its feathers, but it still felt good to lie down. It had been five long days since he'd been able to stretch out to sleep.

He stared at the ceiling, excited about the possibility of a job. *I have to get it. Then I can send for Tatyana.*

A flash of uncertainty swept over him. What would it be like working so far beneath the earth? He quickly pushed aside his anxiety. He couldn't think about that. He had to concentrate on getting the job. It was the only way he and Tatyana could be reunited.

He closed his eyes and pictured his young wife. He smiled. *I will do whatever I have to so she can be with me,* he thought as sleep settled over him.

CHAPTER 3

DIMITRI FINISHED HIS COFFEE and pushed himself away from the table. He'd been hungry after chopping wood and had unashamedly devoured his breakfast of eggs and bacon. The cafe was busier than it had been the previous afternoon. Most of the tables were filled with patrons, and Josephine rushed to keep up with orders. Ready to leave, Dimitri placed his hat on his head and watched as she scribbled on her notepad. She stood very straight and was careful to remain businesslike. He smiled, knowing that only those close to the woman understood her bristles were on the outside.

After taking the order, Josephine tucked her pencil behind her ear, gave the man and woman at the table a brief smile, and returned to the kitchen. As usual, she wore tan slacks and a blouse that she kept tucked in. She'd told Dimitri she didn't care if it was proper for a woman to wear a dress; she liked slacks, and that was that. He smiled as he considered the many raised eyebrows her attire must have prompted over the years.

After leaving a plate of pancakes and one of eggs and toast in front of a young couple, she walked over to Dimitri. "So, you on your way?"

"Yes. If I want that job, I'd better get there early. Thanks for dinner, a place to stay, and the breakfast."

"Don't thank me for your breakfast, thank the owner. It's on him."

Dimitri held out his hand.

Josephine took it and returned his warm handshake.

"I cannot think of a proper way to thank you."

"None is needed. Just come and visit now and then. I'll be praying for you."

Dimitri nodded, tipped his hat, and turned to leave.

"By the way, if you need anything you know where I live," Josephine said.

"I'll remember that." Dimitri smiled and walked out. Pulling the door closed behind him, he looked up at the sky. The previous day's sunshine had disappeared behind a dense layer of clouds. It looked and smelled like rain.

He buttoned his coat. Tucking his hands into his pockets, he stepped onto the street. *I hope I can get a ride,* he thought, scanning the roadway for traffic. It was empty. He walked toward the highway and, glancing at the clouds, hoped he was wrong about the rain.

He hadn't been walking long when a panel truck pulled off the road just ahead of him. Dimitri ran to catch up to it and opened the door.

A man with a heavy mustache and a wool cap pulled over curly, black hair asked, "Where you heading?"

"The Indian Mine."

"It's right on my way. Climb in."

Gratefully, Dimitri slid onto the seat, planted his suitcase on the floor between his feet, and pulled the door closed. The smell of fresh bread permeated the cab. "I really appreciate this."

"Glad I can help."

"It smells good in here. What are you hauling?"

The man grinned. "This is a bakery truck. The back is full of baked goods." He eased onto the road. "So, you a miner?"

"No, but I heard the mine might be hiring."

"You couldn't pay me enough to do that kind of work."

"Why?" Dimitri asked, apprehension needling him.

"Besides the closeness, the dirt, and the darkness, they're always having accidents. Seems someone's getting hurt or killed every time you turn around. Plus, I don't believe man was made to crawl around under the earth. It's a shame people have to risk their lives just to make a living."

Dimitri didn't want to hear about the danger. He needed a job. He pushed aside his fears and said as casually as possible, "Well, these days, work is work."

"I wish you luck," the man said, shaking his head from side to side. He reached out his right hand. "Name's Tom Harrison."

Taking the man's hand and shaking it, Dimitri said, "Dimitri Broido. Good to meet you."

Tom eyed him suspiciously. "You sure got a funny name. And you've kinda got an accent. You a Commie?"

Dimitri was taken aback by the man's question. He'd hoped there would be less bigotry here on the West Coast. Too many times over the years, people had made negative assumptions about him based solely on his heritage.

Biting back anger, he said as calmly as possible, "I am an American citizen and not a Communist. My family came here from Russia eleven years ago. They are not Communists either."

"Good. Wouldn't want to think I'd helped out a Commie." He took a pack of cigarettes and matches out of his shirt pocket. Holding the pack out to Dimitri, he asked, "Smoke?"

"No, thank you."

He shrugged, tapped out a cigarette, then stuck the pack back in his pocket. Keeping one hand on the wheel, he lit a match and held it to the cigarette. He sucked in, and smoke rose into the air. He took another puff, drawing smoke into his lungs, then slowly released it. He looked at Dimitri. "No offense. I just don't trust Communists. If we give them a chance, they'll overrun this country. We've got to stay on guard."

Dimitri didn't know how to respond. He knew very little about Communism. He nodded and stared at the road through the choking haze.

For a while, neither man spoke. Dimitri watched the countryside. The forests were occasionally interrupted by a farm house, most of which had broken-down fences and muddy, slow-moving cows.

A light drizzle began to fall.

"Blast!" Tom said, turning on his wipers. "I was hoping it would hold off." The wipers scraped across the window, making a grating sound. "It would be better if it just rained. When it sprinkles like this, it's a plain nuisance. I've seen it do this for weeks at a time." The wipers continued their irritable swipes, back and forth across the glass.

Dimitri tried to ignore the grating sound. "So, it rains a lot here?"

"It sure does, but too often, it's just this cursed drizzle. I try to remember it's the moisture that keeps everything here so green. I cuss the weather, but I'd sure hate to live in a cotton-pickin' desert."

"What are the winters like?"

"Like this, only colder. We get snow from time to time, but nothing like in the Midwest. I spent my growing-up years in Nebraska, and I wouldn't go back for nothing." He flicked cigarette ashes out his wing window. "This place grows on you. I figure I'll be here until I die."

CHAPTER 3

Gazing at the timber, Dimitri said, "It's nothing like New York. I spent most of my time in the city, but when we visited the country, it was mostly farms. There weren't huge evergreen trees like there are here. At home around this time of year, the oak and maple are turning color—their leaves are bright orange, yellow, and gold." He removed his hat and combed his hair back with his fingers. "From what I have seen, I think I'll like it here. I can get used to country life." He smiled thinking of Tatyana. "My wife grew up on a farm. She'll probably like this better than New York."

"Is she still back there?"

"Yes. I had to leave her when I came out, but as soon as I get a job, I'm going to send for her."

"She might have a long wait. There's not much work."

"What about the mine?"

"You might get on. A lot of guys won't do that kind of work, so there could be a place for you. Like I said, you couldn't pay me enough to spend ten hours a day in a dark hole." He downshifted and slowed the truck. "Speak of the devil. This is it." He pulled into a paved parking lot. "I have to admit, this outfit looks better than most."

Dimitri studied a long row of buildings. Pacific Coast Coal Company was written across the front in bold, black letters. "This isn't the Indian Mine. It says . . ."

"Yeah, I know, but it's the right place. The Pacific Coast Coal Company owns a lot of mines around here. The Indian Mine is one of them."

"Oh." Dimitri grabbed his suitcase. Opening the door, he said, "Thank you for the ride."

"Good luck to you. You're gonna need it," Tom said with a grin. Then he yanked the door closed and waved in a salute as he pulled away.

Dimitri stood in the large lot, uncertain where to go. The building complex was huge. *This must be a good company. Why else would it be so big?* Taking a deep breath, he hefted his bag and headed toward the closest building.

When he found the room with the word Office written over the door, he brushed the dust and dirt from his coat, pulled at the bottom hem to straighten it, and grabbed the door knob. Throwing his shoulders back, he stepped through the heavy door, careful not to let it bang closed behind him. The smell of ink and dust greeted him, along with the click, click, click of a typewriter.

A young woman with strawberry blonde hair sat at a large desk with stacks of files and forms piled all around. She didn't notice the stranger as her hands hurried over the typewriter keys. Dimitri took a deep breath and walked up to the desk. The secretary continued to work. He cleared his throat.

The young woman looked up, her hazel eyes flashing with friendly surprise. "Oh, I'm sorry. I didn't see you standing there." Resting her hands on the edge of the keys, she smiled. "May I help you?"

Dimitri swallowed, trying to wet his dry throat. He needed this job. "I heard you were hiring?"

"Yes, we are. You'll need to talk to our crew boss. Last I heard, he was in the hoist house." She looked around the office until she found a gangly teenage boy with big ears. "Sam, could you take . . . what did you say your name was?"

"Dimitri Broido."

"Could you take Mr. Broido down to see the boss."

The boy grinned, a blush rising in his cheeks as he looked at the secretary. "Right away, Susie," he said eagerly.

Dimitri wondered if the boy had a crush on the young woman.

Taking long strides on spindly legs, Sam headed for the door.

Chapter 3

Leaving the office behind, Dimitri fell into step beside the young man. They followed a pathway alongside the buildings. "You look pretty young to work here."

"I'm supposed to be in school, but I come down and help sometimes. The boss said I'll be able to start mining soon. Then I'll make some real money," he added with a wide grin.

"They let school kids work in the mines?"

"Yeah. Sometimes. It's not like it used to be, though. Now, parents have to sign papers giving permission before the company will let them work. And the kids don't get paid as much. My pa went to work in the mines when he was thirteen. He's still workin', but it's gettin' harder and harder for him. He's got black lung, and it's tough for him to get his breath. After so many years, the coal dust settles in your lungs and . . ." he shrugged his shoulders. "Anyway, he'll probably have to quit soon. My being able to work will help a lot."

The more Dimitri heard about mining, the less he liked the idea. "What is black lung?"

"I'm not sure exactly, but I think coal dust plugs everything up. After a while, you can't do anything without losing your breath and coughing up a storm. Some of the old-timers end up spending their last years in bed. Pa's not so bad as that." He stopped walking. "This is the hoist room." Opening the door, he explained, "The engines that pull the trips to the surface are kept here."

"Trips?" Dimitri asked, stepping into a surprisingly clean room with large pulleys and motors.

"Trips are coal cars being hauled up and down or cars moving the miners in and out of the mine."

A bell sounded, and a man wearing overalls pushed on a lever. Pulleys whirred, and an engine strained as a heavy line wound around a huge spool.

Another man, who wore a dark brown wool suit and a broad-brimmed hat, studied the engine as it worked. He made notations in a tablet.

"Mr. Robinson," the boy called over the grind of machines.

The stocky man looked up and motioned for Dimitri and the boy to join him. "What do you need, Sam?" he called over the noise, glancing at Dimitri.

"Susie said I should bring him out to see you, sir," Sam explained. He stepped back.

Another bell rang, and the man in overalls pulled the stick back. The engine quieted.

"What can I do for you?" Mr. Robinson asked.

"My name's Dimitri Broido." He held out his hand, and Mr. Robinson shook it. "I heard you were hiring workers."

"We are, but we're kinda picky about who we put on. Not just anybody is cut out to work in the mines."

"Yes, sir. I understand."

"Have you done any mining?"

Again, Dimitri considered lying, but said, "No, sir. I haven't, but I have no doubt I can do the work. I learn quick and I'm not afraid."

"Well, if you're not, you should be."

Dimitri said nothing. If the men working in the mines were scared, should he be frightened too? "I'm strong and don't mind long hours. I'll do a good job for you." He looked the man squarely in the eyes.

Mr. Robinson folded his arms across his chest and looked him up and down. Finally, he said, "I've got no room for shirkers. I expect a full day's labor from my men. If you think you can push your work off on another man, you might as well leave right now. I won't put up with it."

"No, sir. I'd never do that."

"Do close places bother you?"

"No." Dimitri's gaze didn't falter, although he didn't know for sure how working in a close setting would affect him. He'd never done it before. All he knew was that he needed a job.

The man studied him. "You're big. How tall are you?"

"Six feet, four inches, the last time I was measured."

The man gave a low whistle. "And how much do you weigh?"

"I don't know for sure. Maybe two hundred and twenty?"

"Well, you ought to be able to do a good day's work." He paused. "All right. I'll give you a chance. You start tomorrow—day shift on the timber crew. Go back to the office and tell Susie. She'll have some paperwork for you to fill out. I'll see you here at 6:30 tomorrow morning."

"I'll be here," Dimitri said with a smile, "at six." He shook the man's hand, turned, and walked out the door. *I have a job!* He wanted to leap and yell but managed to look calm as he headed back to the office. *I'll be able to send for Tatyana!* was his final thought as he stepped through the office door.

Susie looked up from her work and smiled at him. "So, you got the job."

"How did you know?"

"Your grin. No one could miss it." She shuffled through a file folder on her desk, took out two forms, and handed them to him. "Fill these out. One is personal information and work history. The other is for your insurance."

"I'll have insurance?"

"Everyone who works for the Pacific Coast Coal Company has insurance." With a smile, she returned to her typewriter.

Unable to believe his luck, Dimitri sat in a chair against the wall and filled out the form, answering questions like his date of birth, previous work experience, and prior address. Other, more serious questions bombarded his mind. What would it be like to work beneath the earth? Would it be frightening? What if he couldn't handle it? Or what if he got black lung? And what happened if there was a cave in? *Enough!* he told himself. *It's a job. You won't end up at the hobo camp.* He answered the last question on the application and walked back to the desk.

Susie stopped typing and looked at him. "You did that quickly."

Dimitri handed her the forms. He liked the friendly redhead and hoped Tatyana would get a chance to meet her, certain she would like her too.

Susie scanned the forms. "So, you're from back east. Have you been out here long?"

"No. My bus came in yesterday."

"How did you know about the job here?"

"Josephine Simmons from up at Snoqualmie told me. I had a job lined up with a logging company there, but when I showed up, they told me the government contract had been canceled and so was my job."

Susie marked something on the application, then looked at Dimitri. "Do you have a place to stay?"

"No. I don't have any money left. I was counting on the timber outfit."

Susie thought a moment. "Well, my husband and I both work here, days. We can put you up until you get your own place. We live out in Black Diamond. Do you know where that is?"

"No."

"It's about twelve miles from here, back toward the mountains. The company owns houses there. I'm sure that once you start work, you'll be able to move into one of the houses. The rent is deducted from your pay."

"That sounds good. Are you sure your husband won't mind my staying with you?"

"Carl? No. He'll be glad to have another man in the house."

"I want to pay rent. How much do you think is fair?"

"Don't be silly. It's no trouble. And I'm sure you'll be able to get set up in a house almost right away." She paused. "I'll tell Carl as soon as he comes off shift."

"You said he works here?"

"Uh huh. It's been six years now, and he's happy. He started right out of high school. Don't misunderstand, the work is hard and sometimes dangerous, but the truth is, if a job pays well, you have to expect some drawbacks. Besides, these days, a person needs to be thankful just to be working."

"That's true," Dimitri said. "How much *does* it pay?" He felt embarrassed for not asking earlier.

"Three dollars and fifty cents a day."

"How many days a week will I work?"

"Right now, the men are working ten hours, five days a week."

Dimitri couldn't believe his good fortune. The pay was better than the lumber company's. He'd already asked an awful lot of questions and hesitated asking any more. He didn't want to look foolish or too eager, but he needed to know when he could send for Tatyana, so he asked, "Can you tell me when pay days are?"

"Once a month, on the fifth." She glanced at the calendar. "Only a few more days. Until then, I'm sure you can use credit at the company store. Your name will be put on the list of employees."

"The company store?"

"Well, there is only one store in town, and the company owns it. We can charge things there; then the list of charges is sent to the company and deducted from our pay."

"That will be a real help," Dimitri said, marveling at all the extras offered. He would have housing, insurance, and now an account at the store.

"The company is good to its employees. We've been real happy working here."

The door banged closed, and Mr. Robinson walked in.

Susie glanced at him. "I'd better get back to work. I get off at five o'clock. I'll meet you out front then."

"Okay," Dimitri said as he turned and walked toward the door. He nodded and smiled at his new boss as he passed him.

The man nodded back.

When Dimitri stepped into the fresh air, his prior anxieties had lifted. He took a deep breath, relishing the fragrance of rain and wet earth. He felt like jumping and running, shouting his good news. "I have a job!" He watched heavy clouds roll across the sky. Everything had worked out perfectly. He wanted to tell Tatyana they would be able to begin their new life soon, and he wished he could afford a telephone call. A letter would have to do.

He remembered Josephine's words of encouragement and her promise to pray. Glancing skyward, he said, "Maybe you do care about me. Thank you."

CHAPTER 4

THE LIGHTS WENT ON, AND Dimitri pulled his blanket over his eyes.

"Time to get up," a woman said.

He'd heard the voice before but couldn't quite place it. Still more asleep than awake and his vision blurry, he looked at Susie Anderson's smiling face. The previous day's events washed over him—the Indian Mine, his new job, Carl and Susie Anderson's offer of their home. "I'm up," he mumbled, brushing his blonde hair out of his face.

"Coffee's on, and breakfast will be ready in a few minutes." Susie disappeared through the doorway leading to the kitchen.

Still trying to clear his head, Dimitri shifted his legs over the side of the couch and threw the blankets back. The night had been long. Unable to quiet his mind, he'd tossed and turned. His new job, the promise of Tatyana's joining him, and their hopes and dreams, as well as a few qualms about working in a mine, had played and replayed through his mind. He rubbed his face with his hands.

A spring pressed against his thigh as he eased himself up. Grabbing his pants off the end of the couch, he pulled them on. The smell of coffee tantalized his taste buds. Lacing his boots, the reality that he would be going to work in a mine in the next hour jolted him, and butterflies took flight in his stomach. Glancing at the front window, a sheet of blackness lay within its frame. He wished the sun were up. Stretching his arms overhead and yawning, he considered the town of Black Diamond. He liked it. This would be a good place to raise a family.

"Morning. The bathroom is free." Carl walked through the living room to the kitchen.

"Good morning," Dimitri said, pushing himself up and shuffling to the bathroom. Leaning on the sink, he stared at his reflection in the mirror. The last week had taken a toll. He looked drained, the blue of his eyes lifeless, his skin pallid. He turned on the water, and while it was still cold, splashed his face. It burned his cheeks, but he felt more awake. Taking a deep breath, he toweled and gazed in the mirror. "So, this is it. My first day as a miner." The nerves in his body bristled. All he knew about mining was what he'd read, and some of that wasn't good. And yet, along with apprehension, excitement filled him. This was an adventure. He'd be doing something most men never did. Plus, he'd be making a good living for him and Tatyana.

When he entered the kitchen, Carl sat at the table, a cup of coffee warming his hands. Dimitri liked the open, friendly man who seemed to possess no pretension. After discovering his wife had invited a stranger to stay with them, Carl welcomed the newcomer with no reservation.

He looked at Dimitri. "I hope you slept well."

"Not so good. I had a lot to think about."

Smoothing his heavy mustache, Carl nodded. "It's not easy being responsible for a family, especially when they live three thousand miles away."

Susie handed Dimitri a cup of coffee.

"Thank you. It's just what I need." He sat across from Carl. Holding the cup close to his face, he took a deep whiff. "Smells good." Taking a sip, he said, "Mmm, it's perfect."

"Thank you," Susie said. "Do you and Tatyana have any children?"

"No. For now, it's just Tatyana and me."

Carl grinned. "It usually doesn't stay that way for long. Susie and I hope to have a whole houseful of kids one day, God willing."

Spooning hot mush into her husband's bowl, Susie said, "For now, all we have is a calf." She looked at Carl. "How is she this morning?"

"Fine, but I don't know about my shin. She gave me a pretty good kick." His broad face crinkled into a grimace, creasing the freckles across his cheeks. "Some sweetheart," he said sarcastically. "Joe, wasn't quite honest with us when he sold us that calf. She's downright ornery." He looked at Dimitri. "A friend of ours knew we wanted a cow, but we couldn't afford one, so he sold me one of his heifer calves. I wasn't so sure about it, but he assured me she'd be no trouble. It's too bad he didn't tell me she has more than her share of sass."

"Give her some time. She'll gentle with kindness and patience," Susie said, dropping a large spoonful of mush into Dimitri's bowl. "I hope you like hot cereal."

"Looks good," Dimitri said.

Carl folded his hands and bowed his head. "Dear Lord, we thank you for another day and for this food. We pray you will watch over us and keep us in your care. Amen." He looked up and smiled, then swilled down the last of his coffee. "I hope you're right. A full-grown cow with that kind of temperament makes milking a nightmare. And right now, I've got my hands full." He held out his cup for a refill. "Plus, we've probably seen the last of the sunshine for a while. That calf is going to need a shelter."

Susie filled his cup with the dark brew.

"You have bad winters here?" Dimitri asked.

Susie chuckled as she set the percolator back on the stove. "Some years, I forget what the sun looks like." She placed a dish of buttered toast in the center of the table and sat down, nibbling a slice.

"Even in New York, we have our share of bad weather." Dimitri took a bite of cereal. It tasted sweet and felt warm as it went down. "This is good."

Susie smiled and leaned her elbows on the table. "You said your wife came from Russia?"

"Uh huh."

"How long has she been in America?"

"She immigrated more than a year ago." He thought a moment. "I think it's been about a year and a half."

"I can't wait to meet her." Susie's hazel eyes sparkled.

Carl lifted his bowl. "Is there any more mush?"

Taking the pot, Susie scooped more into both men's dishes and took a little for herself.

"The timber crew's a good place to start in the mines," Carl said. "It'll give you time to adjust and get used to how things work. Later, if you want, you can move up to mining."

"Is that better?"

"Absolutely. It pays more." He took a bite of cereal. "And respect comes with the job. Miners don't like working with greenhorns. They don't trust them. It's too easy for newcomers to make a mistake. You get an inexperienced miner down there, doing something he shouldn't, and he can blow everyone to kingdom come." He grinned and scraped out the last of his cereal. "We better get moving or we'll miss the train. Don't forget to bring an extra change of clothes. We shower and change at the mine before coming home."

"Sounds like a good idea," Dimitri said, gulping down his coffee and spooning out his last bite of cereal. Pushing himself away from the table, he said, "Thank you for breakfast, Susie. It was good." He hurried out to the front room, pulled clean clothes from his bag, rolled them into a tight bundle, then stuffed them under one arm. When he returned to the kitchen, Susie held up two round tin pails hanging from metal handles.

"You'll need these," she said. "Otherwise, you'll be awfully hungry by dinner."

Carl took the lunches and handed one to Dimitri. "Don't forget your cap. You'll need it for your light."

Dimitri took his coat and cap from a hook by the back door. Looking at Susie, he said, "You didn't need to fix my lunch."

"Yes I did," Susie said matter-of-factly as she cleared the table and piled the dishes in the sink. "I hope what I fixed doesn't give you heartburn, though. Down in the mine, certain foods don't agree with some of the men." She pulled on her coat, picked up a smaller version of the men's lunch pails, and stepped out the door.

It was still dark as the three headed toward the station. Clearly, Susie and Carl had made the trip many times because the blackness didn't slow their steps.

Dimitri tried to keep up with his new friends; a sense of melancholy settled over him as he watched the easy rapport between the couple. He wished Tatyana was at his side. He stepped into something that squished, and his foot slid. He nearly fell.

Carl grabbed his arm and steadied him.

"For crying out loud! What was that?" Dimitri asked, peering down at his boot.

Carl chuckled. "I would guess a cow pie. You've got to watch for them. Around here, the cows wander free."

"Why?"

"No one has room to keep them, but they need the milk, so they have cows, but let them roam."

Scraping his boot clean against solid ground, Dimitri said, "I've never heard of anything like that before."

"You'll get used to it." Carl slapped Dimitri on the back.

"Some of them scare me. They're not all friendly," Susie said.

Continuing toward the station, Carl asked, "So, how do you feel about going down?"

"A little nervous and excited. I've never been in a mine before. I hope I do a good job."

"You'll be great. And it's normal to be tense. Everyone has butterflies the first time. If I let myself think about it too much, I s'pose I'd still get nervous. After a while, it's like any other job. You get used to it. And the Indian Mine isn't a bad one. We haven't had any trouble with black damp or cave-ins. There's a water problem, but so far they've managed to keep it pumped out."

"What is black damp?"

"Gas, or the absence of oxygen. It can be bad. The trouble is you can't see it or smell it, and by the time you know you're in trouble, it's too late." He planted his hand on Dimitri's shoulder. "All you need to do is listen to your crew boss. Do as he says, and you'll be fine. I think the real danger comes after a fella gets a little comfortable. Sometimes men are cocky. While you're down there, you can never forget where you are. Things are different. The danger is always there, and the rules aren't the same as up here. For instance, no one smokes, ever." He glanced at Dimitri. "Do you smoke?"

"No," Dimitri said, queasiness settling in his stomach.

"Good. If there's gas, one match can blow up the whole works. Another thing, when you're taking a trip . . ."

"A trip? That's a coal car?"

"Yeah, basically. When the cars go up and down, they call it a trip. They haul men, coal, timber, and tools." He switched his lunch pail to his other hand and repositioned his hat. "Like I was saying, wires run above the cars. Don't touch them. They're full of juice. If you forget, you might not see another day, or at the very least, you'll be tasting copper for a week."

Dimitri's butterflies increased and his mouth felt dry. He had a lot to learn.

The train was waiting when the trio arrived. Susie was the first to board. Carl followed her, and then Dimitri. Several men were already seated. Carl and Susie greeted each as they made their way down the aisle. When they sat down, Dimitri took the seat across from them.

Susie glanced at her watch. "How about that, we're five minutes early." She looked at Dimitri. "The train never leaves before six."

"Who's that you've got with you this morning, Carl?" one man asked.

Carl stood up and motioned for Dimitri to do the same. "Everybody, I'd like you to meet a new man on the crew, Dimitri Broido."

Several men offered words of welcome to Dimitri.

Carl nodded at a tall, lean man who was sitting behind him. "Dimitri, Harvey will be your crew leader."

Harvey stood up and extended his hand, and Dimitri shook it. His blue eyes seemed to miss nothing as he looked at the newcomer. "I was told I'd have a new man on my crew today. You ever work the mines before?"

"No." Dimitri wished he didn't have to admit his ignorance in front of the others.

Several men chuckled. "Another greenhorn," one worker said derisively. "Just what we need."

A heavyset man who looked like his stomach had been stuffed into his shirt made his way out of his seat and approached Dimitri. He held out his hand. "Name's Joe Blodgett. Good to have you on the crew."

Thankful for the welcome, Dimitri shook his hand. "Good to meet you, Joe."

"These guys are just giving you a hard time. We're like family. Have to because we depend on each other when we're down there. And we all work hard. There's no other way when you're digging in the dirt."

The train's horn fractured the morning conversation. Couplings clanked and screeched as the train bumped forward and nudged ahead. Gradually it picked up speed, and the men took their seats. Some visited, while others took the opportunity to nap.

As they left Black Diamond, sunlight colored the eastern sky a soft pink. Dark, jagged mountains were silhouetted against the pale background. Dimitri settled back and rested his head against his seat, enjoying the rhythmical clacking of the wheels.

His nerves settled as he thought of Tatyana. The three-hour time difference meant she was already up and probably sitting at the kitchen table sipping coffee and watching the world outside the window. He remembered how they'd spent many mornings visiting at that table. A pang of grief hit him as he contemplated the actual number of days before he would see her. He hoped he would earn enough money by payday to send for her. If he did, he'd have to wire the money, then wait another week for her to travel west. It was too long.

He wondered if it were possible to project his thoughts to Tatyana, and knowing he was being foolish, concentrated very hard. *I love you, Tatyana. I need you,* he thought, hoping that somehow she would know he was thinking about her.

❊ ❊ ❊ ❊ ❊

CHAPTER 4

"I wonder if the men have come up from the night shift yet," Carl said as he walked toward the equipment shed. "I'd just as soon get to work. It's cold up here." He looked at Dimitri. "We've got to wait until they're done before we can get started. First, though, we pick up our batteries. You'll need a light for your hat." They stepped into the shed. The men were quiet as they took batteries and hooked them to their lights.

Harvey Olson, the crew boss, handed Dimitri a light and battery. "You hook this pack to your pants like this." He attached the cell to Dimitri's belt. "The line runs up your back and connects to the globe on your cap. You'll need to take off your coat."

Dimitri shrugged out of his jacket.

Harvey connected the line to his light. "You're all set." He patted Dimitri on the back. "Now all we need to do is catch the man trip down. And you'll need to know some things."

"Sure," Dimitri said, adjusting his cap. His palms felt sweaty, and his heart hammered. He hoped no one noticed his nervousness.

As they walked to the mine entrance, Harvey turned serious. "It's important you listen carefully to what I have to say. Down there, we depend on each other. If one man botches things, it can mean everyone's life. I'm you're boss, and you listen to me. If you have a question, you come to me. Don't decide you know the best thing about anything. You know nothing. Do you understand?"

Dimitri nodded.

After that, Harvey proceeded to give him the mining rules, which were mostly a repeat of what Carl had already told him. When they reached the long train of cars, he said, "If you pay attention, you'll get the hang of everything soon enough. Before long, you'll know all you need to."

Several men were already sitting in the man trip. Harvey climbed over the side of the shallow wooden car and Dimitri followed, sitting on a narrow bench. Inside, there was barely enough room for two men to sit side-by-side. He wedged his feet against the seat in front of him and kept his lunch bucket on his lap.

"Our job is to deliver timbers to the miners," Harvey explained. "We'll be hauling wood all over the mine. You'll know this place better than most of the miners." He studied Dimitri a moment. "You look plenty strong. You shouldn't have any trouble." He sat back. "But, you're gonna have to relax. If you don't, your muscles will cramp up. I don't believe we've ever lost a man on his first day, yet," he said as he chuckled.

Dimitri swallowed hard and tried to smile. His stomach churned. The car jerked forward and moved slowly as they entered the tunnel. The men hunkered down. Dimitri did the same and studied the ceiling as it passed overhead. *I hope it stays put,* he thought.

The trip gradually picked up speed. "You gotta watch your head," Harvey said. "Sometimes the tunnels settle or rise, and there isn't much room. It can get pretty tight."

Dimitri took a deep breath, and the musty, dank smell of the mine swept over him. He exhaled slowly as the outside light disappeared. The only illumination came from an occasional lamp mounted in the gangway wall and the globes on the men's hats. Gradually, his eyes adjusted to the dimness.

The trip moved briskly. Dimitri figured if a man were trying to keep up, he'd have to run to stay abreast of the cars, that is, if there were enough room for a body alongside the trip, which there wasn't. The tunnel pressed in close on both sides, and Dimitri was careful to keep his arms tucked in against his body. For several minutes, the trip remained level. Then, without warning, it dipped downward and descended a steep slope. Their speed remained the same, and Dimitri remembered the pulleys he'd seen in the hoist room the previous day.

The grade angled at about thirty degrees, and he was grateful to have a place to brace his feet. As they continued down, he felt a rising sense of panic. He fought to control it, but couldn't dislodge the image of a mountain of earth and rock lying above him. If it came down, he'd be buried alive.

He closed his eyes, took a deep breath, and thought of Tatyana. She depended on him. She trusted him to make a life for them. He remembered her strength and her trust in God. He needed that trust now. Deliberately, he loosened his grip on his lunch pail. *I am fine,* he told himself.

The trip finally leveled off, traveled on the flat for a few minutes, then headed down another slope. Dimitri had no idea how far below the surface they were, and he wasn't sure he wanted to know. All he needed to think about was doing his job.

When they finally stopped, several men unloaded. Dimitri started to climb out. "No. You stay put," Harvey said. "They've got their timber here. We've got some to deliver on the third level."

Dimitri sat back down. He, Harvey, and one other man were the only ones left in the car as it headed deeper into the mine. After making one more descent, the trip came to a stop, and Harvey climbed out. "Let's get this timber unloaded."

The other man climbed out. He was small and moved with a calm air. Holding out his hand, he said, "My name's Mike."

Dimitri shook his hand. "Dimitri. It's my first day."

Mike grinned. "I know."

"All right, we've got work to do," Harvey said.

Dimitri picked up a timber and rested it across his shoulders, then followed his boss into a smaller tunnel.

"This is the workings," Harvey explained as he headed up a tunnel divided in the middle by wooden slats. Pointing at the wall, he said, "That's the chute. After blasting out the coal, it's channeled through the chute and into cars. They're still blasting coal out of here and need more bracing. It's our job to see they have enough posts and beams." He tossed a timber to the ground.

A miner shoveling coal noticed the newcomers. He stuck his spade into a pile and leaned on the handle. "We've been waiting on you," he said as he grinned. "You better pick up the pace or we'll have the roof coming down on top of us."

Harvey kicked a chunk of coal at the man. "You'll get your wood. I've got a new guy working with me. Got to break him in."

Dimitri dropped his beam beside Harvey's.

His boss placed a hand on his shoulder. "Hey, everybody, this is Dimitri. He'll be hauling timber with us."

The others nodded, and Dimitri returned the gesture. He looked at the work area. Piles of rock and coal as well as a stack of beams were piled alongside an opening that needed bracing. Two men immediately set to work placing the timbers, while the others returned to shoveling. Dimitri watched with interest. If this was going to be his job, he wanted to know all he could.

"We need to get the rest of the lumber unloaded," Harvey said.

Dimitri followed him back to the cars. He felt more relaxed and studied his surroundings. *This isn't so bad,* he decided as he picked up a post and placed it on his shoulder. It felt good to be working.

As the day progressed, Dimitri became comfortable with the dim, close conditions. Unfamiliar noises still raised the goose-flesh on his arms, and he didn't like the sound of dripping water, but for the most part, he felt at ease.

Occasionally the rumble of cars on distant tracks echoed through the chambers, giving Dimitri a sense of familiarity as he realized the mine was very much like an underground city. The labor was hard, and in spite of the cool temperatures, Dimitri worked up a sweat and shed his coat.

Late that morning, he waited in the gangway while charges were set in the coal face. Everything in him told him to run, to get as far away from the explosion as possible. As he looked at the others crouched against the wall, he could see they were calm and knew his fears were unfounded. Yet, he couldn't keep from asking, "What if something goes wrong?"

"They rarely do. And this mine's been holding fine for a long time." Harvey grinned. "But if something does happen, we skedaddle and don't look back."

After that, Dimitri's confidence grew, and he actually began to enjoy the adventure of working in the mine. When he, Harvey, and Mike stopped for lunch, he couldn't believe the hours had passed so quickly. He sat and leaned against the wall. Guzzling water from his jar, he emptied half of it.

"Slow down. You'll need some of that later in the day," Harvey warned.

Dimitri wiped his mouth and screwed the lid back on. "I didn't know I was so thirsty."

"It sneaks up on you," Harvey said and bit into a sandwich.

The dripping of water echoed through the tunnel, and apprehension crept over Dimitri. "Where does the water come from?"

Mike tossed a walnut into his mouth. "Underground springs, or simple condensation, then it leaks through fissures. From time to time, we've had trouble with too much water down here. It's a constant battle. Sometimes they have to pump it out."

Dimitri studied the wall, envisioning a river behind it. "You'd never get a real gusher, would you?"

"Not likely. I've never seen one."

Dimitri devoured the cheese sandwich, apple, and sugar cookies Susie had packed. He felt good. He had a job, Tatyana would be joining him soon, and working in the mine wasn't bad. He took another swig of water. A beam groaned and popped above his head. Dimitri jumped. "What was that?"

Harvey chuckled. "That popping and cracking happens all the time. The beams just need to complain a little. The supports along the gangway are good and strong. We use the heaviest timber along here. They'll last." He shoved the last of his cake into his mouth.

Mike bit into his apple and studied the tunnel. "I've seen some mines so deep the pressure would push the ceilings down. Around here, the ones you need to worry about are the workings where they're taking out the coal. If it's not braced up good, or if there's a lot of coal coming down, you can get into trouble." He patted a beam. "These along here, though, they'll last. Don't get me wrong. Sometimes they need replacing, but you don't have to worry about the whole thing coming down on our heads."

"That's good to know," Dimitri said, glancing up and down the tunnel. "Are there many accidents?"

Harvey pushed the lid onto his lunch pail. "A few. Most are caused by carelessness. But, sometimes you can do everything right, and it still catches you. Over the years, the mines here about have had some bad ones. Men have died."

"Yeah, I lost a brother," Mike said. "Hit his head on a cross beam on his way down. He was riding the bumper of a coal car."

"I'm sorry," Dimitri said. A burning sensation filled his chest. He tried to swallow the pain away, but it only worsened. He stood up and paced.

"Something troubling you?" Harvey asked.

"I have heartburn." He tried to belch.

Harvey grinned. "I should have warned you. Eating down here can do strange things. Some foods just won't set right. Heartburn is a big complaint. I don't seem to have any trouble, but a lot of fellas do. You'll learn what you can and cannot eat."

Mike picked up a small chunk of coal. "I've seen some of the old-timers suck on a piece of coal. They say it settles their stomach right off." He tossed the black chip into the air, caught it, and held it out for Dimitri.

Dimitri raised his hand and shook his head. "Not for me. I'll live with the heartburn."

Harvey pushed himself to his feet. "We better get back to work."

Dimitri climbed onto the trip. Glancing at the electric wires running overhead, he remembered Carl's advice to keep clear of them.

Harvey touched the wires with a stick and looked at Dimitri. "One quick touch and they hear a short bell up top. Tells them to pull us up."

The cars began to move.

Dimitri stared into the tunnel ahead. "It must be real dark down here without the lights."

"You've never seen anything so black," Harvey said. He was quiet for a few moments. "You might as well learn what it's like. This is a good spot. There are no lamps here. Both of you, put out your globes." He turned his off. Mike did the same. "Come on Dimitri," Harvey urged.

Dimitri reached up and put out his light. A deep darkness, like black velvet settled over him. He blinked and stared hard, then held his hand in front of his face, but couldn't see it. The complete absence of light was unlike anything he'd encountered. Panic enveloped him. He felt vulnerable and confused. "Okay. I get the idea. Now, how about some light?" He fumbled with his globe.

"Relax," Harvey said. "You need to know what it's like. Once I had to find my way out of a mine when all the lights had gone out. It happens."

Dimitri forced himself to sit still. He'd never considered how important light could be. Now, sitting in the dark, he remembered his mother telling him Jesus was light in a dark world. He'd never completely comprehended the concept, but now feeling isolated and handicapped, a glimmer of understanding settled over him. He wanted and needed light; he felt lost without it. He promised himself that when he returned to the Andersons' that night, he'd look up the verse in his Bible; then he remembered he didn't know where it was.

CHAPTER 5

STANDING IN THE CROWDED ter-
minal, Tatyana clutched her train ticket. As she looked at her
American family, the sounds of crying children, hurried foot-
steps, and chatter of travelers faded. She couldn't believe the
moment had arrived to say good-bye.

Since she'd arrived in America, the Broidos had been her
family. The forced separation from her Russian home had been
more bearable because of them. Tears burned her eyes, and she
dabbed them with her handkerchief. She glanced at a large clock
on the wall and took an uneven breath. "The train will leave in
twenty minutes."

Pavel placed his hands on her arms. "So, it is time to say
good-bye. You will join our son all the way in Washington State."

Little Ella took Tatyana's hand, turned innocent blue eyes up to her friend, and asked, "Do you have to go?"

Tatyana knelt in front of her. "Dimitri is waiting for me. I must go to him."

The little girl touched the collar of Tatyana's coat, rubbing the rough material between her thumb and forefinger. "I wish you would stay and Dimitri could come home." Her voice sounded small and dismal.

Samuel wrapped his arm around Tatyana's shoulder. "You know what I wish. I wish we could all go. I want to move to . . . to . . . Black Diamond. Dimitri said it is a nice place where people have cows and horses and gardens." He looked up at his father. "Please, Papa, can't we go?"

Pavel placed his hand on the boy's shoulder. "Maybe one day, God willing."

"I think that would be wonderful," Tatyana said as she straightened.

Augusta's brown eyes shimmered. "Maybe it will happen, one day." She tucked Tatyana's upturned collar down and patted it smooth. "Now, you are sure you have everything?"

Tatyana glanced into her traveling bag. A special beef sandwich Flora had made, plus bread, cheese, and apples were neatly packed beside her purse and tickets. A slipcover she'd been embroidering was also neatly folded into the inside pocket. It would be nice to have something to keep her busy on the train. She ran her hand over the blanket her aunt Irina had given her when she'd left Russia, then glanced at Pavel. "The man took my bags? Do you think my records will be all right?"

He nodded. "They will take good care of them."

She looked back at Augusta. "Then, yes, I have everything."

"If I find anything at home, we will send it to you and Dimitri." Her mother-in-law straightened her back and stood as tall as she could. "He is doing so well, my Dimitri. Already he has enough money so you can ride the train. It will be much better than a bus."

Flora, who had been quietly watching the interchange, said in Russian, "I have something for you." She handed Tatyana a small gift-wrapped box.

"Oh, Flora," Tatyana said, taking the gift. "You should not have done this."

Flora shushed her. "Just open it."

Careful not to tear the paper or crumple the ribbon, Tatyana removed the wrapping and lifted the lid off the box. Inside, hidden beneath a piece of tissue paper, lay a white, lace doily. "It is beautiful!" Holding up the delicate cloth, she asked, "You made this?"

Flora nodded. "I meant to give it to you before you finished packing, but every time I tried, I . . ." Her voice broke and her eyes flooded. Wet droplets spilled onto her parchment-like cheeks. She wiped them away. "It has not been so long ago that we met on the ship. And now you are going off to live on the other side of this country. It is like I am losing you to another world."

Tatyana pulled the old woman into her arms. "I will never forget you. You were my first friend after I left my homeland." She held up the doily. "I will keep this in my living room where I can see it every day. I will think of you and my New York home." Tears brimmed over and ran in small rivulets down Tatyana's cheeks. "I will miss you."

Forcing a smile, Flora stepped back and, still speaking Russian, said, "For you, this is not good-bye, but a new beginning. Dimitri is thinking of you and waiting." She sniffled. "Now, it is time for you to think about your new life."

"I am very happy to go to my husband," Tatyana said. "I only wish I did not have to leave all of you behind."

The train's whistle blasted.

"It is time," Pavel said.

Tatyana gave Flora one more kiss.

Augusta stepped up and hugged her daughter-in-law. She held her a moment. "You are like my own daughter." Then she kissed her cheek. "No matter how far away you live, you are my daughter, my *dochka*."

For a brief moment, Tatyana's mother's gentle face filled her mind, and her eyes flooded with fresh tears. "My mother always called me that." She hugged the woman again. "I love you."

Augusta, her chin quivering, smiled and said, "You will give my son a kiss from his mother?"

"Yes. Many kisses."

Ella and Samuel gave her another hug. "We will miss you," Samuel said in his most grown-up way.

Tatyana stood, and for a moment, she looked at her family. "I will miss you so much. I love you all. Please, come and visit."

"We will try," said Augusta, "but soon you will have new friends. When we visit, maybe we will have a grandchild?"

Tatyana blushed. "I hope so."

"Augusta, that is up to God," Pavel said, as he bent and kissed Tatyana on each check. Holding her face in his calloused hands, he added, "When it is the right time, we will be there. We are your family forever."

Resting her hands on his wrists, she studied his kind face through her tears. "You are a special man."

"All aboard!"

Pavel hugged her, then stepped back. "You must go," he said as he wiped his nose.

Augusta took Tatyana's hand as she walked to the train. "We will think of you every day. We will write. And you write to us."

"I promise," Tatyana said, stepping onto the boarding stairs. "Good-bye!" With one last glance at her adopted family, she walked up the steps and made her way to the nearest car. It sounded quiet inside compared to the chaos of the station. Her eyes roamed over the crowded car. A porter stored a bag above the seat of one passenger, a mother tried to restrain a spirited child, and an old man wearing round wire-rimmed glasses stood and tipped his hat to her.

She moved down the aisle toward him.

Smiling, he asked, "Would you like to share a seat with an old man?"

Tatyana was thankful for a friendly face. "Thank you, uh . . ."

"Abner. My name's Abner."

"Thank you, Abner."

"You may sit beside the window if you like."

"You are very kind," Tatyana said and took the seat, placing her bag by her feet and setting the blanket on her lap.

"I travel a lot. It is not such a special thing to sit by the window any more."

Tatyana searched the crowded platform for her family. They were looking for her, too. She waved. When Samuel saw her, he threw his hand into the air and yelled something, but Tatyana couldn't hear. Smiling, everyone waved. Augusta and Flora dabbed at their eyes.

The train vibrated and nudged forward, then stopped. With a jolt, it started again and eased past the station. As the train moved on, leaving the Broidos behind, Tatyana felt a rising panic and turned to watch them. She waved until they were out of sight. A pain cut into her, and she felt alone. *No. I have Dimitri,* she told herself. *He is waiting for me.*

Feeling calmer, she ran her hand over the folded blanket. *So, I am on my way.* A mix of melancholy and excitement filled her. She tried to imagine her arrival in Black Diamond. Dimitri would be there. They would have a wonderful reunion, filled with tears and laughter, embraces and passionate kisses.

Settling deeper into her seat, she wished Dimitri were traveling with her. The last time they'd been on a train together, the circumstances had been very different. She didn't want to think about it and tried to push the memory aside, but it refused to be cast away. Mr. Meyers had been with them. She remembered the gown he'd purchased and the dinner they had shared and how foolish she'd been to trust him. She could still see the outrage on Dimitri's face when he'd come to her rescue.

The memory was painful. She'd been frightened, and both she and Dimitri had lost their jobs, but she'd also discovered the depth of Dimitri's devotion. Her heart warmed as she remembered his gallantry. Tatyana couldn't imagine why it had taken her so long to admit her love for him. Now, it was more powerful and greater than she'd ever imagined love could be. "You are a fine man, Dimitri Broido," she said, unaware she'd uttered the words out loud.

"Pardon me. Did you say something?" the gentleman beside her asked.

She'd nearly forgotten he was there. Wire-rimmed glasses balanced on his long nose and cottony white hair framed his friendly face. When he smiled, his pale blue eyes warmed. "No. I was just talking to myself," she said, blushing.

"Was that your family you were waving to?"

"Yes. Well, no. They are my husband's family."

"Good-byes are always difficult." He settled back in his seat.

Swallowing past the lump in her throat, Tatyana said, "Yes, they are." She wondered how long it would be before she would see them again. "My life seems to be filled with good-byes."

What had become of her family in Russia? It had been a year and a half since she'd left them. After getting on the train in Moscow, she hadn't heard from anyone. Did Aunt Irina and Uncle Alexander still live on the farm? And what about Yuri? Where was he? The last she'd heard, the Russian armies were still battering the people, and Stalin had begun butchering his own government officials. Had any of her family survived? Even as the doubts crowded her mind, she felt an assurance that her brother still lived. In her heart, she knew he was alive, somewhere.

Sighing, Tatyana remembered Flora's words, reminding her to think about new beginnings. *You're going to be reunited with your husband,* she thought, and her spirits lifted. It wouldn't be long before she was with Dimitri, his strong arms around her.

As the train left the city behind, she considered Dimitri's work. She knew very little about mining, but what she did know made her feel uneasy. It could be dangerous. Even Augusta and Pavel were distressed at the news of his job change. The idea of working deep beneath the earth sent shivers through Tatyana, and she wished he were working for the logging company instead. *Father, you know what is best. Please take good care of him.*

Tatyana felt weary and exhausted. Her preparations for the trip had been hurried, and she'd had little time for reflection or ease. Resting her head against the seat, she closed her eyes. Immediately, her mind filled with pictures of Dimitri. She smiled as she recalled his last letter.

He'd written about their house, explaining it was small but nice. Tatyana had been astounded to learn the company provided housing for the employees. They would have to pay rent, but a dollar a month was almost like paying nothing at all. Plus, the house came with a refrigerator and stove and some essential furnishings. She couldn't wait to see it. She'd laughed after reading how Dimitri had bought a cigar when he received his first paycheck. He'd sat on the front step, smoked the cigar, and watched his neighbors as he savored it. *Dimitri must have been feeling very good,* she thought. *He is usually careful with his money.*

Sleep beckoned, and Tatyana thought about their reunion. Dimitri would be waiting at the Black Diamond station, standing alone, anxiously waiting. The moment he saw her, his eyes would light up. He'd run to her, scoop her up, and hold her in a tight embrace. As sleep wrapped itself around her, Tatyana smiled, feeling the strength of his arms.

🐜 🐜 🐜 🐜 🐜

On the third morning, Tatyana fidgeted, frustrated as she tried to find a comfortable position. It was impossible. She'd made several trips up and down the aisles and even to the dining car where she sat at a table sipping tea and watching the flat countryside slide by. Her body ached, and she longed for a bed and bath. Since beginning this journey, she'd only been able to take short naps and was exhausted.

"Are you feeling all right?" the old man asked.

"Not really, Abner. I am tired, and my body hurts. I do not know how you can take it."

"I do all right. You have to remember, before I retired I was a traveling salesman. I'm used to this."

"I do not know if I can stand two more days."

"Actually, three. We still have this one, plus two more."

Tatyana gave him a half smile. "I do not want to think of it."

"Maybe you should ask the porter for another pillow."

"It will not help. What I need is to hear the announcement saying we are in Seattle."

The old man smiled. "You will hear it. Try to be patient. Already two days have passed. And that means you are two days closer to seeing your husband."

"That is a good thing to remember," she said, feeling only slightly better.

The next few hours, Abner slept and Tatyana stared out the window. She wished he'd wake up so she would have someone to talk with. The countryside had little to divert her attention. Barren, parched land stretched out for endless miles. There were no real trees. Instead, brittle sticks stood upright in the dust. At this time of year, one would expect to find a blanket of brightly-colored leaves beneath the trees, but here there were piles of dust and dirt pressed against scrawny trunks. Dried earth and tumbleweeds were heaped along dilapidated fences. Tatyana wondered if the fences had once confined sheep and cattle. There was no livestock now, only blowing wind and fine sand that created a soft haze across the plains.

"Before the drought, these were rolling prairies with deep grass and lush places where trees grew beside lakes and streams. What you see now is a dead world," Abner said sorrowfully.

Tatyana looked at the old man. "I am glad you are awake."

"I only need catnaps," he said with a smile.

"You know what it used to be like?" Tatyana returned to staring at the barren landscape.

"I grew up here."

"It is hard to believe something could change so much. I did not know the drought was this bad. The papers say there is a dust bowl, but I did not know it would be like this."

His eyes were lusterless as he gazed at the land. "I can't even recognize it. It used to be filled with huge farms that grew corn and wheat. The fields would ripple in the wind like a giant green and gold ocean. Now, there's only dust."

"What will happen?" Tatyana asked.

"If the rains return, life will also. If not . . ." He shrugged.

They moved past a farmhouse buried up to its eaves in dust.

"I wonder what happened to the people who lived there?" Abner asked. "Where did they go?"

Tatyana felt a deep sorrow as she considered the family who'd once occupied the house. Like hers, they'd been forced out; the only difference—their enemy was nature. "Hardship comes to everyone I guess," she said softly.

✻ ✻ ✻ ✻ ✻

As the train crossed the country, it stopped in big cities and tiny towns. Some of the small towns were struggling to hang on; they looked like ghost towns, with businesses boarded up and homes abandoned. The stations were deserted and run-down. If rain didn't come soon, the towns would be completely abandoned.

As they pulled away from a nearly deserted town in Kansas, Tatyana noticed a scrawny boy in baggy overalls standing in front of a dilapidated farmhouse. A thin trail of smoke came from its chimney. The child rubbed his hand up and down the nose of a swaybacked horse with jutting hip bones. He watched the train longingly as it moved past. Tatyana felt a tug of her heart as she considered the youngster and wondered what his life must be like.

As they traveled through miles of parched countryside, she began to have trouble imagining anything lush or green. This wasteland seemed to be the only reality. Dimitri had described Washington as a state with great forests, lakes, and grand mountains. It seemed impossible that such a place could exist at the same time as this devastated prairie.

"Oh, my Lord, we're in for it now," Abner said, pushing his glasses up on his nose and peering out the window.

Something in his voice made Tatyana's stomach lurch. She looked in the direction he was staring. What she saw made her heart leap. A monstrous, roiling black cloud filled the horizon. "What is it?"

"A black roller."

"A what?" Her alarm grew as the huge cloud moved toward them. Along its face, small whirlwinds picked up dirt and debris, throwing it into the torrent. Tumbleweeds tossed before it, snagged on fence lines where they gathered into heaps. Tatyana had never seen anything like it. The thick, black curtain moved closer, blocking the sun. "Abner, I am scared. What is it?"

"A dust storm, a big one."

"Are we in danger?" Tatyana couldn't take her eyes off the boiling cloud hurling itself at them.

"Probably not. The ones in trouble are those caught out in it. We'll be safe on the train."

"Will we have to stop?"

"I don't know. I've never been in one of these while traveling." He looked for the porter. When a young man in a white uniform passed, he caught his arm. "Young man, can you tell me what the procedure is for trains caught in dust storms?" He pointed toward the cloud.

The boy's eyes widened. "I'm not sure, sir," he said as he straightened. "But, I'm certain the engineer knows what to do. I'll check," he said, and hurried down the aisle, disappearing through the rear door.

A few moments later a different porter entered the car. "Please, could I have everyone's attention. As most of you already know, a dust storm is moving our way. According to the conductor, we won't be able to avoid it."

A panicked murmur moved through the car.

"Please stay calm. We are perfectly safe. I need you all to place blankets, coats, sweaters, or anything else that will help keep out the dust against the windows." Having said that, he took two pillows and placed them against the door, then stood up and looked at the passengers. "We will do our best to continue traveling despite the storm."

Tatyana tucked her blanket against the window ledge. There was no way to cover the entire window, but she hoped it would help.

It didn't take long for the squall to descend on the train. At first, it seemed nothing more than a lot of wind and dust, splattering tiny bits of sand against the window. Soon, however, the roller engulfed the train, swirling dirt and debris all around. Bits of branches and dried brush hit the windows. The outside world disappeared, and day turned into night. Lightening flashed, followed by booming thunder.

Frightened, Tatyana closed her eyes and huddled in her seat. This was nothing like the snowstorms she had known at home. She sought comfort from her Heavenly Father. *I know I am in your care. Please keep me safe.*

Abner reached out and placed his hand on hers. "It will be all right." He smiled gently, and Tatyana was thankful for his presence.

The wind increased, and dirt and sand hammered the windows. Tatyana prayed they wouldn't break.

The gale howled and the train slowed. Tatyana envisioned piles of dust on the tracks and wondered if they would be able to continue. In spite of their efforts to block it out, dust forced its way inside, and the air smelled and tasted like dirt. Tatyana tucked her blanket more tightly against the window frame. She longed for a drink.

"Let me trade places with you," Abner said and stood up. "It might be better away from the window."

Gratefully, Tatyana changed seats. Wishing she could huddle in her blanket, she shivered from the cold that penetrated the car. *I wish Dimitri were here,* she thought, remembering his strength and how he made her feel safe.

Finally, the storm passed. It left the dry plains much as they had been before; the only difference—a new layer of dark sand now covered the earth.

Abner dusted off his jacket. "It must have started up north. The black dirt comes from Nebraska and Colorado."

"It came from another state?" Tatyana asked incredulously.

"Yes. The Midwest is being blown away one dust particle at a time. Only God knows what will happen if it doesn't rain soon."

"Do you think there will be a drought in Washington State?"

"I don't believe so, but I never thought it would happen here either."

Tatyana wished she could hurry the train. All she wanted was to put this parched land behind her.

"My son says there's no drought in Washington, but they still have their troubles. There's a lot of unemployment like the rest of the country, but so far his business has survived. He told me he could use my assistance." He smiled. "I think he's just helping out his old man."

"I have not been to Washington. I do not know what it is like," Tatyana said.

"It's wet and green."

"That sounds good." She brushed her hair back. It felt gritty. "You remember how I told you my husband is working in a coal mine?"

"Uh-huh."

Tatyana studied her hands. "Do you think it is dangerous?"

Abner knit his bushy gray brows. "I don't know much about mining. Heard it's hard work. I guess it can be dangerous."

"I do not like that he is working in a mine. I am afraid for him." She looked at Abner. "I pray and try to trust God, but I still worry."

"You've got to remember God is bigger than man and any work he might do."

She remembered something her mother had often said. "God is a big God, my *dochka*. There is nothing he cannot do." Galya would smile and caress her daughter's hair. "If he created this world why can't he take care of our little needs?" Her words had always made Tatyana feel better. And now, as they touched her again, she was reminded of the God who oversaw every detail of her life. She could trust him. Why did she have to be reminded so often?

She rested her head on her seat and closed her eyes. *Thank you, Mama.* She hadn't seen her mother since the soldiers had dragged her off, but for a moment, she had seemed so near. A longing for the lost days, of working side-by-side and chatting over a cup of tea, washed over Tatyana.

She glanced out the window at the piles of dust shifting in the wind. In Russia, pillows of snow would be lying beneath trees, and icicles would be reaching down from rooftops. *I don't belong here,* she thought. *Father, how am I going to do this?*

"We'll all just have to trust God more," Abner said softly.

Tatyana looked at him. "What did you say?"

"Just that we have to trust God more. I guess I don't do that enough."

Stunned by the timing of his words, Tatyana knew God was speaking to her. She stared at the distant mountains and felt comforted.

CHAPTER 6

THE TRAIN WOUND ITS WAY through the Cascade range. Clouds swirled atop snowcapped ridges, deep blue lakes lay within their seams, and sparse, crooked pines clung to steep embankments. The tall peaks reminded Tatyana of an icy fortress. After the many miles of desolation, the beauty was like a soothing balm. Her eyes roamed the wide vistas, taking it all in.

As they descended the western slope, the forest became lush. Giant evergreens, their limbs weighted beneath piles of snow, stood along rocky slopes and spread out in wide bands that cut through the highlands. The tracks hugged the edge of the mountain, the cliff face falling away dizzily. Tatyana gazed at an approaching ravine and leaned closer to the window, hoping to get a good look.

The train rumbled across a trestle. Far below, she could see a river and the tops of trees. Milky water washed over rocks and hurried around jagged boulders in a white froth, then swirled into deep pools before snaking though the canyon. At a sweeping bend where the river disappeared, a giant tree, covered with moss, reached out over the water.

"It's beautiful, isn't it," Abner said.

"It is. Do you know why the water is that white color?"

The steward overheard, leaned toward the window, and gazed at the distant river. "It comes from a glacier. When the ice crushes the rock, the minerals in the rock turn the river milky."

"How much longer until we reach Seattle?" Abner asked.

"We should arrive about three o'clock. About another hour and a half."

Excitement welled up in Tatyana. Soon she would see Dimitri!

Abner smiled at Tatyana, his eyes sparkling. "Not long now."

"You must be very excited to see your son."

"Yes. It has been two years. And my grandchildren." His eyes took on a faraway look. "They have been growing. I can't wait to see them."

Tatyana allowed her eyes to roam across distant jagged peaks hooded with snow. "I wonder if it is like this in Seattle?"

"It is a city like others, but there is so much beauty all around. Seattle lies in a big valley." Abner stood up slowly, keeping one hand on the back of the seat. "Oh, I have been sitting too long. My joints are complaining loudly." He smiled at Tatyana. "I could use a cup of tea. Would you like to join me?"

"Yes. Tea sounds good," Tatyana said, stepping into the aisle.

In the dining car, Abner took the chair across from Tatyana. He rested his arms on the table and glanced at the forest rushing by the window. Taking out his wallet, he opened it and removed a photograph. After studying it, he handed it to Tatyana. "This is my son, Tom, and his family."

CHAPTER 6

Tatyana looked at the picture. A tall, slender man with a square jaw and red hair, who looked nothing like Abner, stood with his hand on the shoulder of a short, plump woman with sparkling eyes. Three boys stood in front of the couple. "They are a fine-looking family," she said, handing the photograph back to the old man. "You must be proud."

"I am," Abner said, stuffing the picture into his wallet. "It will be good to see them." A shadow crossed his face. "Since my wife passed on, my life has felt . . . empty." He gazed out the window. "I wish we'd had more time together." Forcing a smile, he looked at Tatyana. "I shouldn't complain. We had forty-five years. That's more than most." He rested his hand on Tatyana's. "I hope you and Dimitri are so fortunate."

Tatyana placed her free hand on his and squeezed gently. "We will be. I know it."

"The years go by so quickly. One day you're saying I do, and the next you're old and saying good-bye." His eyes glistened. He blinked and adjusted his glasses, then cleared his throat. "Love each other. Enjoy each other. Don't wait until tomorrow to live. Do it now."

"I will do my best," Tatyana promised. Resting her arms on the table, she returned to watching the forest. Birch trees now intermingled with pine, cedar, and fir, and patches of red and gold lay between piles of snow. "We will be out of the mountains soon."

❋ ❋ ❋ ❋ ❋

Rain fell, and the leaves of shrubs and berry bushes glistened. Waterlogged evergreen boughs and heavy underbrush drooped from the moisture. Bright-colored leaves plastered the muddy earth. Tatyana wondered if the Northwest was always so sodden.

As the train crested a hill, a broad valley emerged below. A patchwork of green and brown was interspersed with small towns and divided in the center by a large winding river. In the distance, Tatyana could see the fringes of a large city. *At last, we are almost there!* she thought.

As they neared Seattle, Tatyana felt a rush of excitement. She checked her tickets to make sure they were where she'd packed them. After repacking her traveling bag and twice folding the blanket her aunt had given her, she finally set the bag and quilt on her lap and waited.

As the train rolled through the city, a menagerie of buses, cars, and taxis flowed past. As in other cities, humans crowded the sidewalks, seemingly unaware of each other as they hurried to their destinations. Tatyana wondered why city people always seemed in such a hurry. She hoped Black Diamond would be different.

Dimitri had promised to meet her at the bus station in Black Diamond. Still, she searched the crowded landing, hoping he'd changed his mind and had come to greet her. He wasn't there.

The train stopped; Tatyana stood, wanting to be one of the first off. Abner chuckled. "You are certainly in a hurry."

"This is a new beginning for me. I guess I want to get started."

The old man smiled. "I wish I was just beginning."

Tatyana stepped into the aisle and followed the remaining passengers off the train. The station bustled with activity and noise. She watched as travelers greeted one another and hurried to retrieve their baggage.

"There's my son," Abner said, wearing a broad smile and pointing at the man Tatyana had seen in the photograph. The old man took off his hat and bowed slightly. His voice serious, he said, "I must go, but it has been a pleasure knowing you. May you and your young husband have a good life, Tatyana."

Without another word, he walked away. Tatyana watched while Abner greeted his son and family with hugs and pats on the back. When they went on their way, Tatyana felt alone. She retrieved her luggage, and with her traveling bag hanging from her shoulder, her box of beloved records under one arm, and her suitcase in her left hand, she walked to the ticket window.

Standing in the short line, she wondered how long it would be before her bus left, and a fear that it might have already departed needled her. What would she do if it had? Would there be a second one today? She'd seen no buses. Where was she supposed to catch it? One thing at a time, she told herself. *I will ask the woman at the ticket window.*

The clerk was very kind and made certain Tatyana didn't miss her connection. As the young immigrant climbed aboard the nearly full bus, she breathed a sigh of relief. Her trip was nearly over.

"Let me help you with that," the driver said and took her box of records.

Tatyana followed him to the back of the bus. He set the box under a seat, nodded, then returned to the front. Gratefully, Tatyana sat down, placing her suitcase at her feet and her traveling bag and blanket on the bench seat beside her.

As the bus left the city behind, Tatyana stared out the window. Businesses were gradually replaced by homes with well-kept yards. The suburbs eventually disappeared and, once again, Tatyana found herself amidst farms and forests.

Gas fumes seeped into the bus from the exhaust pipe and settled in the back. Tatyana struggled against rising nausea. *I should have sat closer to the front,* she thought dismally and considered opening her window. Glancing at the people around her, she dismissed the idea. It was cold and wet. They would not appreciate a wet breeze. She rested her cheek against the cool glass. It wasn't as good as fresh air, but it helped.

The rain continued in a steady downpour, and Tatyana wondered how the already saturated earth could hold another drop. Evergreens crowded the roadway, and Tatyana felt as if she were traveling through a dark, green cave. Occasionally, the woodlands gave way and the view opened up. Heavy, black clouds rested on nearby foothills, completely obscuring the mountain range she'd just crossed. She wondered what they looked like from this vantage.

They passed a small farm. Smoke drifted up from the chimney, and a large barn stood off to one side. It reminded Tatyana of her Russian home. Knee-deep in mud, two cows and a horse stood with their heads hanging and their heavy coats dripping from the downpour. They looked cold. Tatyana shivered involuntarily.

In the midst of the soggy pasture lay a pond with dense shrubbery on two sides and actually growing into the water. *It is so green and lush here, it must rain all the time,* Tatyana decided, uncertain she liked the idea. What would it be like to live in a place that was always wet? In his last letter, Dimitri told her he liked it here and thought she would too. She hoped he was right.

Her husband's handsome face filled her mind, and she envisioned their meeting. Laughing, he would pick her up and twirl her in his arms. Joyfully, Tatyana would hug him around the neck.

The bus bumped over a section of rough road and jarred Tatyana from her reverie. She gazed outside at the unchanging countryside.

Time dragged as the miles passed and the bus stopped in one small town after another. The light began to fade, and Tatyana knew darkness would soon settle over the countryside. In the dimness, a deer sprinted alongside the bus, then darted into the woods. Tatyana smiled, remembering a hunting trip she'd forced her brother, Yuri, to take her on. He had tried to tell her she wouldn't like it, but she insisted until he finally relented.

They hiked through the forest searching for game. When they came upon a handsome buck, Yuri held his finger to his lips, shushing his little sister, then carefully closing the distance between himself and the animal. Its tail twitching and nose sniffing the air, the deer seemed to sense danger, but he didn't run. When Yuri stood and pulled back his bow, Tatyana couldn't bear to see the animal killed, so she jumped up and hollered for it to run.

Yuri's arrow landed in the earth, and the last they saw of the deer was the flip of its tail as it leaped over a log and darted into thick underbrush. Yuri was angry and made it clear she'd never be allowed to hunt with him again.

She smiled at the memory. He hadn't stayed angry long. Yuri never did.

The bus slowed, pulled off the road, and stopped in front of a small train depot. Tatyana felt a momentary sense of panic. She'd been so deep in thought, had she missed her stop?

"Black Diamond," the driver called.

Tatyana's heart quickened. *I'm here!* She stood and began gathering her things. The driver grabbed her bag and box of records while she took her blanket and traveling bag and followed him.

He set the bags next to the building, tipped his hat, and returned to the bus. Leaving a cloud of black smoke behind, the bus moved on.

Chewing her lower lip, Tatyana stood alone on the landing, just beneath the eaves, to stay out of the rain. A set of railroad tracks ran down the center of the road. Several small businesses were scattered on either side of the street. And a lone cow meandered past the station, not even glancing at her as she moved by. Obviously, Black Diamond was nothing like Seattle.

Hoping to find Dimitri, Tatyana glanced in the dark station. There was no one inside. She looked up and down the roadway, but he wasn't there either. Thick berry bushes grew along the edge of the street; trees rose from their midst, bare limbs reaching toward the gray sky. Smoke drifted from the chimneys of several business establishments and a smattering of houses on the hill above her, but the town felt deserted.

Tatyana wiped wet hair out of her eyes. *Why isn't Dimitri here? He said he would meet me. What if something has happened to him?* She felt the stirrings of fear. *No. He is fine, just late,* she told herself, but her apprehension remained.

A light went on inside the station. Tatyana peered in the window, then walked to the door. With her box wedged beneath her arm, she pushed it open with her hip and stepped inside. Rain dripped off her and formed a puddle at her feet as she looked around the room. A bench ran along the front wall beneath two windows, and a small coal stove stood in the corner.

A ticket agent wearing a black visor and small round glasses looked at her from behind a counter. "I was out back. I've got a lot of freight to get packed. I'm sorry. I should have come out the minute I heard the bus." He studied the drenched woman. "What can I do for you?"

Tatyana set her baggage down and dug into her purse. Locating her ticket stub, she looked at it, but still unable to read much English, she handed it to the man. "Am I in the right place?"

The clerk ran his hand over his balding head and studied the slip. "Sure are. This is Black Diamond all right." He handed the ticket back to Tatyana.

She put it in her purse and looked out the window. It was nearly dark. Looking back at the man, she said, "My husband said he would meet me. His name is Dimitri Broido. Do you know him?" Chilled from the rain, she shivered.

Pushing his glasses up on his nose, he thought. "Can't say that I do. We get newcomers through here all the time." He nodded at the bench. "You can wait here if you like."

"Thank you." With her arms folded over her chest, she studied the steady downpour, then sat on the bench.

CHAPTER 6

The man eyed Tatyana. "I could get you a cup of coffee from the confectionery across the street."

"Is it open?"

"Yeah. Loretta's open most days."

"You do not have to go. I can," Tatyana said, standing up.

"No. You're already wet. Besides, I could use a cup myself. It will just take a minute. I'll be right back." He pulled on a coat, grabbed an umbrella, and disappeared out the door.

Grateful at his generosity, Tatyana watched as he hurried across the street, skillfully skirting puddles while holding the umbrella over his head. He disappeared inside a small shop with a sign over the door that read, "Black Diamond Confectionery."

Tatyana glanced up and down the road. Still no Dimitri. *Where could he be? What if something has happened to him? Then what will I do?* She looked through her purse and counted out her money. She had eight dollars. *It should be plenty for a hotel and a meal.*

Still shivering, she walked over to the stove and held her hands close to it. Heat radiated against her palms and warmed her face. Taking off her wet coat, she draped it over the end of the bench nearest the stove, hoping it would dry; then she returned to standing in front of the firebox.

The door creaked, and Tatyana turned around expectantly, hoping to see Dimitri. It was only the kind man who'd gone for coffee.

He smiled, his eyes crinkling. Holding up a sweet roll, he said, "Loretta thought you might be hungry, so she sent this over. She makes the best cinnamon rolls around." He handed the drink and roll to Tatyana. "By the way, my name is Hubert Martin."

"I am Tatyana Broido. How much do I owe you?"

He waved his hand to ward off her offer. "It's on the house. My treat." He took a drink of coffee, returned to his desk, and shed his coat, hanging it on a hook.

"That is very kind. Thank you." Tatyana gazed out the window.

"I'm sure your husband will be here soon."

Tatyana smiled at the man, hoping he was right. She sipped her coffee. It was very hot and burned her tongue, but she took another drink. It warmed her as it went down. She wasn't hungry but didn't want to offend Mr. Martin, so she bit into the roll. The cinnamon sweetness tasted good. She swallowed. "This is delicious. Please tell your friend."

"Sure will," Mr. Martin said. "Loretta takes pride in her cooking. She'll be glad you liked it." He studied Tatyana for a moment, unable to keep his brows from knitting together in worry. "If you'll excuse me, I have some more things that need boxing up. I'll be in the back room." He disappeared through a door on the back wall.

Tatyana finished the roll and coffee, then returned to the bench. She sat with her hands in her lap, her back straight, and stared at the stove. Rain pounded the rooftop as darkness settled over the town.

With each passing minute, her apprehension grew. *Please, Dimitri, step through the door,* she willed him. But he didn't come. She wanted to cry. What reason could he have for not being here?

Soon she would be forced to make hotel arrangements.

Balancing several boxes, Mr. Martin returned and set them on the counter.

"Sir, is that large building across the street and down a block a hotel?"

"Yes it is."

"Do you know how much it costs to stay one night?"

"Last I heard, they were asking $1.50." He studied her a moment. "If you stay at a boarding house, you might be able to get a cheaper room. Maybe $1.00 a night." He glanced at the clock. "I'm going to have to close. My wife will start worrying."

CHAPTER 6

Tatyana stood. "I am sorry. I did not mean for you to stay late." She bent and picked up her box, when a rumbling came from outside.

"Ah, the train. I can load these packages tonight," Mr. Martin said.

"Train? I thought there was no train in Black Diamond."

"The passenger train doesn't run anymore, but the miners ride back on a coach. They must have worked late today."

"The miners?" Tatyana asked, her heart pounding with excitement. "My husband is a miner."

"Well, that must be where he is then," Mr. Martin said grinning.

Tatyana hurried to the door and yanked it open just as the train rolled in amidst a blast of steam. Even before it stopped, she saw him. Dimitri stood in a doorway and leaped to the landing. With his bright blue eyes locked on hers, he closed the distance in long strides.

"Dimitri!" Tatyana yelled. "Oh, Dimitri! Dimitri!" She rushed toward him.

He scooped her up into his arms and pulled her close. "Tatyana, I have missed you." He caressed her hair, kissed each cheek, her forehead, then her mouth. For a long while, they stood in each other's arms.

Tears coursed down Tatyana's cheeks. "I love you. I love you." She smiled up at him. "I was afraid you were not coming for me, that something had happened to you, or . . ."

He quieted her with a kiss. "I am sorry. Never, never would I not come for you. When I wrote, I didn't know that today I would be working over. I couldn't get here sooner. Did you have to wait long?"

"Long enough, I'd say," Mr. Martin cut in. He leaned on the doorway, his arms folded across his chest. "Seems to me, you might have sent someone for her."

"I wanted to, but everyone I know works at the mine."

Mr. Martin pursed his lips and said nothing more.

"I didn't know I would be so late. I am sorry." He cupped Tatyana's face in his hands. "Please forgive me."

Tatyana smiled. "I could not be angry. I am too happy."

He grinned and kissed the tip of her nose. "My friends live very close. We can walk." He picked up her bag and the box of records. "Susie went straight home to fix us some dinner. You'll like her and Carl. They are good people. I wrote you about them." He wrapped his free arm around her waist. "After dinner, we can go home."

Tatyana snuggled against Dimitri. "Home sounds wonderful."

CHAPTER 7

TATYANA LIKED SUSIE AND
Carl. They were warm and friendly and made her feel welcome.
She did her best to remain attentive through dinner, but after
days of traveling, she had difficulty staying awake.

Finally, over dessert, Susie said, "Dimitri, I think you need to
get your wife home. Otherwise, she's going to fall asleep at the
table."

Tatyana could feel her cheeks flush. "I am fine."

"You've been on a train for days. You must be exhausted."
Susie stood up. "You need sleep. I'd be out on my feet."

"Susie's right." Dimitri stood, took Tatyana's arm, and helped
her up.

"I am very tired," Tatyana admitted.

Dimitri slipped his arm around his wife. Looking at Susie, he said, "Thank you. Dinner was delicious."

Tatyana smiled. "Yes. It was very good. Thank you."

"I was happy to do it." Susie looked at Tatyana. "I'm glad you're here."

Tatyana smiled at the friendly redhead. "When I am settled, you and Carl will come to our house for dinner."

"We'd like that," Carl said.

Dimitri retrieved Tatyana's coat from the closet and slipped it over her shoulders. "Our place is only five doors down." He pulled on his own coat, picked up the box of records and Tatyana's suitcase, and headed for the door.

Tatyana took her traveling bag and blanket and followed.

"I hope I'm not intruding too much, but I've been wondering what's in the box?" Carl asked.

"Carl," Susie said, giving him a playful slap on the arm.

Carl's face turned red, and then he grinned. "I was just wondering."

"It is beautiful music. My uncle packed my family records in that box. Mama, Papa, Yuri, and I used to listen to them every day. I hope one day I will have a phonograph, so I can listen to them again."

"I have a phonograph," Susie said. "You can bring them here."

"I would like that."

Dimitri opened the door and ushered Tatyana outside. "I'll see you two tomorrow."

"Tomorrow," Carl said.

Standing in the doorway, Susie watched as Dimitri and Tatyana walked down the front path. "Goodnight."

The storm had relented, and a silver thread of moonlight reached through the clouds. Keeping the box of records braced under his right arm, Dimitri transferred the suitcase to his right hand and took Tatyana's hand.

The feel of his rough palm and the strength of his grip made Tatyana feel secure. She savored the cold air. Taking a deep breath, she caught an unfamiliar but pleasant fragrance. "What is that smell? It is sweet . . . lovely."

"That's the pine and cedar trees. When it rains, they always smell stronger." He squeezed her hand. "So, what do you think of Black Diamond?"

Tatyana had to admit that in the moonlight, the little town held a special, cozy appeal, but she hadn't forgotten the dark, soggy woods and the gloom from the heavy cloud cover. "I have not seen very much yet," she hedged. "It was raining hard when I got here."

"It rains a lot, but that's what makes it so green. You'll get used to it. I think I already have. You know, the trees are huge here. I've seen some so big, it would take at least five men with their arms linked to circle it."

"I would like to see a tree like that."

Dimitri stopped in front of a tiny house. It was dark inside. This is it. Still holding Tatyana's hand, he led her around a large puddle and up to the porch. Wearing a playful smile, he set her box and suitcase down. "I heard a husband is supposed to carry his wife over the threshold when they enter their first home." He scooped Tatyana up in his arms, held her a moment, then kissed her tenderly. "I am so glad you are here. I have missed you."

Tatyana wrapped her arms around his neck and hugged him. "I missed you too. I love you."

Dimitri didn't move but held her tighter. Gazing down at her, he stood with his wife cradled in his arms.

"Maybe you should take me in?" Tatyana finally asked.

"Oh. Yes." Dimitri fumbled with the knob, pushed the door open, and stepped inside. Flipping on the light, he said, "It isn't fancy, but we can fix it up."

Tatyana gazed at the small front room. The hardwood flooring gave it a feeling of warmth, and the two windows in front would let in morning sunlight. There were no window coverings, but it wouldn't take much to make a set of curtains. A wooden rocker rested beside the windows, and she imagined one day spending hours in it rocking children. A small coal stove on the far wall would provide plenty of heat for the house. A threadbare chair stood beside a doorway. The house was very much like Carl and Susie's, so Tatyana guessed the door led into the kitchen. And a floor lamp with a wrought iron stand and scalloped shade had been placed beside the chair. It was the only other source of light in the room except for the ceiling light.

Tatyana sighed and kissed Dimitri's cheek. "This is our home, and I love it."

Carefully, he set her on her feet.

Tatyana placed her hands on her husband's chest and looked into his eyes. "I do not know how to be a wife, but I will try to be a good one. I will do my best to make a nice home for you."

Dimitri wrapped his arms around her and pulled her close. "We will do it together."

Tatyana rested her cheek against Dimitri's chest. She felt safe. It didn't matter if Black Diamond was wet and dreary. Dimitri was here, and they would be happy.

"We will have a good life," Dimitri said, brushing his lips against her hair.

"I am so happy, Dimitri."

Without warning, her brother's face flashed into her mind. She hoped he was happy too. Closing her eyes, she prayed, *Father, please take good care of Yuri. Allow him to know joy as I do.*

❋ ❋ ❋ ❋ ❋

Yuri stared at the words carved in the wooden beam beside his bed. It said simply, "WHY?" He wondered about the man who'd written it. What had happened to him? *He's dead,* Yuri decided. In the four months since he'd come to the camp, he'd never seen anyone released.

He rolled onto his back, rested his head on his arms, and stared at the blackened wood ceiling. To endure the camp, each day he had to make a new commitment to survive. At times he believed death would be preferable to life. Guards delighted in torturing and murdering prisoners—always eager to release the wolf dogs that paced the compound perimeters. At the slightest provocation, the animals were ordered to bring down those suspected of attempting escape. He'd seen them converge on helpless inmates, while the guards stood back and watched the animals maul their victims.

Starvation and disease took many. As the winter progressed, the pile of bodies at the edge of the camp had grown. The first time Yuri witnessed guards tossing stiff corpses onto the pile like animal carcasses, he'd embarrassed himself by losing his breakfast. He'd been told the victims remained until the spring thaw, then mass graves would be dug and the bodies buried.

Hunger never left Yuri; its pain consumed his thoughts. There was never enough to eat, and what food was available smelled and tasted rotted. And yet, men fought over it, their hunger intensified by hours of hard labor.

Yuri knew that if he ever regained his freedom, the images he'd seen here would remain with him. He could never be free of the sorrow and hopelessness he'd witnessed.

He rolled onto his side. A man in a nearby bunk struggled for breath, his gasps raspy and shallow. *Pneumonia,* Yuri thought. *He won't last long. Even if he recovers, it won't matter. He won't get food rations while he's unable to work. Either way, he'll die.*

Yuri balled his hand into a fist and pounded his straw mattress. *I won't end up that way. I'll show them. Somehow I'll survive. Then Elena and I will find Tatyana. Life will be good again. There will be enough to eat, and I'll sleep in a warm bed.* But, even as he imagined his future, the pain in his belly reminded him how absurd the fantasy was. Like the others, he would weaken and die.

He scratched his arm. The itching had begun again. His body was covered with red welts. Even in winter, bed bugs tormented the inmates. The nights were the worst. Sometimes, Yuri thought he'd go mad. He'd want to scream and beat his body, but he didn't dare draw attention to himself and give the guards a reason to beat him. He pressed his body hard against the bed, hoping the pressure would relieve the itch. It didn't help. Finally, he relented and scratched, gritting his teeth as his nails dug into his inflamed skin.

Shivering, he pulled his thin blanket more tightly around him. The mattress was packed down so hard that his bony shoulders and hips felt bruised.

He studied Alexander's back. His friend's even breathing told Yuri he slept. *How do you find peace?* he wondered. Even as he asked the question, he knew the answer. In the four months since he'd met Alexander, he'd never known him to lose faith in God. No matter the circumstance, he remained strong and trusted in a God of love. Even when Alexander had been beaten, he didn't complain or say anything evil about the men who'd battered him. Openly, Yuri thought him foolish, but secretly, he wished he could be more like Alexander. He remembered that once he'd lived a life of assurance based on God's goodness. Since his arrest, his faith had been elusive. The place within him where God once resided felt shriveled and spent.

I am lost. My life will end here. He took a deep breath. *I will never see my family again. I'll never hold Elena, beautiful Elena.* He squeezed his eyes shut. *God, why have you abandoned me? I was a faithful servant. Why would you allow me to die here?* He tucked the blanket tighter under his chin. *I want a life. Hear me! I want a life!*

The familiar zing of the metal clasps that hooked the wolf dogs tethers to their wire cables sang, and Yuri knew the restless dogs paced.

CHAPTER 7

The word *escape* whirled through his mind. So often, he'd considered it. If only it were possible. But he'd thought and thought and could find no way. He'd never heard of a prisoner who made it to freedom. If a *zek* made it past the dogs, he would be hunted down and shot. And in the midst of a Siberian winter, a bullet provided a more merciful death than one found on the frozen plains.

Please, God, remember me. Please. Finally, Yuri slept, but the brutal world he lived in joined him in his dreams. He could find no relief from his anguish.

※ ※ ※ ※ ※

The next morning, even before daylight, Yuri was roused from bed by the bellowing of a guard. As always, he forced himself upright and swung his legs over the side of his bed. Would this be the day he succumbed to some disease? He rubbed his eyes and made a mental checklist of his body's health. He seemed relatively fit.

He didn't need to dress. Because of the cold, he slept in his clothes, including his coat. He pulled on his boots, wound the laces around his ankles, and tied them. As the other prisoners awakened, the usual sniffling, coughing, and groaning filled the barracks.

"So, did you sleep?" Alexander asked.

"Not so good. But some."

"Everyone out!" shouted the guards. They herded the men outside where they relieved themselves in the snow. After that, they formed a line and were steered toward the mess tent. There, they waited in the wind and cold while a few at a time went in. That way, each man showed his ration card and was given only the portion he'd earned.

Yuri huddled in his coat, trying to keep out the icy wind. His stomach cramped with hunger as he waited. Finally, his turn came, and he stepped inside. He held out his ration card. The server checked it, then dipped out a large spoonful of *balanda*. It smelled foul, and fish scales floated on the top of the broth, but Yuri took it gladly along with a thick slice of hard bread.

"Eat! Eat!" a guard ordered.

Yuri sat at a table, fished the bones out of his soup, and swilled down the greasy liquid. It felt hot in his belly, and he could feel the warmth spread through his body. He chewed the bones, crunching them into tiny pieces before swallowing them. The pain in his belly was only slightly relieved when he was hurried out the door.

Carefully guarding his bread, he sat on the frozen ground beside the building. Tucking his legs up to his chest, he pulled his coat close, trying to keep out the wind. Ignoring the mold, he tore off a chunk of crust. It tasted like wood pulp, but he ate it just the same. It would help fill his hollow stomach.

"Good morning, Comrade," Alexander said as he sat beside Yuri. Shivering, he tore into his own bread.

"Good morning." Yuri studied his friend. If it were possible, his eyes seemed more sunken, his body more emaciated than the day before. Yuri wondered how he must look. He hadn't seen himself for many months. He could feel his matted blonde hair and knew his youthful face was buried in a heavy beard. He guessed his face was haggard like the others.

"Will today be a good day, do you think?" Alexander asked.

"How can any day be good?"

"Some are better than others," Alexander smiled. "When a man hangs on to his anger, life is more difficult."

"You think I should not be angry? We are slaves, breaking our backs for evil men who only understand torture." He took another bite of bread. Looking Alexander straight in the eyes, he said, "We will die here, you know." He held his gaze a moment, then eyed the guards. "They do not care. No one will care." Yuri's voice rose with his anger.

CHAPTER 7

"Shh. They will hear. You do not want to end up in the isolator."

Yuri closed his mouth. He knew better than to give them a reason to throw him into the icy cell cut into the earth. He'd seen more than one man hauled out of the frozen hole. *If* you were still alive, it might take days or weeks to recover. Some died later. He glanced at the guards. "I will not give them that pleasure."

Alexander studied Yuri's face. "I believe, at one time, your blue eyes were kind and not hard. I hope one day I will see that again."

Yuri didn't respond. He did not like to be reminded of the bitterness that held him. He couldn't rid himself of it. And even if he could, the Stalinists didn't deserve his charity.

Shoving the last bite of bread in his mouth, Yuri chewed slowly. He remembered how good his mother's fresh, hot bread had tasted. When he was a boy and it was time for the bread to come out of the oven, he'd stand by the stove, waiting for a piece. The house would be filled with its aroma. He always asked, "Mama, can I have some?" She'd smile and, with the steam rising from the loaf, cut an end piece for him. If they had butter, she'd spread it on the wedge. His mouth watered at the memory. How much circumstances had changed! He was different now. That boy had ceased to exist. He longed for that time—a time of wonder and innocence.

"To work! To work!" the team leader shouted. "Up! Everybody up!"

Reluctantly, Yuri released the memory and pushed himself to his feet. He was no longer strong but still could fulfill his quota. He wondered how much longer before he faltered. He shuffled on heavy feet to the line of workers.

"Keep your heads down and no talking!"

Several men were chosen to pull sleds and were put into harnesses, two to a sled. They led the procession of workers away from the lights of camp and into the nearby forest. The short winter days forced the prisoners to leave before daylight and return long after the pale winter sun had set.

At the work site, the men were assigned duties. Some felled timber; others cut away the limbs of downed trees, then gathered the branches into bundles and carried them to fires where they were burned. The most difficult job was hauling logs to waiting sleds and loading them. Today Yuri chopped limbs and hauled them to the fire.

He didn't mind working, if only there weren't quotas to be filled. It helped him maintain some of his strength, filled the days, and gave him something to think about besides his stomach. Plus, the exertion warmed him.

As the hours passed, weariness settled over him and he struggled to maintain his pace. Not meeting his quota meant his food ration would be cut. He couldn't let that happen. Once a man's food was decreased, he became weaker, making it more difficult to make quotas, and a downward spiral was set in motion—less food, more weakness, greater ration cutbacks, more weakness, and so on. Eventually, death put an end to the cycle.

The crack of a saw blade fractured the air. The men stopped their work and looked to see who had broken a whipsaw. It was easy to find the responsible pair. One member of the team, with a portion of the blade in his hands, stared fearfully at the guards. The other defended the accident. "It was not our fault. The blade was weak. You cannot cut back my ration!" His voice was sharp and panicked.

The guard lashed him with a whip. "Stupid man!" He snatched the broken blade from the other prisoner and threw it at the one who had spoken.

The man tried to move out of the way, but the blade caught him across the shoulder and sliced open his coat. Immediately, red stained the material. He grabbed his arm and blood seeped through his fingers.

Yuri felt momentary grief for the two but knew he needed to take care of himself and returned to chopping a limb.

"Back to work!" the guard ordered.

Without interrupting his work, Yuri glanced at the men. Another saw had been issued, and the injured prisoner pulled it across the tree.

Limbing was the job Yuri liked best. After cutting several branches, he bundled them and carried the stack to the fire. He tossed them into the bonfire, the flame's heat warming him.

While he worked, he searched for food. Larvae, slugs, and snails could be found beneath the bark. Yuri remembered the first time he'd seen an inmate eat a slug. He vowed he would never become so desperate. That was before he knew the hungry fire in his belly. He wanted to live. The first time he'd put a snail in his mouth had been hardest, but after that it got easier.

"Get back to work!" a guard shouted.

Yuri jumped. He'd been daydreaming. Quickly, he picked up his axe and cut away a limb.

"Tomorrow, your ration will be cut," the guard said, his voice hard.

Yuri looked at the man, balled his hands into fists, and clamped his jaw tight. Everything in him wanted to show the soldier how much he hated him.

The guard's eyes shifted toward Yuri's hands, and he grinned.

Yuri maintained his stare. He knew his actions were foolish but couldn't stop himself.

"No more burning brush." The soldier grabbed another man. "You will haul it," he ordered, shoving the man toward Yuri. He glared at the insolent prisoner. "Using only your axe, you will fall timber. I like the sound it makes against the trunk of a tree," he said with a smirk. "You make sure I hear it." He kept his rifle pointed at Yuri's chest.

Forcing back his anger, Yuri stood before a large spruce. Swinging his axe hard, he sunk the blade into the trunk.

The guard returned to walking the perimeter of the work area.

The man who'd taken Yuri's job was careful to keep his head down and his face turned away from Yuri. Hurriedly, he piled limbs and brush. Something about him looked familiar. He glanced up once, and Yuri caught a glimpse of pale blue eyes. He knew those eyes. He searched his mind. Where had he known this man?

After throwing a load of brush on the fire, the stranger returned to piling branches. Yuri tried not to think about the man but couldn't dismiss him from his thoughts. He knew him from somewhere. He turned to look and found the prisoner staring at him. Their eyes locked for a moment, then the man grabbed a large branch and hauled it toward the fire.

Who are you? I know you, Yuri thought. Unexpectedly, the memory of a card game and betrayal flooded him. *Saodat! It is Saodat!* This *zek* had turned him in to the NKVD in Moscow. Because of him, Yuri lived this miserable existence. Before he knew what he was doing, Yuri screamed "Saodat!"

The man with pasty, white skin and frightened, pale blue eyes gazed at Yuri. His arms loaded with brush, he took a step back.

Now, Yuri remembered those eyes. He'd once studied them over a deck of cards and trusted the man. "You! It is you!" Months of anger and bitterness boiled to the surface as he lunged toward the little man. "You did this to me! I'll kill you!"

Alexander called, "Yuri! No!"

All Yuri knew was rage. Saodat deserved to die.

His eyes wide with terror, Saodat edged backwards away from Yuri. "I . . . I did nothing. I do not know you."

Yuri wasn't fooled. He threw himself at the man and gripped his throat.

His eyes bulging, Saodat grabbed Yuri's hands and tried to pry them loose. A strange hissing squeak came from his mouth, but Yuri only tightened his hold.

Alexander pulled at his friend from behind, and Saodat broke free. He searched frantically for a compassionate face. "Help me," he begged as he lumbered into deep snow. Glancing over his shoulder, he cried, "Please! I have done nothing! I have done nothing!"

Looking strangely detached, the prisoners watched. Smirking, the guards folded their arms over their chests and waited.

Yuri grabbed his axe and tore after the traitor. He could feel the blood pump through his body. For too long, he'd kept his rage in check. Now it was time to get even for all he had endured. He raised the axe over his head. "You did this to me! Now you'll pay!"

Using a tree as a shield, Saodat stopped and looked at Yuri. "I am sorry. I did not know this is what would happen. I only wanted to protect myself. Can you blame a man for wanting to save his life?"

Deaf to the man's pleading, Yuri continued toward him, his feet sinking into deep snow.

"You will stop! Now!" In a small corner of his mind, Yuri heard the guard's order but ignored it.

Saodat turned to run but stumbled. Scrambling to his hands and knees, he looked over his shoulder. "Please. I did no wrong."

Gulping for air, Yuri stood over him, his axe raised above his head. "Before you die, you will tell me why you betrayed me."

Saodat cowered. "Please. I did nothing." He started to cry.

Yuri swung the axe back.

"Okay. Okay. I turned you in, but I did not know this would happen. I only wanted to protect myself. I was told to turn in dissenters. Each man must do what he can to live." He glanced around. With a grimace, he said, "You can see it did me no good. Like you, I was betrayed."

Unexpectedly, Yuri's hatred diminished. He looked at the cowering man, and for the first time saw another victim.

He heard the crunch of snow behind him, but before he could turn to look, his head exploded with pain and blackness was all he knew.

CHAPTER 8

Yuri struggled to open his eyes. Light penetrated the back of his eyes, and pain roared through his head. As he pressed his hands against the sides of his skull, he rolled onto his back. His muscles and joints ached and felt stiff. He held still and waited for the pain to pass.

Carefully removing his hands, he opened his eyes and tried to focus. Were the walls frozen? He pushed himself up on one arm, but the throbbing in his head thundered and the room spun wildly as nausea swept over him. Immediately, he laid back down, pressed his fists against his eyes, and tried to stop the whirling.

Every place his body touched the floor, he could feel its icy chill. Shivering from the cold, he did his best to hold still. It increased the pain, but he couldn't stop the convulsive shaking.

His hands felt the frozen floor. He had to get up. Bracing against the return of spinning and nausea, he rolled over and pushed himself to his hands and knees. The room whirled, and he waited for it to pass. Gradually, it lessened, and he pushed himself to his feet. He closed his eyes for a moment, hoping the throbbing in his head would ease. When it didn't, he guardedly opened them and studied his surroundings more closely. He stood in a small chamber overlaid with ice. The walls reached up above him to about ten feet, but there was no ceiling. He could see wispy clouds laced across a blue sky. *The isolator! I'm in the isolator!*

He tried to think back, but his thoughts were muddled. *Why am I here?* He could see Saodat's face in his mind; then he remembered standing over the frightened man, holding an axe. Saodat had begged for his life. He couldn't recall anything after that. Had he killed him? Yuri groaned and leaned against the wall. "How could I have been so foolish? They'll never let me out. I'll die here."

He slid down the wall and sat with his legs tucked close to his body. Only then did he realize he no longer wore his coat and boots. A wool blanket lay in a heap. Moving slowly, he took it and, sitting on a corner of it, pulled the rest around his body. Gritting his teeth, he fought to control his shaking.

He peered up at the small patch of sky. It was a pale blue. That meant the temperature would plummet at nightfall. He had to get out! He would die here! Standing, he reached his hands up the wall and shouted, "Let me out! Let me out!"

A guard appeared above. "So, you want out," he taunted. "Tell me, why I should help you? Is there something you can do for me?" He laughed. "Is there? Come on, tell me."

Yuri looked at the man but said nothing.

"We don't tolerate murderers here."

"I didn't kill anyone," Yuri said, hoping his words were true.

"You would have. If we let you prisoners get away with murder, we'd have chaos. And we couldn't have that, now could we?"

"I just went a little crazy. It will never happen again." Yuri hated himself for begging, but he wanted to live. "Let me out, and I will show you."

"You're right. You won't do anything like that again because by the time we drag you out of there, you won't be able to tie your own shoes, let alone threaten anyone." The man disappeared for a moment, then tossed down a chunk of heavy bread. "Here. Enjoy." His cruel laughter echoed from above.

Yuri picked up the bread and stared at it, then took a bite. It was dry and hard to swallow. He was thirsty, but there was no water. "Please, can I have some water?"

There was no answer from above.

Yuri finished the bread, tucked the blanket around him, then sat, leaning against the wall, and tried to sleep. He felt alone and hated the silence. Still unable to quiet his shaking, he pulled his legs tightly against his chest, laid his arms across his knees, and held them tight. *God, how could you allow a man's life to come to this?*

His mind wandered back over his days on the farm. He longed for the warmth of the sun and smell of fresh-cut hay. He smiled as he pictured his father atop the wagon, calling for him to toss up more hay. No matter how hard Yuri worked, he could never keep up with him.

Those had been good times. Now they seemed unreal, like a distant dream.

Yuri slept. When he woke, the sky was dark. Still shivering, he looked around his cell. He could see nothing in the blackness. Curled up in the corner of the icy cell, he focused his attention on the upper edge of the hole where the camp lights gave a little illumination. *How will I live?* he asked himself as he looked at the heavens. He could see no stars. *Keep moving. Keep moving,* he repeated.

Tearing off strips of blanket, he tied the cloth around his feet and pushed himself upright. His head pounded, and the cubicle spun. Pressing his hand against the wall, he struggled to keep from retching, refusing to give back any nourishment. *I will show them. I will live.*

The back of his head ached and he gingerly touched his scalp. His hair was matted and sticky. *Probably used the butt of a rifle on me,* he thought.

His anger rose. The guards relished savagery. He pounded his fist into the palm of his other hand. "You will not win," he almost shouted, his voice echoing in the deep pit. Even as he spoke, he remembered his own inhumanity and felt sick inside. When he'd gone after Saodat, he would have killed him if he hadn't been stopped.

Feeling his way in the dark, he took three steps to the wall, then turned and took three steps back. He continued his strange march, knowing inactivity would mean death. His breath froze to his beard and mustache.

He thought of Saodat. As he considered the man, guilt prodded Yuri. He tried to push the emotion away, telling himself that he deserved to die, but he felt no conviction. Wasn't Saodat a victim just as he was? Like so many others, the little man had believed Joseph Stalin's persuasive words. And now he had become one of the madman's casualties as the leader played his cruel game.

Yuri's anger faltered, and he heard a voice in his mind say, "Forgive." He didn't want to listen, but the voice persisted. "You must forgive or you are no better than your enemy."

Yuri pressed his hands against his ears. "I can't. I can't." He looked up at the sky, wondering if the voice belonged to God. "Is it you? God, is it you?"

CHAPTER *8*

A light shown above. "Are you looking for God?" a guard said laughingly. "He's not here. He's forgotten you."

Biting back an angry response, Yuri glared at the man. He wanted to tell him how he hated him but knew better. He'd seen irate guards throw water down on prisoners locked in the isolator.

He returned to pacing. "He's right. God isn't here," he muttered under his breath. "You're stupid, Yuri. You've killed yourself."

The light disappeared, and Yuri heard the guard leave. Through the night, he ignored the pain in his body and continued to walk. Finally, exhausted, he slid to the floor and pulled the blanket around him. "God, do you know I am here?" he asked, despair enveloping him.

His mind filled with images of Elena. She was so beautiful. He smiled as he remembered her strength. When she'd been beside him facing the possibility of execution, she didn't plead for mercy or cry but had stood bravely. Her flashing brown eyes and proud smile haunted him, and he felt empty, knowing that he might never see her again.

As he tried to sleep, he thought of Tatyana. The last time he'd seen her was at the Moscow train station. She'd begged him to let her stay. "Thank God I made you go," he whispered. He tried to envision what her life was like in America but couldn't imagine it.

Resting his head on his knees, he closed his eyes. Even though the cold penetrated his blanket, he finally slept. When he woke, the darkness remained. Huddling in the blackness, he tried to ignore his gnawing hunger. But worse than that was his thirst. No matter how hard he tried, it couldn't be restrained. He needed something, anything to wet his tongue. Desperately, he dug his fingernails into the frozen wall and chipped off a piece of ice. He shoved it in his mouth. It tasted of mildew and dirt, but as it melted, his thirst eased.

Two days passed. All Yuri knew was cold, pain, thirst, and hunger. He slept more and walked less. His strength was failing.

Twice a day, bread was tossed down and, hands trembling, he snatched it up and ate it. He forced himself to take tiny bites, making it last longer. It did little to ease the ache in his stomach.

The morning of the third day, Yuri knew it would be his last. He had no strength to walk, and his thirst couldn't be satiated with the small bits of ice he managed to chip from the wall. Plus, he'd started coughing the day before, and his lungs hurt. He wouldn't make it through another night. Huddled on the frigid floor, he prayed, "God, I can't do this. I can't fight anymore. It hurts too much. I want to die. Let me die. *Please,* let me die."

Death stood waiting and promised him peace.

When bread was thrown down that day, he made no move to pick it up. He stared at it, then closed his eyes.

If only Alexander were here, I would be all right. I wouldn't have to die alone. As Yuri considered his friend, he almost smiled. He was an unusual man, possessing a magic that each day brought renewed hope. He had often rankled Yuri, his constant unwavering faith a reminder of what Yuri didn't possess. But now, he yearned for the man's soothing and powerful words.

Painful hacking coughs shook his body, and Yuri struggled to breathe. When the coughing subsided, he tried to imagine that his friend was with him. *I need you, Alexander,* he thought.

"No. You need me," came the calm voice Yuri had heard before.

He opened his eyes. Was there someone in the cell with him? There was no one. Could it be God? No. God didn't love him anymore. How could he? After all, Yuri had turned his back on him. Yuri looked at the gray sky, afraid to hope. "God, are you here?" He closed his eyes. "I need you. I have failed you. Please forgive me."

Again, he heard the voice, "I never stopped loving you. I will never leave you nor forsake you."

Yuri felt peace wash over him, and he slept.

The next thing he knew, arms jerked him off the floor. They dragged him up a ladder, then across the grounds and into the barracks. He tried to open his eyes, but they were crusted shut. He was tossed onto a bed and left.

Yuri lay still. To even move his legs was too difficult. They felt disconnected from his body. The blackness closed in again, and he tried to hold it back, but despite his efforts, he knew no more.

When he gradually regained consciousness, he heard Alexander's hushed voice.

"You will be all right, my friend. God is with you."

Yuri could feel a blanket being tucked around him, and he tried to open his eyes, but they were stuck closed. Cold, he shivered, and the pain in his joints swelled. A cough from deep in his lungs choked him, and someone lifted his shoulders up. He could feel a soothing hand on his face.

"Father, Yuri is yours. I trust him to you," Alexander prayed.

Yuri managed to open his eyes a little. Peering through slits, he saw Alexander sitting on the bed beside him. "I will live," he whispered. Another cough shook his body.

Keeping his arm around Yuri, Alexander said, "God loves you. He has a plan for you. Hang on."

Numb, Yuri tried to comprehend the words. *A plan? How can that be? I betrayed God. He has no plans for me.* Grief washed over him. He'd been so far from God for so long. "I'm sorry. I'm sorry. Forgive me."

"God has forgiven you," Alexander said gently.

Yuri strained to remain alert. "Alexander? I needed you, but you weren't there."

"I'm here now." His voice tender, it reminded Yuri of his mother's. Oh, how he missed her.

"Here, drink this." Alexander gently pressed a bowl against his lips.

It smelled like *balanda*. Yuri sipped the hot liquid. It tasted of fish.

"A little more."

He tried to take more, but the darkness pressed in again and his head rolled back.

"Yuri, you must try," he said firmly.

Yuri lifted his head and opened his mouth, allowing the soup to flow down his throat. Unable to swallow fast enough, he sputtered and choked. Pushing the dish aside, he said, "No more."

"All right." Alexander lowered him to the mattress.

Yuri sank into the blessed sanctuary of sleep.

Hours later, when he awoke, Yuri felt stronger. His eyes were still crusted, so he wet his finger and rubbed it back and forth across his eyelids. Blinking, his vision was still blurry. He stared hard at a hazy image beside his bed. "Is that you, Alexander?" he asked in a raspy voice.

"It is." The tall, lean man sat on the edge of the bed. "You look better." He smiled. "I have food. Can you eat?"

"I think so." A cough shuddered through Yuri. After it quieted, Alexander helped him to sit up. His vision cleared a little, and he studied the barracks. It looked foreign, as if he'd been gone a long time. Sunlight flowed through an open door and cut a wedge across the muddy floor. He focused on Alexander's face. "Why aren't you working?"

"It is our resting day." With a furtive glance at the doors, Alexander held out a small chunk of meat. "Eat this."

Yuri looked at the food in amazement. "Where did you get meat?" He shoved it in his mouth and chewed slowly; the effort almost too much.

Alexander ignored the question and gave him another bite.

Yuri took it gratefully.

"I saved a little bread for you too. I couldn't sneak out any soup. Here." He handed his friend a crust of heavy bread.

Yuri ate it, then laid back. "Thank you." He quickly fell asleep.

The next time he woke, Yuri felt better and pushed himself up on one arm. His head spun, but the dizziness quickly subsided. The barracks were empty, and sunlight no longer brightened the dreary, empty building.

Everyone is working, he decided and tried to sit up, but it was too much, and he laid back down. The effort brought on a coughing fit, and a sharp pain stabbed his lungs. He pressed his hand against his chest. *Pneumonia.* He knew the symptoms. He'd seen many succumb, especially after being punished in the isolator. To live would be a miracle. Trying to close out the cold, he pulled his blankets up under his chin. Had he imagined his meeting with God or had it been real? *I must have been delirious,* he decided, depression settling over him.

When Alexander came in with the work crew that night, Yuri was able to sit up in his bunk. He ate the bread Alexander brought him.

"The man you attacked, who is he?" Alexander asked.

Yuri took an unsteady breath. He dared not breathe too deeply or set off coughing spasms. "His name is Saodat. He's the one who turned me in to the NKVD." He looked at the floor. "I didn't know I hated him so much, but when I saw him . . . I'm ashamed of what I did."

Alexander rested his hand on Yuri's forearm. "It wasn't the hate of one man, but the bitterness you carry from injustices to you and your family. I understand. You have experienced overwhelming pain, and you allowed it to grow. With each additional wrong, your hatred has swelled and festered like a boil within you."

Yuri handed the bowl to Alexander and laid down. "I know, but how can I not hate?"

"God can help you."

Yuri still didn't know if his experience in the *isolator* was real or imagined. He wasn't ready to talk about it. He needed time to think. He pulled his blankets up beneath his chin and realized he had an extra cover. He looked at Alexander. "Is this yours?"

His friend didn't answer.

Yuri threw the blanket back. "I cannot keep it. You need it."

"I do not. You are the one with a lung infection. When you are better, you will return it."

Yuri was too weak to argue. "You are a good man." Remembering the meat, he wondered if he'd dreamed eating it. "Did I imagine you gave me meat?"

"No."

"Where did you get it?"

Alexander raised one eyebrow and half grinned. "Are you certain you want to know?"

Yuri nodded.

"I have a friend who taught me how to trap rats. It's not difficult once you know how."

"Rats?" Yuri couldn't believe he'd eaten rat meat. Since being imprisoned, he'd eaten things he'd never imagined, but he had always believed rats were vermin and filthy. "I . . . I never thought of eating them." He looked at his friend. With a half smile, he added, "It did taste good. You will have to teach me how to catch them."

Alexander rested his hand on Yuri's shoulder. "God supplies our needs, sometimes not the way we want or expect, but he takes care of us."

Yuri wished he would stop bringing up God. He still didn't know what he believed. Had God been with him in the *isolator?* Once he'd known God, but now? He looked at Alexander. "I am not certain I know where God is. Or if he cares about any of us."

"He is here, and he cares. Are you still alive?"

"Yes, but . . ."

"And did he not provide someone to care for you?"

"Yes," Yuri had to admit.

"We will live one day at a time, and he will reveal himself to us."

"Do you think he would help us escape?" Yuri grabbed Alexander's hand. In a whisper, he said, "We must escape." His eyes roamed over the barracks. "There has to be a way."

"No. We *must* wait on God. He has a purpose for our being here."

Disbelief swept over Yuri. "Here? What can we do here? It is a place of torture and death."

"That is what I mean. We're needed."

"I do not think I'm ready to be part of a saintly calling."

"When *will* you be ready?" He held the young man's gaze.

Yuri looked away.

"You cannot run from God. Once his, you always belong to him."

"I'm not sure what I believe anymore. I lost my family and friends. I watched as my uncle was dragged off to be shot." He turned and looked at Alexander. "Why didn't God help us then? How can you expect me to serve a God who abandoned the people I love?"

"You can't. Not until you forgive," Alexander said evenly. "Hating is poison, Yuri. It will destroy you."

Yuri stared at Alexander. He had no rebuttal. He could feel the toxin of bitterness within himself.

"Yuri, have you ever considered that you might be blaming the wrong one for your suffering? God did not cause any of it. He didn't want puppets, so he gave man the freedom to choose good or evil. In this world, we live with the choices of others. Stalin's insanity touches us all. But it is not God." He stood up. "You must choose. Whom will you serve?"

Still not looking at Alexander, Yuri said quietly, "How can I choose God when all that's around me is evil?"

"You must search for goodness. You cannot see if your heart is closed. Look for God."

"Once, that was all I saw. After I was arrested and he left me in prison . . ." his voice trailed off. "All that is left is evil . . . except for you. I see God in you. I do not know what would have happened to me if you weren't here."

Alexander gazed out the doorway. "This is an evil place, but it doesn't mean God has ceased to exist. Even in the midst of depravity, he seeks hearts that long for him and have compassion for others." Alexander looked back at Yuri. "God gave everything he had for us. Jesus allowed himself to be hung on a cross, took on the sins of the world, and died because he knew you would need him. He didn't have to. He is God." His voice shook with emotion. "Those who belong to the Lord have a higher calling. God has a purpose for our being here."

Alexander's words pierced Yuri's heart. God *was* real and living and had never forsaken him or his family. He'd always been there beside them. *How could I have been so deceived?* The words of his parents flowed over him. "Never let down your guard. When you do, the enemy will ambush you," they'd said many times. Yuri had forgotten their warning and lowered his defenses. And when bitterness took root, it devoured God's goodness in him.

Anguish spread through Yuri, and he closed his eyes. *I have hated you. Please, forgive me.* Tears coursed down his cheeks. God's deep love blanketed him, and joy replaced torment. Yuri knew he would no longer feel alone.

He felt a touch on his shoulder and looked up. Alexander stood over him, compassion on his face. Gently, he said, "Who shall separate us from the love of Christ? Shall tribulation, or distress, or persecution, or famine, or nakedness, or peril, or sword? As it is written: For your sake we are killed all day long; we are accounted as sheep for the slaughter. Yet in all these things we are more than conquerors through Him who loved us."

CHAPTER 9

Doing his best to keep up with the line of workers, Yuri stumbled, still weak from his ordeal in the isolator. His lungs burned with each breath, his body ached, and fever caused bouts of dizziness. He should have been in bed.

Yuri gripped his axe handle, determined to work and live. Glancing heavenward, he prayed for strength. Smiling, he thought about his recovery. Although it had been only a few days, it was a time of rebuilding. God had used Alexander to provide physical care as well as spiritual nurturing, and Yuri had grown stronger. He glanced at the tall, gaunt man. He'd truly been an example of Christ's compassion and mercy. If not for his kindness, Yuri knew he would never have made it. He would have remained incapacitated and been transferred to the infirmary. There, patients died with little or no care. *Thank you for Alexander,* he prayed.

He turned his attention to the path, grateful for those who went before him and packed it down. He placed one foot in front of the other, careful to stay out of the deep snow.

"Move!" shouted a guard. "If you want to make your quotas for the day, you'll have to move faster!"

The prisoners increased their pace. The man's voice grated on Yuri, and anger surged once again. But this time, instead of allowing it to grab hold, he prayed and asked for God's help in releasing it. Immediately, his hostility ebbed.

He gazed over the plain of white stretching endlessly in three directions, stopping only at the nearby forest. A shimmering sun rested just above the horizon. It gave little warmth yet fed the soul. Yuri contemplated God and how he had known the heart of man as he set the heavens in place. In setting such splendor before humankind, he'd nourished the spirit as well as confirmed his very existence. *How can anyone look upon creation and not believe in the Creator?* Yuri wondered and was immediately reminded of his own blindness.

"Don't stare too long," Alexander warned. "You'll hurt your eyes."

Yuri looked at his friend. He was a blur of light. Blinking, he laughed. "You're right. Either that or you're an angel."

"It's good to see you laugh." Alexander clapped Yuri on the shoulder.

"It feels good." He shook his head. "I've missed so much, locked inside my hatred. It's amazing how it blinded me. I've been here months and never seen any beauty. Today, I see God's glory. He's given me new eyes."

"My heart is warmed by your words," Alexander said, his voice breaking. "The angels in heaven rejoice."

When they reached the forest, Yuri felt anxious. What if he couldn't complete his quota? He studied the timber that needed to be loaded onto the sleds and prayed silently, *Father, I need your strength.*

A guard pointed at Yuri and three others. "You, you, you, and you will carry limbs and brush."

Relieved, Yuri immediately began picking through the scrap.

"You," he pointed at Yuri again. "Work with him," he said and nodded at a man hunched over a pile of brush. Folding his arms across his chest, the guard grinned maliciously.

The other prisoner straightened and stared at Yuri through frightened eyes. Saodat!

Yuri studied the frail, thin man. Saodat couldn't hide his wounds, his bereft face revealing his hopelessness. His gauntness and sorrowful eyes told of his wretchedness. Instead of the anticipated hatred, compassion welled up within Yuri.

As he wondered how to ease Saodat's anguish, he realized God's love had truly transformed him. The power of the Almighty could do the impossible. He said nothing as he began piling brush.

Throughout the day, Saodat kept as much distance between himself and Yuri as possible. More than once, Yuri found the man watching him suspiciously. Wishing to convey his remorse over the earlier attack, Yuri tried to hold his gaze, but Saodat always averted his eyes. Once he smiled, but Saodat obviously misunderstood the gesture. Fear flickered across the man's face, and he moved several paces further away.

Undaunted, Yuri watched and waited for an opportunity. When Saodat lugged an armload of branches to the fire, Yuri followed. Standing close to the man, he threw his load into the blaze and whispered, "Please do not be frightened. I will not hurt you. I am sorry for what I did."

Saodat glared at Yuri, then glanced back at the overseers. No one seemed to be paying attention. "You can't deceive me so easily. I know how things work. You'll wait until my defenses are down and then get your revenge. Do you think me to be so stupid?" he spat and hurried away.

Yuri wanted to be angry. After all, he'd done everything he could, and still, the man was contemptuous. Even as the thoughts came, he knew they were wrong. He needed to try harder. If not, Saodat might never know the hope of Christ. Yuri decided to wait for God to provide an opportunity and stopped thinking about him.

As the day wore on, Yuri's strength waned, and his body refused to obey. Each step became a struggle. His fever rose, and the cold air burned his lungs. He coughed and coughed, trying to clear away thick mucous clogging his airways. Unable to work steadily, it became clear he'd never make his quota, and his food ration would be small.

As darkness gathered over the frigid plain, Yuri moved toward the fire. His mind confused by fever, he carelessly cut a new path through deep snow. Finally, dropping his armload of brush into the flames, he took a deep breath. Pain seared his lungs, and a strangled cough escaped his lips. He struggled for air, and his legs buckled. Resting on his knees, he stared into the flames, knowing the guards would soon be upon him.

"You! Get back to work!"

Yuri didn't look up.

"I said, get to work!"

Finally, Yuri stared at the man. There was no compassion in his eyes. "I just need to rest a little."

"He is fine," Alexander said amiably as he approached. Putting his hands under Yuri's armpits, he hefted him to his feet. "The day is nearly through," he whispered. "You must continue. You can do it."

Yuri nodded. "I can do it," he repeated. "I will work." Leaning on his friend, he made his way back to the waiting brush.

Before returning to his saw, Alexander said, "God is all powerful. Remember he will enable you to do what you cannot. He has not forsaken you."

Yuri nodded. As he picked up branches, his mind pulsed with the words, *God enables, God enables . . .* Sweat broke out on his forehead and trickled into his eyes.

"You will stop!" shouted a guard.

Yuri looked to see who was the guard's target. Several yards beyond the fire, a man plowed through the snow and headed toward the vast plain. Buried to his knees, he lunged toward freedom. Pulling one leg free from the deep snow, he leaped in a lopsided way and was buried to his thighs. Forced to stop, he glanced over his shoulder and tried to push through.

"Stop!"

The man clawed at the frozen field and managed to put one leg in front of him.

"Stop! I will shoot!" The soldier placed his rifle on his shoulder and sighted in on the man.

The prisoner continued to struggle forward.

"Don't shoot!" Yuri heard himself cry.

A sharp report splintered the barren, white world. The man stumbled but didn't stop.

Yuri wished he could hurry him and leaned forward as he mentally urged the man on. *Go. Go. Faster.*

Another blast came from the gun, and the prisoner pitched forward. Blood bubbled from a wound on his forehead, coloring the snow crimson. He didn't move.

Yuri went after him, following the trail he'd cut through the deep powder. All he could think about was the man dying alone and how wrong that would be.

"You will be still," a guard ordered.

Yuri stopped. "He needs help."

"He is beyond that. Back to work."

Yuri stared at the officer, then glanced at the injured man. There was no movement from his body. He looked back at the soldier, feeling the old loathing surge. For a moment, he clung to the insidious emotion, wanting to hate, but the voice in his mind said, "No." Instead, he prayed, *Lord, help me to be like Christ. Help me to love.* He glanced at the guard. "May God forgive you," he said quietly and headed back to his work.

"What did you say?"

Yuri took a slow, even breath. He knew that speaking the truth could mean death. But he turned and faced the man saying, "God forgive you. I will pray he has mercy on you."

Holding the rifle across his chest, the guard stared at his prisoner but said nothing. Yuri detected a glimmer of interest behind his eyes and was reminded that the enemy is not flesh and blood, but powers and principalities. The battle could not be won in the flesh.

As if knowing he'd revealed his humanity, the guard pointed his rifle at Yuri and spat, "Back to work."

Yuri turned away but couldn't help smiling. God had given him a glimpse of truth. Clearly, the enemy was not man, but Satan.

Psalm 103 played through Yuri's mind. Often as a child, he'd sung it with his family. As he worked, the music filled his thoughts. He hummed quietly to himself, then, without realizing it, the tune flowed from him, his tenor voice faltering and weak. As he sang of God's mercy and love, strength returned to his vocal chords, and the pain in his lungs diminished. Momentarily, some of the men stopped their work and listened. Yuri didn't notice as he sang louder. The guards said nothing. The song echoed throughout the woods, bringing with it a sense of serenity. The men worked more steadily and quickly, and there were no further disruptions.

When the guards ordered the prisoners back to camp, Yuri rejoiced that he'd made it through the day. When he looked at his work area, he realized he'd filled his quota.

The trip back to camp was difficult. Yuri could feel the sickness in his lungs, although not as badly as before. He sucked at thin air, yet he didn't feel defeated. To Alexander who walked beside him, he said, "I wish I had opened my eyes sooner."

"God's timing is perfect, Comrade," Alexander said, just as his foot dropped into a deep trough of snow and he tumbled onto his face. Pulling himself upright, he offered Yuri a wry grin and said, "There are surprises everywhere."

A line of new prisoners marched toward the front gate. As the zeks drew closer, Yuri realized they were all women. Eyes wide with fear, they stood waiting for permission to pass through the entrance and into a world they could not imagine. Ragged clothing hung on bony frames. Shivering, many huddled together, desperation and hopelessness etched into their faces.

One woman caught Yuri's attention. Very pregnant, she stood unwavering, cradling her swollen belly. Sorrow enveloped him, and he mourned over what she faced. *Lord, help her.*

The woman looked at Yuri, and their eyes locked. Surprisingly, Yuri didn't see fear there, but steadiness. He was reminded of the first time he'd met Alexander. She had the same look. He knew she believed.

She smiled softly.

Yuri nodded slightly and smiled back. A need to hold a woman in his arms, to love and be loved, swept over him. He wanted to spend time with her and talk of their faith in God. Keeping his eyes on hers, he thought, *I will pray for you.* He hoped that somehow she understood.

The guards ogled the women and yelled obscenities.

The pregnant one blushed and looked at the ground. A large woman bumped into her, knocking her to her knees. "Watch out," she said. "Stay out of my way."

Without thinking, Yuri took a step toward the woman, intent on her defense.

Alexander grabbed his arm. "There is nothing you can do."

"What will happen to her?" asked Yuri.

Alexander didn't answer for a long moment. Then, his voice quiet, he said, "We cannot know, but God does. She is not alone."

"She will probably die. And the baby . . ."

"Remember, God is here. And death is not the end, but a new beginning. If she believes, and *if* her life ends here, she will find freedom from the shackles she wears." He took a deep breath. "Death will come to each of us. Until then, we must do all we can to serve God."

As Yuri watched, he anguished over the young woman. When she pushed herself to her feet, she looked kindly into her assailant's eyes and said something. For a moment, it looked like the large woman would hit her, but she finally backed off and found another place in line.

Yuri felt a proud sort of sorrow spread through him. Clearly, this woman was a child of God. He understood her life would probably be short, but as Alexander had said, heaven waited, a place where she would never hunger or thirst, a place of matchless love.

The guards herded Yuri and the other prisoners past the women. He found the young woman's eyes one more time and smiled encouragement. She nodded.

※ ※ ※ ※ ※

That night, as Yuri lay in his bunk, he thought of the woman. *Father, take good care of her and the baby. I pray it is your will that they live long lives, but if you claim them soon, do not let them suffer unduly.*

He thought of Daniel and Tanya and wondered where they were and if they had avoided arrest. He missed them and longed for the times when they'd sat around the table sharing stories of God's faithfulness. Elena's exquisite face haunted him. Sorrow had always hidden behind her brown eyes. Without the Savior, how would she face the inevitable struggles? She must be frightened. He hoped that one day they would talk of spiritual things and he could share how real God was and how much God longed for her to know him.

In order for him to see his loved ones, Yuri knew it would take a miracle, but he also understood that miracles were not beyond God's ability, if he chose to do them. He wondered if Elena were in a prison somewhere. The thought wrenched at him. He couldn't bear for her to suffer. *I give her to you, Father,* he prayed.

As his eyes grew heavy and sleep beckoned, Tatyana filled his mind, and he hoped she was living a good life in America. He smiled, wondering what adventures she'd had. *One day, we will be reunited. If not here, then in heaven. I love you, little sister,* was his last thought as sleep overtook him.

CHAPTER *10*

TATYANA PULLED ON A SWEATER. These days, she could never get warm. Arms folded across her chest, she stared out the front window. The rain had stopped. "I better go now before it begins again," she said with a sigh.

Taking her coat from the hook by the door, she pulled it on, then grabbed her hat and placed it on her head. She looked in the mirror and pinned the hat. Taking crumpled gloves from her coat pocket, she pulled them on.

Hurriedly, she crossed to the kitchen and grabbed her change purse from the table. Dropping it into a shopping basket, she hung the wicker container over her arm and walked out the front door.

She stopped for a moment on the porch and took a deep breath, enjoying the crispness in the air. A slate gray sky promised snow. *I hope it does snow. A white blanket would brighten the dreariness.* She studied the curtain of clouds where she'd been told the mountain stood. Since arriving in Black Diamond three weeks before, heavy clouds had clung to the hillsides, concealing the mountain range, and she'd never seen it.

Mount Rainier was one of the tallest peaks in America, and people were proud of it. Many described it as a benevolent sentinel standing guard over the foothills and lowlands of the Green River Valley. Tatyana wished it would reveal itself.

Adjusting her gloves, she stepped onto the gravel path and headed toward the company store on Railroad Avenue. Being outdoors made her feel more energetic. Taking long strides and swinging her free arm, she lifted her head and smiled.

Among patches of bushes, bright red and black berries still clung to their vines, remnants left from the summer crop. Picking berries during the summer would be fun. She could make jams and pies. Dimitri loved pie.

Some homes had thick green yards with neat flowerbeds, now devoid of blossoms, framing the houses and edges of their lots. Tatyana imagined how her home would look when spring arrived and her own flowers bloomed. Of course, she'd have to plant some. *I will ask Susie what kinds grow here.*

The wind bent a tall cedar; its top seemed to reach nearly to the clouds. She thought how much more beautiful it must look on a sunny day. Although many living here loved the greenery, she would prefer more sunshine and less foliage. The constant wetness and dreary days felt oppressive, and she longed for more sunshine. Even heating the house was a greater chore here than in New York. Dampness permeated every corner, and it never felt warm. When she moved into the home, mold had to be scrubbed off the walls. She'd been told that before winter passed, the chore would have to be repeated more than once.

Just that morning, Dimitri had smiled broadly and hugged her, saying, "It's only lush like this because of the rain. We can't have one without the other." She hadn't said anything, only reached up and gently brushed aside the blonde curl that always fell onto his forehead. Smiling at the memory, she thought, *Rain or not, I love being with Dimitri.* He loved the abundant greenery, and she needed to try harder to appreciate what God had given.

She considered the handsome man who's life she shared. He worked hard but hadn't forsaken his enjoyment of life. He liked to tease, and she loved how he made her laugh. Since her arrival, they had grown even more comfortable with each other, exchanging new ideas, hopes, and fears. *I can tell him anything and he'll understand,* she told herself. Even as she said it, she knew she wasn't being completely truthful. Why couldn't she talk to him about how she missed her homeland and family?

It would only hurt him, she decided. *There is no reason to do that. For now, it is enough to be his wife.*

She'd done all she knew to make a nice home for Dimitri, making sure to have dinner ready when he came in from work and keeping the house spotlessly clean. She even baked his favorite dessert, apple pie, when Susie gave them some fall apples.

Susie had become a good friend, helping in any way she could. She gave Tatyana two feed sacks with a yellow background and red paisley design and showed her how to make draperies from them. Using Susie's sewing machine, the two women completed the set in one afternoon. When they finished, the curtains no longer looked anything like feed sacks, and they dressed up the front windows beautifully.

Tatyana enjoyed being in charge of her home, and as the days passed, gained confidence. But, she missed her family in New York and the constant bustle of activity. Her house felt empty in comparison. One day she and Dimitri would share it with their children. Smiling, she imagined the noise and laughter of towheaded youngsters.

A group of three girls, each carrying a lunch pail in one hand and school books in the other, approached. They smiled shyly. "Good morning," one of them said, her freckled face brightening with her smile.

"Good morning," Tatyana said, thinking, *One day, my children will walk to school just like these girls.* She watched them as they stopped and admired two older boys crossing the street. Giggling, they followed the boys, careful to stay a safe distance behind. The young fellows looked over their shoulders but didn't hurry their steps.

A drop of rain splattered her cheek. The sky had darkened. "I'd better hurry," she said, picking up her pace.

When she reached the company store, the rain still fell in sporadic drops. Maybe it would hold off until she made it home.

Her boots echoed on the wooden boardwalk. Excited, she stared in the front window. She didn't plan to buy much, but she still enjoyed looking at all the merchandise. On her first visit, she'd been surprised at the array of items the store carried. She hadn't expected to find so much in a small town. Shelves were piled with beautiful coverlets, throw rugs, pots and pans, clothing, food, sewing supplies, hardware, and even toys. One particular item caught her eye, a phonograph set in an oak case. Each time she visited, Tatyana stood in front of the machine admiring it and thinking about how the music it played would warm her home.

The bell over the door jingled, and Tatyana looked up. She'd been daydreaming. Blushing, she looked at the proprietor, Tom Robertson, standing in the doorway.

"So, do you plan to do your shopping from out here?" he asked with a friendly smile.

"Good morning, Mr. Robertson. I was just thinking." She stepped inside. Watching the robust man make his way to the back of the store, she smiled. From her first visit, she'd liked him. His round face always looked flushed, as if he'd spent too much time in the sun, and he always seemed to be smiling. His eyes were warm and spirited, as if containing some secret delight.

When she first visited the shop, he'd told her how things worked at the company store. He showed her the ledger where he wrote the amounts of her purchases and explained that the money was deducted from her husband's pay.

Tatyana wandered through the store and, before she realized it, found herself back at the front window where the phonograph stood. She ran her hand over the rich wood.

"You sure do like that, don't you?"

Tatyana felt heat flush her cheeks. "It is beautiful. I have records from my homeland. They would sound wonderful on this." Keeping her hand on it, she stepped back a little. "Maybe one day."

"Sometimes, items in the store go on sale. Maybe this will, one day."

"On sale?"

"That means we lower the price for a few days."

Tatyana was puzzled over such an arrangement. "Why do you do that?"

"It helps sell items that have been on the shelf too long. Or, if we need to make room for new supplies, then we have to sell things in a hurry. The company lets me know when to mark down prices."

Tatyana liked the idea. "You will tell me when you have a sale?"

"Absolutely. I'll make a note of it." He took out a pad and wrote in it, then looked back at Tatyana. "Now, what can I get for you today?"

"I need butter and cheese."

Heading back toward the counter, Mr. Robertson asked, "How much?"

Tatyana followed him. "I think a pound of butter and two pounds of cheese will be enough. Dimitri likes to eat a cheese sandwich for his lunch."

The door bell jingled as someone entered the store. Tatyana turned, and when she saw it was Susie, smiled and said, "Good morning."

"How are you, Susie?" Mr. Robertson asked.

"Good." She looked at Tatyana. "I was hoping I might see you today."

"Why are you not at work?" Tatyana asked.

"I wasn't feeling well this morning, so I stayed in bed. I'm much better now." She scanned the shelves behind Mr. Robertson. "I was hoping you had some saltines."

"Saltines? I sure do." He studied her, his eyes sparkling mischievously. "Saltines, huh?"

Susie ignored the comment.

Mr. Robertson looked at Tatyana. "The cheese and butter are in the cooler. I'll be right back." Tightening his apron, he stepped through a door in the back wall.

Susie took Tatyana's hands in hers and, her face bright, said, "I just have to tell someone! You promise not to say a thing?"

Tatyana nodded.

"I think I'm going to have a baby!"

"That is wonderful news!" Tatyana gave her friend a hug. "When?"

"Early summer, maybe."

"That is a very good time."

"It's perfect."

Mr. Robertson returned with a hunk of cheese and butter. He cut two sheets of paper off a roll and wrapped the items, then taped them closed. Setting them on the counter, he wrote the purchases in his ledger. "Let me know if you need anything else."

"Thank you," Tatyana said, putting the items in her basket.

Tom set a tin of crackers on the counter, and Susie picked them up. "Thank you." Then she turned to Tatyana. "Why don't you come to my house, and I'll make us some tea?"

"I would like that." Then she looked at Mr. Robertson and said, "Thank you, again."

"You're welcome. Have a good day, and say hello to that young husband of yours."

"Bye, Tom," Susie said, taking Tatyana's arm and leading her out of the store.

"In America, stores are such a wonder. Here, people go in and buy what they need. It is not so easy in Russia. There is never enough."

"What did you do?"

"The government took most of what we had, and we lived with less. Many were hungry." Not wanting to talk about Russia and sorry she'd brought up the subject, Tatyana asked, "What will you do when the baby comes? About your job?"

"I'll have to quit to take care of the baby. Money will be tighter. I'll have to change my shopping habits, but it's worth it." She glanced at the sky. "Looks like snow. I always liked snow. It would be nice for Thanksgiving."

"I remember Thanksgiving. Last year I had a nice Thanksgiving with the Broidos."

"Maybe we could celebrate it together. My parents will be here. I would love for them to meet you and Dimitri."

"That sounds fun. I will ask Dimitri."

Tatyana liked Susie's home. The shelves were filled with dusty knickknacks, and bright afghans were haphazardly flung over chairs. A hodgepodge of colors and textures, Susie's house wasn't the most orderly, but Tatyana felt comfortable and welcomed there. As she took off her hat and gloves, she studied a painting of a snowcapped mountain shaded by clouds and a valley stretching out below. "I have not seen this before. Did you paint it?"

Susie took off her coat and hung it in the closet. "Oh, no. I don't have a bit of talent. My mother did it. Last time we went into Seattle, she gave it to me. She loves the countryside, especially the mountain."

"It is beautiful. It is Mount Rainier?"

"Yes. I know it's hard to believe, but it really does exist. One day, you'll see it."

"Do you visit your mother often?"

"No. Carl and I don't like going into the city. And even if we did, it's not easy to make the time."

"Does she know about the baby?"

"No. I don't even know for sure yet, but if I am pregnant, I can't wait to tell her. She'll just bust. She's been wanting grandchildren." Susie went to the kitchen and filled the kettle with water. Taking a tin from the cupboard, she measured tea into cheesecloth, tied it off, and set it in the kettle.

Tatyana slipped off her coat and draped it over the end of the couch beside a pile of laundry, then joined Susie in the kitchen. She sat at the table.

Susie glanced out the window. "It sure looks like snow."

"It was raining a little this morning," Tatyana said as she folded her hands in front of her and looked around the room. "I like your kitchen. It has more light than mine."

"That's because we have two windows on this wall. You have one. Most of the places only have one. That's why I picked this house."

A vase with an assortment of green plants and cattails sat on the window sill. "That looks pretty. Where did you get it?"

Susie followed Tatyana's gaze. "I found the plants down by Lake Fourteen. I thought they'd look nice in the window."

Tatyana stood and crossed to the window. Touching the cattails, she said, "They feel like soft wood." She gently caressed a fern.

CHAPTER *10*

Susie studied the arrangement. "I like to bring the outside in." She took the whistling kettle off the heat, then set two teacups on the table. "Would you like some sugar or honey?"

"Thank you. I would like a little sugar."

Pouring tea into the cups, Susie said, "I still don't know much about you, Tatyana, except that you're from Russia and you met Dimitri in New York. Does your family live in New York?"

Tatyana sat down. Scooping out a half teaspoon of sugar, she stirred it into her tea. "My adopted family, Dimitri's family, is in New York." She set her spoon on the edge of the saucer.

Susie sat across from Tatyana.

Her voice very quiet, Tatyana continued, "I do not know what has become of my family in Russia. I am afraid they are dead." She took a sip of tea. "In 1930, soldiers came to our farm and took my mama and papa. I never saw them again." A gust of wind moaned, and a spindly rose branch scraped the window. "In Russia, many people disappear."

Susie reached out and placed her hand on Tatyana's. "I am so sorry. It must have been awful."

"Yes." She gazed at her tea. "My brother Yuri and I lived with our aunt and uncle. They were good to us, but times got worse, and people were dying because there was no food. That is when my brother sent me to America."

"You came here all by yourself?"

Tatyana nodded. "On the boat, I met Flora Leipman." She smiled as she said her name. "She is Dimitri's aunt. That is how I got to know Dimitri and his family. They helped me when I came to New York." Leaning her elbows on the table, she cradled her chin in her hands. "When I first knew Dimitri, I thought he was very arrogant and brash. Not at all a good Russian. He flirted with me, and I was shocked. I decided it would be a mistake to get to know him." She picked up her cup. "But, God had a different plan," she said smiling. "I was so wrong about Dimitri. He is a good man, and I am very glad I am his wife." She sipped her tea.

Susie leveled a serious look at Tatyana. "I know you are happy, but sometimes I see sadness in you. Is it because of what happened in Russia?"

Tatyana studied her hands, then looked at Susie. Her eyes glistened with tears. "Yes, but more. It is very hard to talk about. You will not say anything? Not even to Carl?"

Susie laid her hand over her chest and said, "I swear, not a word."

"I am happy to be Dimitri's wife, but this is not my home. I miss Russia and my family very much. I have not heard from my brother or aunt and uncle since I left. I am afraid for them." She wiped a tear. "And when I married Dimitri, I thought I would feel better. Now I see how silly I was to believe my pain would go away because I am married. I still miss my family and Russia. It is very different here."

"It takes time to adjust, Tatyana. It always does." Susie patted her friend's hand. "You'll get used to it. You'll see." She took a drink of tea.

"I want to believe you."

"Then do." Susie sat up straighter and smiled. "So, what was Tom saying about a phonograph?"

"Oh. He has a beautiful one in his store. I would like very much to own it and play the music from my homeland."

Susie brightened. "We have one. We keep it in the bedroom most of the time because we love to lay in each other's arms and listen to music." She leaned forward with a mischievous expression. "Don't tell anyone; the men will never stop teasing Carl if they know."

Tatyana laughed. "I will say nothing."

"I think you should get your records and bring them over. I mostly listen to Duke Ellington and Guy Lombardo. I'm afraid I know nothing about Russian composers."

"Russian music is beautiful. You would really like to hear?"

"Yes."

"Then I will go and get them."

*   *   *   *   *

Tatyana set the box of records on Susie's bed. For a moment, she stared at it. "I have not opened this since I left Russia." She looked at Susie. "I will need something to pull out the nails."

"I'll get it," Susie said, jumping up and running out of the room. A few moments later, she returned, carrying a hammer. "This will do the trick."

Tatyana pried out the nails. Lifting the lid, she dug through wood shavings. "I hope none are broken." When she came to the first record, she carefully lifted it out and removed the jacket. Tenderly, she ran her fingers over the grooves.

"What record is that?"

"The composer is Peter Tchaikovsky."

Susie took it, placed it on the turntable, then pushed the switch and the record began to turn. She gently set the needle on the furthest outside ridge, stepped back, and sat on the bed beside Tatyana, who had her hands tucked between her knees.

The sweet harmonic sound of a symphony filled the room. The notes washed over Tatyana, and she closed her eyes. Transported back to her family's home, she could see her mother standing in the kitchen, apron tied snugly about her tiny waist, smiling as she swayed gently to the music. Leaning back in his chair, eyes closed, her father held his pipe in one hand and counted beats with the other. She could see Yuri standing beside the phonograph, impatient to move on to the next piece of music. He'd always been so eager. And then Tatyana saw herself, young, blonde hair flowing, pirouetting around the room, her skirt swirling away from her legs.

The scene was so vivid, that for a moment, she felt as if she were truly there. She opened her eyes, expecting to be in her snug Russian cottage.

Susie's face, flowered wallpaper, and the gray outdoors framed within the window startled her into painful reality. "Please. Please, turn it off." She cried in a strangled voice and ran out of the room.

Susie quickly removed the needle from the record and followed. "Tatyana. Wait. What is it?"

Hugging her waist, Tatyana stood at the window and stared at the unfamiliar wet world. Home had seemed so close. Without looking at Susie, she said, "I am sorry. I did not know the music would affect me so. I felt like I was home with my family. It seemed so real." She wiped away a tear. "I thought I was doing okay. I did not know . . . Sometimes, I feel lost here. America is a wonderful place, but . . ." She turned and looked at her friend. Concern creased the redhead's face. "I do thank God for his goodness, but . . ." Tatyana didn't know how to share her heart without sounding ungrateful. "Sometimes Russia calls to me, and I long to return."

Susie stepped close and put her arm around Tatyana's shoulders. "I can't know what you're feeling, but I believe if you give yourself time, this place won't feel so strange, and it will become home."

Her eyes still brimming with tears, Tatyana looked at her friend. "Do you think so?"

Susie nodded.

"I hope you are right." Tatyana sniffled and wiped away the last of her tears. "I better go." She picked up her coat and pulled it on. "We will listen to the music another time. You may keep the records for now and listen to them whenever you want."

"Thank you. I will. Already I can tell it is special, very beautiful."

"Peter Tchaikovsky is one of my favorites." Tatyana didn't bother to put on her hat and gloves. "Thank you for being my friend." With a quick hug, she stepped outside and pulled the door closed.

As Tatyana headed toward her home, the music and sadness stayed with her. Was it true? Would this place become home? She contemplated her fantasy and, with each step, realized she missed more than her homeland and family. She yearned for something she could never again have—childhood, a magical time when everything was possible. It was not something she could recapture. No one could.

She shivered. The temperature had dropped and the slate-colored clouds looked dense. A white flake drifted from the sky, and Tatyana watched until it touched the ground. Another one followed, then another and another until white crystals filled the air. She turned her face up and closed her eyes. The snow felt cold against her skin. She hurried her steps. By now, the coal had burned down, and the house would be cold. She'd need to rebuild the fire.

Turning onto the walkway, she stopped. A very large black and white cow stood in front of the porch. Unaware of the intruder, the cow yanked a mouthful of grass out of the ground. Chewing slowly, she swung her head around and stared at Tatyana.

Tatyana had dealt with cows before, but she didn't know this one, so she approached the animal cautiously. With her hand outstretched, she said, "Now, what are you doing in my yard?"

The cow watched her with baleful eyes, then lowered her head and took a menacing step toward Tatyana.

Tatyana waved her hands. "Shoo. Go home, cow." The beast didn't move. Searching for a switch, Tatyana found a thin, birch branch. She picked it up and whipped the air with it. "Go on. Move." The cow held her ground. Tatyana swatted its bony rump and finally, with an injured expression, the bovine lumbered away.

"No wonder people here have fences around their houses," Tatyana said as she stepped onto the porch. She'd have to write the Broidos and tell them about the cows that wandered the streets. Her family in Russia would be astonished at such a thing. Farmers there were more careful with their animals. She watched the falling snow. In Russia, animals were kept in barns during the harsh winters. Sometimes she had helped Yuri with feeding and milking. She always enjoyed working with him. Outside the wind howled, but in the great barn she had felt secure. The sound of cows munching and the smell of hay had always given her a feeling of contentment.

As she stepped inside her home, she longed for that same comfort and wondered if it would be forever out of reach.

CHAPTER 11

DIMITRI'S TRAIN CAME TO A
stop beside the mine complex. Wind had blown snow into piles
along the walls and blanketed the rooftops with white. Long icicles hung from the eaves, reaching toward the ground. Except
for the smokestacks, which seemed deeper black against the
white, the buildings looked brighter.

Susie was the only woman who rode the train down with
the men. The other secretary came up from the valley on the
bus. As always, the workers filed out after Susie.

Dimitri hurried down the steps, placed his foot on the platform, and slipped. If he hadn't grabbed the railing, he would
have found himself flat out. He laughed. "Sometimes it's hard to
see ice. I'm glad there's none down below. We'd have a heck of
a time."

"It would be a strange sight, though, with everything all white," Carl said.

"At least it wouldn't be so dark," Susie teased.

Carl took his wife's arm. "Ah, it would just melt and make a mess of things. We'd be slopping around in black mud. I don't figure anybody would enjoy that."

The bus from Renton pulled in, and the men from the valley unloaded.

Ignoring it, Dimitri scooped up a handful of snow and pressed it tightly between his palms. The cold tingled against his skin, and he hurled the ball at Carl.

It splattered against the back of his head. "What the . . . ?" He twirled around and looked at Dimitri.

Blowing into his hands, Dimitri said, "Cold stuff, snow." He grinned.

Carl quickly grabbed up a handful and threw it at Dimitri.

Soon the two were dashing around flinging snowballs at each other.

A voice cut into their fun. "Broido. Dimitri Broido." It was the mine superintendent.

Immediately, Carl and Dimitri stopped their play. Sticking his hands in his coat pockets, Dimitri turned and faced Mr. Goodman. "Yes, sir." He couldn't imagine what the boss wanted with him. Had he done something wrong?

Mr. Goodman remained on the sidewalk, his brows knit. "In my office. I need to talk to you." He turned and retreated indoors.

Dimitri looked at Carl. "What do you think? He didn't look very happy."

Carl shrugged. "All you can do is talk to him."

With trepidation, Dimitri knocked the snow off his boots and stepped into the office. Mr. Goodman was sitting behind his desk, papers in his hand. He looked at Dimitri and pointed at a chair.

Hat in hand, Dimitri sat.

"One of the miners called in this morning and quit." He shook his head slowly. "Not even a two-week notice. It's hard to believe that in these tough times a man would give up a good job." He leaned forward on his desk and looked squarely at Dimitri. "You haven't been with us long, but I need a man to replace him. I've had good reports on you. Harvey thinks you can handle the work. I realize you don't know a lot about mining, and that could be a problem. The men depend on each other down there. Broido, you're sharp, and they'll teach you, but you've got to listen." He paused. "So, what do you think? You want to give it a try?"

Dimitri's heart beat fast. Being a miner would mean more money, but also more danger. He took a slow breath. "If you think I'm ready, I am."

His expression stern, Mr. Goodman stood. "Just do exactly what you're told. That way nobody will get hurt. And you better count on the men not trusting you at first. You'll have to earn that."

Dimitri pushed his chair back and straightened. "I'll do my best, sir," he said, wondering why he'd been chosen. There were others who'd been working for the mine longer.

"Do better than your best. You'll be working for Carl. He's a good man."

Dimitri nodded. "Thank you, sir," he said and shook his boss's hand.

Carl waited beside the trip. His eyes brightened when he saw Dimitri. "Heard you are going to join us," he said with a smile.

"I'm supposed to work with you."

"I'm glad to have you. Figure if the boss trusts you, so can I."

"I'm ready to learn," is all he said, but inside he worried, *What if I make a mistake? I could get someone killed.* His stomach lurched at the thought.

"Stick with me. I'll show you everything I know." Carl said grinning.

Dimitri went to work shoveling. When it was time to blast out more coal, he sat on the ground beside Carl. His legs bent and arms wrapped around his knees, he pressed his back against the mine wall. "Why do they blast to get at the coal?"

"It's the easiest and fastest way," Carl said as he looked at his friend in the half light. "The men know what they're doing. They've been setting charges a long time, and they're not about to get themselves killed."

"Have you ever been on a crew that had an accident while blasting?"

"No. It happens, but I've never had any problems like that." He glanced down the line. "After the charges go off and the dust clears, we get the coal running down the chute and into the cars. Then, we clear things out for more charges."

Dimitri stared at the far wall, his eyes following the tiny cracks running through it. Taking a deep breath, he tried to quiet his racing heart. He didn't know why he was nervous. Over the last weeks, he'd heard a lot of blasts and had hauled wood into the work sites. There'd never been any trouble. In fact, he liked his job, enjoying the hard labor. He didn't even mind the dark, close quarters anymore. But, things were different today. Now he was part of the mining crew.

The two men who'd gone in to set the charges raced out of the tunnel and crouched against the wall. A few moments later, a muffled boom reverberated from within the tunnel, and the ground shook. Dust poured into the passageway. When it cleared, the crew headed back to the workings.

"See, nothing to it," Carl said.

Dimitri felt embarrassed about his jitters. An overhead beam groaned, and his heart quickened.

Glancing at the beam, Carl grinned. Reaching beneath his cap and scratching his head, he said, "I'm not so jumpy these days, just do my job. You'll learn what means trouble and what doesn't. I've heard when things are getting ready to go, a man's hair stands up on his neck. Kind of a sixth sense, I guess. I've had my share of scares, but never anything real bad." When he reached the barricade holding back the coal, he opened it up, allowing the coal to run down to the cars.

"I'll pull down the loose stuff," Carl said. "You shovel what's on the floor." Using a pick, he went to work knocking out the coal.

Dust still filled the air. Dimitri could taste it. Working side-by-side, Carl picked, and he shoveled. Dimitri saw something fly at his face, then felt a sharp pain just above his right eye. Dropping his shovel, he covered his eye with his hand. Blood seeped through his fingers and down his arm.

Carl stopped working. "What's wrong? Are you all right?" He lifted Dimitri's hand. "Let me take a look." He peered at the injury. "You've got a sliver of coal in there."

"It felt like a piece of glass hit me." Dimitri blinked, making sure he could see.

Carl looked closer. "It missed your eye. I'm sorry. I should have warned you to stay further back. Sometimes, pieces fly. It's a pretty deep gash and bleeding good. You're gonna' need a few stitches. You better hitch a ride up on the next trip and see the nurse."

He rested his hand on Dimitri's shoulder. "God must be watching over you. You could've lost an eye."

"I guess he is."

✹ ✹ ✹ ✹ ✹

The nurse removed a chip of coal, cleaned the laceration, and put three stitches in. Placing a bandage over the wound, she said, "You're a lucky young man. A quarter of an inch lower and you would've lost that eye." She laid the last piece of tape over the gauze.

It pulled when he lifted his brow.

"You'll want to be careful when you change the bandages. It'll pull. The best way is to do it quickly. Come back in about a week, and I'll take the stitches out."

"Thanks," Dimitri said as he stood.

"You have some iodine at home?"

"Don't think so."

"I'll get you some." She disappeared out the door.

Dimitri studied a picture of a doctor in a brown suit with a large syringe and a boy with his pants partially down, his rump exposed. The child was clearly unaware of the doctor's intentions. Dimitri smiled and looked closer to read the artist's name. "Norman Rockwell. I never heard of him." He glanced in the mirror but couldn't see anything through the large bandage that covered one eye. He touched it gingerly. The sutures stung. *What will Tatyana think when she sees this?* He knew she already worried about his working in the mine, even though she'd said very little.

He couldn't deny the danger, but there was something about mining he enjoyed. He liked hard work, but it was more than that. Knowing he was doing something most men wouldn't made him feel unique; plus, facing danger each day was stimulating. He also enjoyed the camaraderie among the men. They joked among themselves and shared stories about their pasts. Working as a team, they watched out for each other, carried tools for one another, and double-checked equipment to make certain it was working properly. And always, they watched for danger, ready to help. Dimitri smiled as he remembered the several offers from men to ride up with him. The unique partnership carried over into their lives outside work, touching even the miners' families. And above all the rest, he was thankful for a job. It was difficult to find one, especially one that paid well.

When Dimitri returned to work, he reported back to Carl.

CHAPTER 11

"Good to see you. You sure you can work with only one eye?"

"Sure. It's not a problem."

Hanging on to his pick with one hand, he studied Dimitri's dressing. "That's a pretty big bandage."

"It's just three stitches."

"Glad you're back," he said. "We've got coal to clear out of here before we can shoot again." Using his pick, he pulled out more coal.

Dimitri scooped it into the shoot, wondering, *Why am I on the mining crew? I don't deserve it. Others have more time in than me.* Susie's bright face came to mind. *I wonder if she had anything to do with it?*

* * * * *

That evening, when the train arrived in Black Diamond, all Dimitri could think of was a soak in a hot bath. As he headed toward home, his body felt tired. Although he'd been working timber, mining forced different muscles into use, and they were sore.

Carl laughed. "You look beat."

"I am."

"You'll get used to it, but tomorrow you'll be hurting."

Dimitri grimaced. "That doesn't make me feel better."

When he stepped into the house, Tatyana took one look at him and gasped. "Dimitri! What happened? You are injured!" She reached out and gently touched his wound.

"It's nothing. A piece of coal flew out and hit me. Just needed a few stitches. I'm fine." He took off his coat and hat and hung them on the hooks inside the closet. "Something smells good. What are you cooking?"

"Stew. And I made fresh bread. Are you hungry?"

Dimitri pulled her into his arms and held her close. "Starving." He buried his face in her hair. "I love the way you smell."

Tatyana rested her head against his chest and wrapped her arms around him. She squeezed him tightly, then stepped back and looked at his bandage. "How close is it to your eye?"

"Just below my eyebrow."

"Oh, Dimitri, you could have lost your eye."

Dimitri grinned. "I know. You're not the first person to tell me that."

"And then what would you have done?"

"I'd have been the one-eyed Russian who works in the mines," he said with a wry grin.

"It is not funny," Tatyana said as she folded her arms over her chest. "You should not make fun of such a thing."

"What good will it do to think about the what-ifs?"

"Dimitri, I do not think you take the danger you face seriously. There are men who work the mines who get hurt. Some die. I heard of a man who was riding up on one of the cars and a beam hit him in the head. He died instantly. Another man broke his back when he was knocked off a car. And there are stories about black damp. It kills you before you know there is trouble. It is not only explosions and cave-ins that kill men."

"Would it be better if I worried every moment?"

Tatyana stepped close again and burrowed against his chest. "It is just that I do not know what I would do without you."

Dimitri caressed her hair. "Nothing will happen to me. I will be more careful."

"I have met women who have lost husbands or sons. And there are children who have no fathers." She searched his face. "I do not want to become a widow."

"Mining is dangerous. Sometimes, I worry too. But, that's why the money is so good. Besides, it's not as bad as you think.

The men watch out for each other. The longer I work there, the more I'll know and the safer it will be."

Dimitri held her close, wishing he could offer her more comfort. "You pray for me, and my mother prays for me. I think I am protected."

"Yes, we pray. Do you?"

Dimitri caressed her back. "I figure your prayers are more than enough."

Tatyana felt a stab of concern. Before she married Dimitri, she thought he was a Christian; but she wasn't so certain now. Although he faithfully accompanied her to church on Sunday mornings, he didn't seem to have a personal relationship with Christ. *Father, if he doesn't know you, show yourself to him,* she prayed. She looked into his eyes. "It is a good thing the company has a shower room. Otherwise, it would not be so nice to hold you when you come home." She gently wiped a smudge off his face. "But, you missed a spot today."

"I had to be careful because of my bandage," Dimitri said, then kissed her. "One of the miners quit, and the boss gave me his job. It means more money, plus I'm working with Carl."

"That is good. And I am glad you will be with Carl." Stepping back, she said, "Now, let me look at your cut."

Dutifully Dimitri followed her into the kitchen and sat at the table. "The nurse took care of it."

"I still want to check." Without warning, she stripped away the bandage.

"Ouch!" He looked at his wife. "You should tell a person before you do that."

Tatyana smiled. "And would it hurt less?" She looked closely at the wound. "It is not bad. The nurse did a good job." She went to the sink and moistened a cloth. "There is dried blood all around the gash." Gently she wiped it away. "Our neighbor, Mrs. Johnson told me there was an accident at the mine last week."

"Yes, but it was the man's own fault. He was goofing off, and you can't do that. You've got to be alert all the time."

"And how can you? Some days a person is tired or not feeling good. Tomorrow, your head will hurt." She dabbed at the wound.

"The nurse gave me some extra gauze and some iodine. They're in my lunch bucket. I left it in the front room." He moved to get up.

"I will get it." She disappeared, then returned a few moments later with the gauze and iodine in one hand and scissors in the other.

After dabbing some iodine on the wound, she placed a fresh dressing over it and taped it securely.

"That is good. It will stay clean, at least until you go to work." She sat across from Dimitri and, taking a deep breath, said, "I was not going to say anything, but . . ."

"Go ahead."

"You know I respect you and the work you do. But I am afraid for you. The more I learn about mining, the more I worry." She leveled an even gaze on her husband. "I wish you would find other work."

Dimitri folded his hands on the table in front of him. He studied them a moment, then looked at his wife. "Tatyana, when I started at the mine, I was scared." He gave her a sideways grin. "I didn't want you to know. But now, I like what I do. And there aren't many jobs around. This one pays well. I can take care of you." He reached out and took her hands. "I do not believe anything will happen to me. I know it must be difficult for you to understand, but I like mining."

Tatyana studied her husband. He was a good man. She squeezed his hands. "You do what you must," she said, forcing a smile. "I will love you and support you, no matter what work you do."

Dimitri leaned across the table, lifted Tatyana's hands to his lips, and kissed them. "I will do my best for you. One day, we will have children, and I want to give them a good life."

Tatyana took a slow, deep breath. *Yes, me too,* she thought. *I just want to make sure you are here to share it with us.*

CHAPTER 12

S<small>WEAT BEADED ON</small> D<small>IMITRI'S</small> forehead and ran into his eyes. Standing his shovel in a pile of coal, he took a handkerchief from his back pocket and wiped his face. He could feel the scar above his right eye. It was still tender. Shoving his handkerchief back into his pocket, he studied the timbers bracing the workings. A long crack ran along the main beam. *It must not be dangerous; otherwise someone would say something,* he told himself. He grabbed his shovel and dug into the coal.

"Hey, Carl, isn't it time for a break?" Jack Miller asked.

Carl stopped working and looked at his watch. "You're right. You men go ahead. Take your break. I'm gonna' finish filling this last car."

"I'll give ya a hand," said Joe Dexter.

"Me too," Mike Clark added.

"Thanks," Carl said and returned to work.

The rest of the men walked down into the gangway where they'd left their lunch pails.

Dimitri picked up the water jug he'd left in the tunnel and swigged several gulps of water. Leaning against the coal chute, he screwed the lid back on and studied the three remaining workers. He admired Carl. He not only worked harder than his crew, but was an honest, sensible man, trusted and liked by the workers. Dimitri knew if he ever needed anything Carl would be the one he sought out. Even those who smirked at his Christian faith trusted his judgment.

"You guys gonna' take a break?" Dimitri asked.

Carl glanced at Dimitri. "Yeah. Just wanted to get this finished first."

Dimitri rotated his aching shoulders. "What time is it?"

Carl chuckled. "Why, you tired?"

Dimitri grinned and nodded. "I'm not used to this kind of work like the rest of you."

"It's two o'clock. Only a couple more hours."

"These ten-hour days could kill a man," Dimitri said as he rubbed his arm. "A long soak would feel good."

"Maybe you can talk your wife into giving you a massage when you get home." He winked. "She's a good woman."

"I have to agree with you. At one time, I didn't think she'd ever be my wife. In the beginning, she was so set on returning to Russia she wouldn't have anything to do with me."

Carl leaned his pick against the wall. "Hey, guys, this rock will be here when we get back. Take a break."

"Sure, in a minute. You go ahead," said Mike.

"We'll shovel out the last of this," Joe said.

"Suit yourself." Carl joined Dimitri and the two stepped into the gangway. "It's hard to believe that at one time she wasn't smitten with you. Nowadays, it's clear to see she loves you. I can't imagine her refusing your offer of marriage."

Dimitri could feel the blood rush to his face and was thankful for the dirt that hid it. "I'm blessed all right, but sometimes I still worry how she feels about living here and being so far from her homeland. Although she doesn't talk about it, I know she misses Russia and her family."

"You're probably worrying about nothing. She made her decision when she married you." Carl bent and picked up his water jug. Opening it, he drank several mouthfuls. Wiping his mouth with the back of his hand, he replaced the lid. "Maybe you should talk about it."

"We need to, but I'm afraid she might say something I don't want to hear, like she wants to move back to Russia. Then what would I do? I can't leave America. You know the reports coming from over there. It would be suicide. When she talks about home, she's remembering a fantasy. She's not being realistic." A thought he'd refused to consider spiraled through his mind. *What if she left me and returned alone?*

Carl clamped his hand on Dimitri's shoulder. "I think Tatyana's more sensible than you give her credit for. We all remember our pasts as being better than they really were. And just because people dream doesn't mean they're going to do anything about it. Tatyana loves you." He squeezed his friend's shoulder. "Susie says she talks about you all the time. Sometimes she speaks of Russia, but as far as I know has never even hinted she'd return."

"I know, but . . ."

Dimitri heard a deep rumble from within the tunnel. The ground shook, and a thundering roar resounded from the workings.

"Cave in!" Joe cried. A muffled, "Ahhh!" followed.

"Get out of here!" Carl pushed Dimitri toward the cars. "Joe! Mike!" he shouted and peered through the dust. The only answer was the sound of falling rock and an advancing black cloud.

Dimitri's feet felt heavy as he ran toward the man trip. When he made it to the cars, he catapulted himself into a seat. The others were already inside.

His mouth covered with a handkerchief, Carl ran up, grabbed a stick, and touched the wires. As he climbed in, the cars moved upward toward the surface. Black dust rolled out of the tunnel, spilling into the gangway. Choking and feeling as if he might suffocate, Dimitri mentally commanded the cars to hurry. Even with his handkerchief covering his mouth and nose, he could taste grit and dirt. His heart hammered. Gripping the edge of the car, he couldn't keep from shaking.

Carl grabbed his forearm. "We'll make it."

"What about Joe and Mike?"

His face glum, Carl said, "I don't know. I couldn't see anything. As soon as we know its safe, we'll send down a rescue crew."

Dimitri felt sick. Were they still alive, buried beneath piles of black coal and dirt? He looked back, hoping to find them chasing after the cars, but all he could see was a thick, black cloud. He looked at Carl. "Was there anybody else?"

"I don't think so." Carl counted the miners in the trip. "Everyone is here except for Mike and Joe."

When they reached the surface, Dimitri gulped fresh air, grateful to be alive.

The miners were assembled, and a roll call was taken to make certain every man was accounted for. Only Joe and Mike were missing.

A rescue team was called in.

"Why don't they go down now and get them?" Dimitri asked, his fear growing for the men left behind.

"They will, but they've got to make sure it's safe first. We don't want to lose anyone else," Carl said soberly.

Dimitri nodded. He looked at Carl. "Was there anything we could have done?"

"It's hard to say. When a place starts coming down . . ." Carl wiped his face with his hand. "You don't know how bad it is or if there's gas or fire. You just have to get out."

"Carl!" Susie ran to him and threw her arms around her husband. Crying, she held him for several minutes before stepping back and looking at him. "I was afraid you were still down there." She kissed him hard on the lips, then hugged him. "Thank God you're all right." Then she looked at Dimitri and reached out and touched his arm. "You too."

Word quickly traveled to Black Diamond. The mine parking lot filled with buses and cars as families came looking for their men. As loved ones were reunited, there were cries of thanksgiving. Dimitri searched the faces for Tatyana. He needed to hold her, to tell her he was all right and that he loved her.

A plain woman with brown hair knotted into a bun stumbled as she stepped off the bus. She ran toward the mine entrance and the throng of people. Her eyes searched the crowd. "Joe! Joe!" When she found Carl, she gripped his arm. "Have you seen Joe?"

His eyes grave, Carl looked at her. "Eleanor, Joe didn't come up with us."

The woman's face went ashen.

"He and Mike were in the workings when . . . it happened."

She swayed and grabbed Carl's arm.

Susie put her arms around Eleanor and held her as she wept. Smoothing her hair, she said, "They'll find him. He'll be all right."

Eleanor gave Carl a pleading look. "Please, please save him."

"We'll do our best. A rescue team is going down now."

Her face lined with grief, Eleanor nodded. Another woman joined her and, clinging to each other, they shuffled to the mine entrance. They waited there, and Eleanor quietly wept into a handkerchief.

Another bus pulled into the lot, and Dimitri pushed through the crowd, searching for his wife. When he found her tormented face, he waved and shouted, "Tatyana! Tatyana!"

Hope replacing anguish, Tatyana scanned the throng for the source of the voice. When she spotted Dimitri, she smiled broadly and ran into his arms. Resting her face against his blackened shirt, she held him tightly. "Dimitri. Dimitri. I was so afraid." For a few minutes, she cried softly, then stepped back and looked at her husband. "Are you all right?"

Dimitri wiped dirt from her face. "Yes. I'm fine and glad you're here."

Susie ran up to the couple and grabbed Dimitri's arm. "Have you seen Carl?" Her voice sounded shrill.

"He said something about helping the rescue team."

Susie turned and stared at the mine entrance. Her arms encircled her waist. "I knew it."

Tatyana rubbed her friend's back. "He will be all right."

Susie's eyes filled with tears, and she looked at Tatyana. "He doesn't know about the baby. I should have told him. Maybe he would have stayed up top." She glanced back at the mine. "I should have told him."

A woman's shrill cry rose above the murmur of the crowd. Tatyana gripped her friend's hand. She was grateful it wasn't her loved one trapped beneath the earth.

Families and friends continued to gather as the vigil lasted into the night. Joe's children had joined their mother. Clinging to each other, their eyes large with fear, they stared at the entrance as if willing their father to emerge. Mike's parents and his fiancée stood in a small huddle, praying and weeping.

Fires flickered from within rusted barrels and cast strange wavering shadows. People huddled around them, bundled deep in their coats. Women Tatyana had never seen handed out hot coffee and did their best to comfort the frightened and grieving.

In the darkness, the scene became surreal, and Tatyana wished she could make it go away. She felt trapped within a nightmare and longed to wake up. She closed her eyes. *Father, hear our prayers. Please, bring the men out safely. Let them live.*

※ ※ ※ ※ ※

With the passing hours, word spread, and newspaper reporters joined those waiting. They prodded people for information while photographers snapped pictures. One man with a cigar clenched between his teeth and a notepad in hand, approached Tatyana. "Do you know who the trapped men are?"

She glanced at the man, then returned to staring at the mine entrance. "No."

"Does your husband work in the mine?"

"Yes." Wishing he would go away, she didn't look at him.

"Was he down there when it all happened?"

Irritated, Tatyana looked at the man. "Please, sir. We are praying. I do not have time for your questions."

The man eyed her suspiciously. "Are you from Russia?"

Tatyana stared at the reporter. "Yes. I am."

"You a Communist?"

"No. I am not." Now she was angry. Clamping her teeth together, she returned to watching the mine.

The reporter took the offensive cigar out of his mouth, tapped it, and spilled the ashes on the ground. He nodded at Tatyana and walked away to probe another onlooker.

Tatyana leaned against Dimitri. "Why do the news people have to be here?"

"It's their job."

Susie seemed unaware of the reporters. Instead, she stared at the cave, and pressing her fist against her lips, said, "I wish they would hurry. They've been down there a long time. What is taking so long?" A sob escaped her lips. "Why did Carl have to go back down?" Tears washed her cheeks. "I don't think I could stand it if anything . . ."

Tatyana wrapped her arm around her friend and held her. "God is with him."

"Carl knew the dangers. He did what he thought was right," Dimitri said.

"There could be black damp down there or more cave-ins or . . ."

"That is enough," Tatyana said gently, stepping in front of Susie and placing her hands on the woman's shoulders. "None of those thing will happen. God is watching over him."

Susie wiped her wet cheeks. "I know you're right. I'm just so afraid." She let her head rest against Tatyana's shoulder.

"They're coming up!" someone called.

Onlookers crowded closer to the entrance. The front car rolled out into the lights.

"Where is Carl? I can't see him," Susie said, her voice shrill.

The rest of the trip cleared the tunnel.

"Is that him?" Tatyana asked, pointing to a man in the second car. He was so black with dirt he was nearly unrecognizable.

Holding a man against his chest, Carl looked up, his face streaked where tears had washed away the black.

Eleanor's cries of "No! No! Oh, God, no," carried over the hushed crowd. People made room as she made her way to the cars.

"I'm sorry. I'm sorry," Carl said as he struggled to stand.

Two men lifted Joe out of the car.

As the men carried another body from the last car, Mike's family cried out in anguish. Tatyana's legs went weak, and she felt sick. Feeling faint, she leaned against Dimitri. She could feel his arms tighten around her.

"Are you all right?" he asked.

"No. Are you?"

Dimitri didn't answer.

"My son! How could this happen?" a man demanded. He stared down at Mike, then glared at Carl. "My son is dead! Who did this? It's the company, isn't it? They never think about the men who work for them. All they can think of is how much coal they can get out and how much money they can make!"

A small woman kneeling beside Mike stood. She placed her hand on the angry man's arm. "Please, Tim, not now. Please."

Tim looked at the woman. His face crumpled into anguish, and he pulled her to him. Shoulders heaving, he sobbed his grief.

✦ ✦ ✦ ✦ ✦

Three days later, two wagons carrying the men's caskets rolled through town. Family, friends, and the men who worked with them walked behind the wagons. Others followed as they made their slow march to the cemetery.

Her feet feeling like heavy weights, Tatyana gripped Dimitri's hand as she walked. She glanced at her husband. *It could have been you,* she thought. *I could have lost you.* She studied the bent shoulders of Joe's wife and children, Mike's fiancée, both sets of parents, and other family members. She knew what it was like to lose people you love. Pain swelled in her chest, and her throat tightened as tears spilled onto her cheeks.

After a minister spoke words of comfort and farewell, the bodies were lowered into the ground. More prayers and tears followed. As family members sprinkled the caskets with dirt, final farewells were said and people silently moved away, migrating to the church hall.

Dimitri stood over Joe's grave, his face creased with grief. Gripping Tatyana's hand, he said, "I never thought anything would actually happen." He paused, then continued, his voice haunted. "I saw a cracked beam. I should have said something."

Tatyana squeezed his hand. "You couldn't have stopped the accident."

A woman Tatyana had never seen before stepped up to them and laid her hand on Dimitri's arm. "I'm sorry."

Dimitri looked at her. "Josephine?" He almost smiled. "It is good to see you."

The tiny woman reached up and hugged Dimitri. "These were your friends?"

"Yes. Part of my crew." His voice trembled. "I was there when it happened."

"Praise God you're alive."

His eyes brimming with tears, Dimitri looked at Tatyana. "Why did they die and I didn't?"

Tatyana reached her arm around his neck and pulled him close. "We cannot know God's ways," she said softly.

Dimitri stepped back and looked at the open graves. "I just don't understand. They were good men. Why would God allow this?"

"Some things we cannot understand," Josephine said. "Still, we need to trust him."

Dimitri wiped at his tears. "It is not so easy to do."

"Give yourself time." The old woman looked at Tatyana. "Is this the beautiful wife you told me about?"

Sniffling and forcing a half smile, Dimitri placed his arm across his wife's shoulders. "Yes. Tatyana, this is Josephine Simmons. Josephine, this is Tatyana."

"You are as beautiful as he said." Her gray, blue eyes warmed as she smiled. Soft creases etched her face.

"Josephine is the woman who took me in when I first came here," Dimitri explained.

Tatyana smiled. "Oh, yes. Thank you for your help."

"I was glad to do it."

A large woman wearing heavy-rimmed glasses atop her more than generous nose joined the threesome. Tucking a strand of gray hair into a bun at the nape of her neck, she said, "Josephine, I'm sorry, dear, but we need to go. We're helping with the refreshments at the reception."

Josephine smiled. "Miranda, I'd like you to meet my friends Dimitri and Tatyana . . ." she hesitated, "Broido. Is that right?"

Dimitri nodded.

"This is my sister, Miranda Harms. She lives here in Black Diamond. These men were friends of hers."

Miranda's eyes teared. "Like my Charlie, they were too young to die."

"Was your husband killed in a mining accident?" Tatyana asked.

Miranda pushed her glasses further up on her nose. "Yes. He was killed in the Ravensdale accident."

"That's right. Josephine told me," Dimitri said.

Tatyana felt a surge of fear.

Josephine laid her hand on her sister's arm and said, "That was a long time ago." Then she looked back at Dimitri. "It was so good to see you, Dimitri, and wonderful to meet you, Tatyana. Are you coming up to the church for refreshments?"

Dimitri glanced at Tatyana. "Yes. We'll be there."

"Good. We'll see you in a bit, then?"

Dimitri nodded.

As they made their way up the street, Tatyana held Dimitri's hand tightly. She didn't want to let go. After hearing about the Ravensdale disaster, she was afraid. Dread had prodded her since the accident, but she'd managed to keep it at bay. Now, it grew and choked her. She kept seeing Dimitri lying in a coffin, kept hearing Joe's widow wail. Her voice barely audible, she said, "It could have been you they laid in the ground."

Dimitri took a deep breath. "I know, but it wasn't."

Tatyana stopped. Her eyes brimming with tears, she looked up at her husband. "I don't know what I would do without you."

Dimitri pulled her into his arms. "I'm here, and I plan to be here a long time."

Anger replaced Tatyana's fear. She stepped back. "Joe and Mike believed the same thing! And they are dead!"

Dimitri gripped Tatyana's forearms. "A person can't know what lies ahead. We can only do our best to live until death comes. It is part of living. We all must face it, and I can't live fearing it. I won't."

Tatyana knew he was right, but fear still gripped her. She looked intently at her husband. "We do not need to seek death. I am afraid you will die young when you do not have to."

Dimitri met his wife's gaze. "You are the one who always talks about trusting God. Do you or don't you?"

Tatyana was stunned and didn't know how to respond. She looked at her hands. "I want to trust, but . . ." Doing her best to control her tears, she gazed into her husband's eyes. "Please do not go back to work in that mine."

CHAPTER 13

TIGHTENING HER SCARF, TATYANA pulled the front door closed and stepped onto the frost-covered yard. Icy wind caught at her coat, the cold blast bending bushes along the roadside and sweeping thin wisps of cloud across a pale blue sky. Chimney smoke swirled over rooftops. Mt. Rainier glistened white beneath the winter sun, deep snow concealing jagged peaks and giving broad valleys the look of vanilla ice cream.

Tatyana stared at the huge mountain. Like so many others, each time she stepped outside she looked toward the mountain, hoping to see it. Although many miles away, its immensity dwarfed the town of Black Diamond. After waiting weeks for its first appearance, she hadn't been disappointed in the brilliant white jewel standing guard over Black Diamond and the Green River Valley.

One day, I will visit the park, Tatyana decided, as she headed toward the company store, her shopping basket swinging from her left arm. During the summer months, many people trekked into the mountains. She'd been told about meadows ablaze with wild flowers and lakes that sparkled so clear, they reflected the peaks around them. Visitors picnicked, and some even climbed to the glacier. *I would like to do that.*

Remembering her reason for going into town, her stomach lurched in anticipation. If only she was right. The doctor would know. *A baby. I hope I am pregnant,* she thought, resting her hand on her abdomen. It seemed unbelievable a life might be growing within her. Of course, Dimitri would be thrilled. She couldn't wait to tell him the wonderful news. But, even as she considered this, a dark cloud settled over her. He still worked in the mine. What if something happened? He would not only leave her, but his child too. Fighting against the fear, she tipped her chin into the air and told herself, *No. He must work. I must trust God.*

She forced her mind to think about other things. Christmas was only three days away. She still hadn't purchased baking goods, and she wanted to buy something special for Dimitri.

The frozen ground crunched beneath her boots. Feeling playful, she stomped on a large, frozen puddle to see if she could break the ice. It held, so she glided across it.

A neighbor stepped onto her porch, a throw rug in hand. She waved. "Good day to you Mrs. Broido."

"Good day, Mrs. Johnson."

"How are you and your husband?"

"We are fine. Thank you."

The woman gazed at the sky and pulled her sweater closed. "It's a cold one."

"It is."

Mrs. Johnson smiled. "By the sparkle in your eyes, I'd say the cold suits you."

"I love it. In Russia, the winters were bitter. Here, the cold is a nice change from the rain."

"I've seen enough rain for a good long while," Mrs. Johnson said as she shook out a rug and folded it over her arm. "Have a nice day."

"And you," Tatyana said as she watched the door swing closed. A baby cried inside. Tatyana smiled. If she was right, soon she would have a child of her own. Mrs. Johnson had five. *I do not think I want that many,* Tatyana thought and walked on.

Children skipped past her, shoving and laughing. A woman hurried by with three youngsters walking in a straight row behind her. As she passed, she smiled and nodded. Tatyana returned the gesture.

She liked Black Diamond. Most of the residents were friendly, although there were those who made it clear she didn't belong. One who'd always been kind was Mr. Robertson at the store. He'd gone out of his way to help her understand the system, and helped her make purchases. And although Mr. Boseman at the post office kept a close eye on her mail, which made her a little uncomfortable, he'd always made sure she didn't miss any letters from New York.

She wished she felt like a real part of the community. The kind of caring that existed between the citizens of Black Diamond became especially clear after the mining accident. The townspeople provided food and money to Joe's and Mike's families. Men made regular stops to keep up the work on the families' homes, and the women stopped to chat and offer comfort. The outpouring of compassion and concern touched Tatyana, reminding her how things had once been in Russia before Stalin had infused the nation with mistrust and suspicion. People had forgotten how to trust. She wondered if her homeland could ever be the way it once was.

However, one aspect about the town's reaction puzzled Tatyana. The townspeople went on with their lives much as they had before and said little about what had happened, as if pretending everything was fine would make it so. Even Susie, who'd been so distraught during the disaster, returned to work seemingly unaffected by Carl's position there. Tatyana needed to talk about it, but when she broached the subject with Susie, her friend was clearly uncomfortable and quickly changed the topic.

Tatyana gradually began to understand that the townspeople accepted accidents as part of mining and believed talking about them would do nothing but stir up fear and resentment. She would simply have to cope. It was not easy, but Tatyana pushed aside her fears and returned to caring for their home, preparing meals, and praying for Dimitri.

As she approached Railroad Avenue, she was surprised by the crowds. Women, their arms full of packages, some with children hanging on their skirts, hurried from store to store. Although the bakery was a popular stop, clearly the company store seemed to be doing the most business. One little girl stepped out of the confectionery, a stick of hard candy in her mouth. She looked at Tatyana and grinned. Tatyana smiled back.

As she walked toward the general store, her shoes made a hollow clicking on the wooden sidewalk. Enjoying the sound, she purposely made her steps quick and sharp. When she reached the store, she stopped and admired the window dressings. Tinsel hung from the frame, and bright colored ribbons and packages decorated the shelf. Stepping inside, the aroma of spice and sugar greeted her. *Christmas in America is a wonderful time,* she thought.

"Good morning," an old woman Tatyana had occasionally seen at church said with a warm smile. "Town is certainly busy today."

"It is." Tatyana frantically searched her mind for the woman's name.

CHAPTER *13*

"Will you be going to the Christmas celebration at the theater?"

"Yes. I was told it is a special time."

"Oh, yes. We have a community sing and Santa will be there with gifts for the children. And there will be lots of delicious foods." Her eyes sparkled.

"Dimitri and I are excited to go," Tatyana said, still unable to recall her name.

"I will look for you." The woman smiled and moved past her.

Tatyana wandered among the displays, looking for a gift for Dimitri. The store had so many things, but most were too expensive. She picked up a pair of wool socks. *Dimitri could certainly use these,* she thought. Setting them back on the rack, she looked at a pair of leather boots, remembering the repeated repairs to Dimitri's worn work boots. But they were much too expensive, and sadly she returned them to the shelf.

As always, she stopped in front of the phonograph. Although she knew it was impossible, she envisioned how perfect it would look in their home. How wonderful it would be to find it wrapped for her on Christmas morning. "Stop being ridiculous," she told herself and moved on.

Several knives were displayed in a glass case. She gazed at them through the glass. One had a wooden handle with intricate carvings and a leather sheath to attach it to a belt. Dimitri had talked about hunting with Carl and how he'd need a knife to butcher and skin out his kill.

"Have you found something you like?" asked Mr. Robertson.

"I am looking for a gift for Dimitri."

"Well, we have some mighty fine knives."

She pointed to the one she liked.

Mr. Robertson took it out of the case and set it on top of the glass. "The handle is hand-carved, and the blade is made of the best steel. It's a good hunting knife and will hold an edge." He handed it to Tatyana.

Turning it over in her hands, she felt the weight and carefully touched the blade. "How much?"

"Four dollars and fifty cents."

"That is a lot of money," Tatyana said, unable to disguise her disappointment.

"The case alone is worth two dollars." He studied Tatyana a moment. "Let me take a look and see if the company has recommended I put it on sale. I might have forgotten to mark it." He returned to the front counter and looked in a journal. Smiling, he walked back to the display. "Well, how about that. I did forget to mark it down." He looked at her. "It's only two dollars and fifty cents."

Tatyana studied the knife. It was beautiful. Two dollars and fifty cents wasn't so much. *Dimitri would like this.* "It is nice," she said. "And Dimitri needs one." She looked it over again. "I will buy it."

"It's a good knife for that price. I think you'll be pleased with it. I have a box I can put it in. That way you'll be able to wrap it for Christmas." Returning to the front of the store, Mr. Robertson made his way through shoppers, giving each a pleasant greeting. Tatyana followed. Once at the counter, he asked, "Is there anything else I can get for you?"

"I need five pounds of sugar and ten pounds of flour," Tatyana said as she scanned the shelves. "Do you have chocolate?"

"The best," Mr. Robertson said as he took a tin of cocoa from the cupboard and placed it in front of Tatyana.

"Good. Thank you." She looked back at the display of wool socks. *Dimitri really needs some.* "One more thing," she said as she walked back to the rack. Picking them up, Tatyana returned to Mr. Robertson and placed the socks on the counter. "I would like these also." Colorful wrapping paper and ribbons brightened a nearby shelf. Tatyana wished she could afford to buy some.

Chapter 13

"The wrapping paper and ribbons are on sale," Mr. Robertson said. "Only ten cents for a roll of paper and the ribbon is five cents a yard."

Tatyana chewed her lower lip. She knew it was an extravagance, but her presents would look so much nicer if they were wrapped. She picked up a roll of green and red paper and red ribbon and added them to her purchases.

Mr. Robertson smiled. "Your packages will look real pretty." He added up the total and marked it in his ledger. "You're a careful shopper. Dimitri must be proud of the way you manage the household."

"I am still learning, but I do my best." She glanced at the wall clock. The doctor would certainly be open by now. Quickly placing her purchases in her basket, she said, "Thank you. Have a good day." Then she hurried out of the store and headed down the street.

Taking a deep, calming breath, Tatyana stepped into Dr. Logan's office. Cold air swept into the room, shuffling the pages of a magazine sitting on a table.

A tall, thin woman wearing a white uniform sat at the front desk. "It certainly feels like winter."

"Yes, it does."

"Everyone at my house is hoping for a white Christmas."

Hesitantly, Tatyana approached the desk. "My name is Tatyana Broido. I would like to see the doctor."

"Have you been here before?"

"No."

The nurse took a form from a file and handed it to Tatyana. "Have a seat and fill this out."

Tatyana stared at the paper. She could read only a little English. This was much too difficult. She looked at the woman. "I cannot read this. I have not been in this country very long."

"Oh, I'm sorry. Why don't I ask the questions, and you can tell me what to write down."

Tatyana nodded gratefully.

The form was simple and took only a few minutes to complete. The nurse disappeared into a back room and Tatyana sat down to wait, her stomach doing somersaults. The odor of alcohol and disinfectant permeated the office, and she could hear a child's cries. She threw one leg over the other and nervously swung her foot back and forth. What would the exam be like? She'd never had one before.

The door to the back offices opened, and she jumped. A little girl with tears still on her face and a sucker in her mouth ran into the outer office.

"Have a good day, Jennifer," the nurse said, smiling at the child.

"I will." Jennifer waved, then took her mother's hand as they left the office.

The nurse looked at Tatyana. "The doctor will see you."

Tatyana thought she might be sick, and her legs felt weak as she stood. Forcing a smile, she followed the woman into a small examining room.

※ ※ ※ ※ ※

Leaving the doctor's office behind her, Tatyana strode toward home. *A baby! I am going to have a baby! How will I tell Dimitri?* She considered several possibilities, then decided to wait until Christmas. It would be a wonderful gift, and she would only have to wait three days.

※ ※ ※ ※ ※

On Christmas Eve, the cold still clung to Black Diamond. Snowflakes fell as Tatyana and Dimitri walked hand in hand toward the theater. Tatyana thought about her news, cherishing her secret. Since seeing the doctor, she'd nearly given in and told Dimitri several times. Once again, she wanted to tell him but bit her tongue. The timing needed to be perfect.

This was their first Christmas together as husband and wife, and walking beside her husband, Tatyana knew it would become a cherished memory. With the frosty night all around and her secret tucked away, she knew she'd been blessed.

They climbed the steps leading to the second story of the theater, and as they entered the upstairs hall, they were greeted by the mingled fragrance of pine, spices, and candies. Already, the room was crowded with people. Women stood in small clutches sharing recipes and their children's latest accomplishments. Men talked of fishing, hunting, and work. Youngsters squealed and laughed as they chased each other around the adults and dessert-laden tables. Some of the younger children stood at the foot of an immense evergreen tree, gazing at the colorful decorations hanging from the limbs and the gifts piled beneath it.

Dimitri joined the men, and Tatyana was quickly drawn into conversations with her new friends and neighbors. She and Dimitri caught each other's eyes occasionally throughout the evening. At one point, he joined her and whispered close to her ear, "Is everything all right? You look like you have something on your mind."

"I am fine. We can talk later," Tatyana answered and smiled, thinking what it would be like when she gave him her news.

Unexpectedly, a round, jolly Santa entered the room. "Ho! Ho! Ho!" he bellowed, and the children gathered around him. He patted the closest one on the head and asked, "Have you been a good little boy, Billy?" Then he did the same with Martha, Jimmy, Jane, and the others. The children wore bright smiles, and their eyes sparkled. One little boy reached out and tugged on Santa's whiskers. His eyes widened in surprise when the beard didn't budge. "I'm sorry, Santa," he rushed to apologize.

Santa simply laughed and added a few more ho, ho, ho's.

Tatyana decided she liked this custom very much.

Santa handed out gifts, and the children tore through wrapping paper and boxes. Boys found footballs and baseball bats, balls, and gloves. Girls discovered beautiful dolls and roller skates. Some children received stick horses and immediately began romping around the room astride their new steeds. In addition, each child received candy, fruit, and nuts.

"Where do the presents come from?" Tatyana asked Susie.

"Each man in the union donates a dollar, and the company contributes the rest. That way, every child in town gets something nice."

"Oh, Dimitri did not tell me." Tatyana smiled as she watched the children show their gifts to their parents, then run off to play with the new toys. *One day our son or daughter will be here.*

After all the gifts were distributed, everyone sang Christmas carols. Tatyana had heard many of the songs the previous year and knew some of the words. She and Dimitri intertwined their arms as they lifted their voices and sang of the blessings of Christmas.

Her heart full, Tatyana wished the Broidos and her family in Russia were here to share this special time. She closed her eyes and prayed, *May God keep you all safe this night and may you rejoice in the birth of our Savior.*

After the singing ended, everyone gathered around the table and sampled the delicious desserts. Tatyana found sugar cookies that looked very much like the ones she'd once made. Memories of days spent in the kitchen with her mother flooded her, and tears burned the back of her eyes. Those had been special times, and she hadn't realized it at the time.

Dimitri placed his hand on her shoulder. "Are you all right?"

Tatyana forced a smile. "Yes. I was just thinking of home and my childhood." She took her husband's hand. "I want to talk to you. Could we go outside?"

Donning coats and gloves, Dimitri and Tatyana left the party and walked out into the cold night air. They snuggled close. With the chatter and laughter sounding far away, they watched the snow fall, its brightness lighting the darkness with a soft glow.

"What did you want to talk about?" Dimitri asked. "You've been keeping something from me for days." His voice sounded strained.

"What I have to say will change our lives."

His face lined with concern, Dimitri looked at Tatyana. "I know you miss your home and family. I miss mine too. But we have each other. We are building a new life here. I could not bear for you to leave . . ."

"Leave? Is that what you think I want to talk about?" she said chuckling. "If I were not so happy, I would be angry at you for having so little faith in me." She paused and took a breath. Facing him and holding both his hands in hers, she looked into his eyes. "Dimitri, I have wonderful news. We are going to have a baby."

Stunned silence filled the air.

"A baby?" Dimitri finally said.

Tatyana laughed. "Yes! A baby! I saw the doctor, and he told me we will have our baby in the summer."

He broke into a broad smile, wrapped his arms around his wife, and lifted her. He kissed her face, her forehead, her cheeks, and lips. "I am going to be a father!" Setting her back on her feet, he cradled her face in his hands. "I love you. Thank you." He pulled her close and held her tight. "I can hardly believe it, a father."

As Tatyana laid her head against his chest, her joy seemed almost too much to contain. Listening to his beating heart, she felt content. Watching the snow fall and cuddling close to her husband, she wondered how she could ever have worried that moving here could be a bad thing.

CHAPTER 14

THE DREAM STARTED AS IT always did. Yuri could see a familiar-looking woman and was drawn to her. He struggled forward, but his legs wouldn't cooperate. They felt heavy, and he fought for every step. The woman walked into light, but he still couldn't see her face.

"Who are you?" he asked. She didn't answer. He took another step. Slowly, the woman turned toward him and smiled kindly. It was his mother.

"Mama?" His heart pounded.

Still wearing the devoted smile, she held her arms out toward him.

"Mama, I thought you were dead." Yuri propelled himself forward, his legs growing heavier with each step. The more he tried to hurry, the slower he moved. He needed her. "Help me," he cried, knowing that just as she came into reach, she would disappear. She always did.

This time, it was different. His mother spoke to him. "Do not be afraid."

"I try, but it is so hard."

"I know it is difficult, but you can do it," his mother reassured him. "We are waiting for you. One day you will join us and we will have a glorious reunion."

"Where are you? I want to be with you." He continued to struggle forward, unable to close the distance.

"First, you have work to do, then you will come." The image began to fade.

"Mama, don't leave!" Panic swelled. "No! Mama! Mama! Please stay!"

She disappeared.

Legs suddenly free of their weight, Yuri ran to the place his mother had stood, but she was gone. He fell on his face and wept. "I need you. Please come back. Come back."

Something pushed against Yuri's shoulder. He was being shaken.

"Yuri. Wake up. Wake up."

Forcing himself back to reality, Yuri blinked and tried to focus on Alexander's face.

"You were having a dream."

Yuri glanced around the nearly dark barracks. As he came awake, he shivered. The cold penetrated his consciousness, and he thought sorrowfully, *It was only a dream.* "I saw my mother," he said. "But I couldn't reach her."

Alexander sat on the edge of the bunk. "Shh. We'll wake up the other prisoners," he whispered.

"It was so real." Yuri sat up and dropped his legs over the side of the bed and rested his forearms on his thighs. Closing his eyes, he tried to reclaim the image of his mother. For a moment, he could see her intense green eyes. They looked at him sternly, the way they had when he'd been a disobedient boy. He knew he needed to put an end to his self-pity. Immediately her eyes warmed, and he lost the image. Straightening, he said, "She was so beautiful. She could be strict, but she loved us." He looked at Alexander. "I miss her. Sometimes I can't believe she's gone."

"But not gone forever."

"I know." Yuri scrubbed his face with his hands. "Still, there are times when it feels like forever." Taking a deep breath, he rubbed his eyes. "I've had the dream before, but this time it was different. She talked to me and told me I have work to do."

Alexander smiled. "You do. Maybe God is speaking to you through your dreams."

"Does he still do that?"

"Sometimes."

"But why me?" he whispered. "For so long I turned away from God. I was useless. Ever since the isolator, I've done better, but I still fail. Every day I fight my anger. Hatred calls to me, and I want to answer. I'm so weak."

Alexander's eyes filled with compassion. "You speak the truth. We are all weak and not worthy to serve God, but he forgives us our weaknesses and asks us to follow him in spite of them." He gripped Yuri's forearm. "What is done is done. Do not let the past corrupt the present. Instead, use it to learn and grow. You're doing well. I've watched you, and you're not the same."

"But you don't understand. I want to hate. I want my old life back," He said as he stood.

Alexander folded his arms over his chest and smiled. "And when you feel this way, what do you do?"

Yuri swept his hair off his forehead. "If I could only say I immediately let it go, that I'm always strong, but that's not true. The feelings sweep over me, and sometimes I can release them, but other times I hang onto them and don't want to let go." He sat back down. "Usually, in the end, I pray and ask God to help me."

"And what happens?"

"He answers my prayers and frees me from the feelings."

"What more do you want? Remember, it is not us, but God in us who is our strength." He smiled and patted Yuri's back. "Do you think you can do this on your own?"

"No, but I still get angry with myself. And what will happen when I can't let it go? I'm afraid the hatred will return and stay; then the battle will be over. I *know* how weak I am. Couldn't it happen again?"

His voice calm and steady, Alexander said, "God brought you through great affliction, and you're stronger now."

"Sometimes I don't feel strong. When I'm tempted, I think, this is it, I will fail."

"You will." Alexander stood straighter. "If you think you're above failure, you're being arrogant."

Yuri stared at his friend. His throat constricted as the realization of his pride sank in.

"Yuri, all believers struggle. Do you think you're the only one?"

"But you always seem peaceful and strong."

"Some days, I fight just to make it through another minute." He clamped his hand on Yuri's shoulder. "We all fall short of God's perfection. As long as we live in this world, we will never be as good as him. Perfection only comes when we stand face to face with our Lord."

Remorse over his pride welled up, and Yuri buried his face in his hands and cried. With the tears came freedom from guilt as Yuri accepted God's forgiveness and was able to forgive himself.

"All God asks is that we have willing hearts. And you do."

Footfalls crunched on the frozen ground outside. Yuri and Alexander stood motionless, barely breathing. Finally, the steps moved away, and the men breathed freely.

Whispering, Alexander asked, "Do you remember the verses about the time Jesus walked on the lake and Peter had so much faith that he, too, stepped out on the water?"

Yuri nodded.

"The lesson for us isn't how much faith Peter had, but how he faltered when he took his eyes off Jesus and began to look at the waves around him and focused on himself and his fears. Only then did he sink." He grabbed Yuri's hand. "We must keep our eyes on Jesus and not the storm all around us."

"Sometimes I think about how I denied the Lord, and I wonder how God sees me. Does he trust me?"

"When Jesus prayed in the Garden of Gethsemane on the night of his arrest, not one of his disciples stayed with him. They fell asleep, even after he asked them to watch with him. And Peter, the one who had said he'd die for him, denied he even knew Jesus after the Lord was arrested."

Yuri knew the story and felt assurance of God's forgiveness stir within him.

Alexander tightened his hold on Yuri's hand. "Peter was afraid even to admit he knew Jesus, and yet, God forgave him and trusted him to help establish the church. And in the end, he gave his life for his Lord."

"But, he was strong."

"Peter wasn't strong. God was. He's the one who lifted him up and set him on firm ground. God gave his disciple the name 'rock' for a reason. He knew Peter would help build the church. God believed in him." Alexander placed his hand on Yuri's shoulder. "We can be rocks if we have faith and obey."

"I know what you say is true." Yuri felt strength kindle within him. "God *can* work through me."

Alexander went to his bed and returned a moment later with something hidden beneath his shirt. "Do you know what day this is?"

"No."

"It's Christmas."

Yuri felt shocked. "No. It cannot be." He shook his head slowly. How could so much time have passed? He had spent last Christmas with friends—it seemed so long ago. It had been a time of merrymaking and joy; they had gone to the ballet. It felt like a dream. He looked around the dismal barracks. No wonder he'd forgotten. Here, there was no hint of the holiday. "I didn't know," he said, his voice flat.

"I thought you might not have remembered," Alexander said, excitement in his voice. "I have something." From beneath his shirt, he took out a wine bottle with less than a half cup of liquid in it and a small hunk of bread. "Today is a holy day and a time to celebrate communion."

"Where did you get wine?"

"One of the cooks for the officers is a friend and brother in the faith." His expression serious, Alexander knelt beside the bed and Yuri joined him. "The night before Jesus was arrested, he shared a last meal with his disciples. Jesus took bread, broke it in half, and taking a piece, ate it, then passed it to the others, saying, 'This is My body which is given for you; do this in remembrance of Me.'" Alexander tore the bread into two pieces and handed one to Yuri. "Lord, we thank you for giving your life so we could live." He placed the bread in his mouth and chewed.

Yuri did the same. Closing his eyes, he could see Jesus bending and picking up a child, reaching out and healing the lepers, and sitting at a table with sinners. The Lord had never turned away from anyone. Instead, he offered life to all who sought him. Fresh understanding filled Yuri. He finally grasped that no matter what he had done or would do, he belonged to the Lord. He wept and whispered, "Thank you."

Alexander held up the wine. "After supper, Jesus also took the cup, saying, 'This cup is the new covenant in My blood, which is shed for you.'" Alexander handed the bottle to Yuri; he drank from it, then handed it back to his friend. Alexander took the last swallow and closed his eyes for a few moments. The two men prayed silently.

"It is because of his blood that we have life," Alexander finally said, setting the bottle down. "I wish I had a Bible. For me, just to read the Scriptures again would be like water to a man dying of thirst." His eyes held a look of longing. "What a miracle that would be."

Tears wetting his face, Yuri said, "I used to smuggle the Scriptures to people. Even then, I took my Bible for granted. I took so much for granted. But no more." With a small sob, he continued, "Whatever time I have left here on earth, I will trust you, Jesus, and do everything I can to be like you and serve others."

Leaning against each other, both men cried, and Yuri prayed, "Father, I've spent so much time apart from you. I know you never left me. I understand it was I who walked away from you. Now, I place my life in your hands. May I be worthy of your love."

For a long while, the men prayed, first silently, then openly. When they looked at each other, they knew life would never be the same between them and understood that no matter what paths they took, they would forever be brothers.

🐾 🐾 🐾 🐾 🐾

Almost immediately, Yuri's newfound faith was put to the test. The following day, Saodat was assigned to work with Yuri. When they'd been forced into partnership before, God had given Yuri compassion for the man who'd once betrayed him, but Yuri knew it wasn't enough. He hadn't loved Saodat with the sacrificial love God wanted from him.

Saodat's hands were bare. Yuri knew the man's fingers could freeze without gloves. He looked at his own gloved hands. *I could give him mine. No, that would be foolish; then my own hands will freeze.* Try as he might, he couldn't dismiss the idea. Could God be speaking to him? *Father, what should I do?* At that moment, he realized that giving him one glove might work. Each man could transfer the glove back and forth, and neither hand would have to freeze. *Still, they might,* he argued.

The words he'd spoken the night before came back to him. *Whatever time I have left on earth, I will trust you, Jesus, and will do everything I can to be like you, serving others.* He inhaled deeply, the cold searing his lungs. His breath hung in the air as he slowly exhaled. He knew what he needed to do.

No guards were nearby, so he cautiously approached Saodat. As before, the man stared at him with fear. He looked feverish, his skin and eyes too bright. "Why are your hands bare?" Yuri asked.

"My gloves were stolen, and the guards wouldn't give me another pair."

Stripping off one glove, Yuri held it out. "You may use mine."

Saodat stared at the glove.

"Take it," Yuri urged. "You can move it from one hand to the other. That way, maybe your fingers won't freeze."

The frail man eyed Yuri suspiciously. "What do you want for it?"

"Nothing. We are prisoners together. We should help each other."

"Why would you do such a thing?"

Yuri placed the glove in Saodat's hands. "God told me to."

Saodat closed his fingers around the glove. "He spoke to you? And what is it he said?" he asked with a smirk. "Why would he want you to help me? I've done nothing for him. I do not even believe in him." Suspicion returned to his face.

"Even so, he loves you." Yuri said as he turned and walked away. With his gloved hand, he picked up his axe and chopped limbs. He looked at Saodat.

The man wore a puzzled expression as he studied the glove. He pulled it on, then shot a wary look at Yuri. Unexpectedly, his face softened, and he bent to pick up loose branches.

A surprising rush of acceptance and love for Saodat washed over Yuri. He didn't know how God accomplished the warming of his heart; he only knew that he did. Excitement swept over him as he realized that even in these abysmal circumstances, God was working, and he, Yuri Letinof, was privileged to be a part of the Almighty's plans.

CHAPTER 15

Hᴉs ᴀʀᴍs ᴀᴄʜɪɴɢ, Yᴜʀɪ ᴘᴜʟʟᴇᴅ the whipsaw toward him. Falling was difficult work, and despite the cold, sweat dampened his clothing.

"That's it," said the man on the other end of the saw. "It's ready to go."

Hanging onto the saw, the two backed away from the tree as it splintered from the trunk and tipped sideways. It smashed through limbs of other trees, snapping them off as it plunged toward earth. The ground shook as it hit, its weight so great there was no bounce. The pungent aroma of spruce filled the air along with tiny dust particles and needles.

Every time a tree came down, Yuri's adrenaline surged. The sight was exciting but also frightening. Looking down the length of the spruce, he placed his foot against its rough bark. It had been mighty. Feeling a pang of regret, Yuri wondered how long it had stood, reaching through the forest for the light.

"We have to keep working," his partner said.

Leaving the conifer to the tree limbers, they moved on. There was no time to admire God's creation. There were quotas to fulfill.

The pair moved to the next tree, Yuri changed his glove to his bare hand. As he did, he realized he hadn't experienced discomfort from the cold on his skin. He'd been so busy working, he hadn't noticed the air had warmed. Remarkably, the customary brittle cold had relented. Stuffing his bare hand into his pocket, he looked for Saodat. Across the field of downed trees, he spotted him carrying a bundle of branches to the fire. The man didn't notice Yuri watching him. He seemed winded and limped slightly. Yuri wondered if Saodat was sick.

"I need you on the other side of this saw," Yuri's partner called.

"I'm sorry." He picked up his end, placed it against the tree, and pulled. A slit opened, and the men dragged the blade across it again and again, exposing pale flesh beneath the bark. Yuri's muscles cried for relief, but unable to stop even to wipe sweat from his brow, he forced himself to continue. Panting for breath and praying for strength, he ignored his pain. When the sharp blast of a whistle sounded, Yuri immediately let loose of the saw and dropped his arms, grateful for a rest.

The prisoners trudged to the lunch sled and waited for their portion of bread and water. Yuri took his, walked to a downed tree, and sitting on boughs, pressed his back against it.

Alexander slowly lowered himself to the ground beside Yuri. "How are you, Comrade?"

"Weary," Yuri answered. "You?" he asked, eyeing his friend.

Alexander smiled. "I keep reminding myself that my body is a temporary vessel, and I won't have to carry it around with me forever."

CHAPTER *15*

"You're looking thinner, and you move too carefully. I'm worried about you."

"I will have to trap more rats," Alexander jested.

Yuri gave him a half smile. If Alexander became too weak, he wouldn't be able to keep up his quota. Yuri couldn't imagine surviving in this place without his friend. Life would be unbearable. *Father, please don't let him die.* He closed his eyes and rested the back of his head against the tree.

The snow crunched, and Yuri forced his eyes open. Saodat stood in front of him, a look of contrition on his face. For a long moment, the two stared at each other, neither speaking. Finally, Saodat took a slow deep breath. His voice barely audible, he said, "I wish to thank you." He held up his gloved hand.

Yuri nodded. "Are your hands all right?"

Saodat held them out, turned them palm up, then palm down. "Yes." He looked up at Yuri. "Because of you."

"No. Because of God. He told me to give you the glove."

Jutting out his chin, Saodat struggled to control his emotions. "I'm sorry for what I did."

"I forgive you. It is in the past."

"But I sent you to your death."

Yuri looked down at himself. "It seems I'm still alive."

"But . . ."

Yuri raised his hand. "Please, say no more. I understand. You wish you could undo what happened, but that cannot be. We are where we are, and God is with us."

Saodat swayed and sat on the fallen tree. "But I don't even believe in God."

"He believes in you," Alexander interjected.

Saodat said no more. He stood and walked away.

Alexander gave Yuri's leg a playful slap. "You did a good thing. I wondered what happened to your other glove."

"It was what God wanted me to do. And I will not ignore him again." Yuri ate his last bite of bread and drank his water.

"Oh, for the days of meaty stews and berry pies." He glanced at the nearby underbrush. "There should be berries in the summer."

"Yes. And I will pick every one I see," Alexander said with a grin.

Yuri glanced at an approaching guard. "And how will you do that?"

Alexander shrugged. "I will find a way."

"Back to work!" the guard shouted, and the men pushed themselves to their feet.

⚜ ⚜ ⚜ ⚜ ⚜

That night, exhausted, Yuri gratefully fell onto his bed and closed his eyes.

From the bunk next to him, Alexander said sleepily, "You've come a long way, Yuri. I remember when I first saw you on the prison train. You were so angry and afraid. You'd built such a strong wall around you, I didn't know if you would ever let anyone in. I prayed for you."

"I know you did. Thank you." Yuri rolled onto his side and looked at Alexander. "I remember you too. Your face appeared like a quiet pool in a raging river. And I wondered how you could have such peace. I wanted it." He placed his arm under his cheek. "I wonder if my sister has found peace in America."

"As you said, she is the Lord's. You can trust him to take care of her."

"More and more, her face haunts me. I want to know where she is and what she is doing. Since sending her away, I have never heard a word. It would be so good to see and talk to her." He sighed heavily. "I believe we will not meet again until heaven."

"You may be right, but do not forget that God has a way of doing the unexpected."

"He would have to get me out of here. Can we escape?"

"Even if we made it beyond the gates, there's the tundra. We'd die out there. We must wait on God. I want his plan, and it may not be escape. He will do what is best."

Yuri nodded. "I agree."

A deep, rattling cough came from a nearby bed.

"Another one sick," Yuri said. "There is no end." He looked upward. "God, I know you are here and that you love us, but there are those who have no comfort. They don't know you care about them. Who will help them?"

"We will," Alexander said quietly.

"More bodies are added to the dead pile every day." Yuri tried to wrench the image of heaped corpses from his mind. He sat up, pulled his legs against his chest, and wrapped his arms around his knees.

His voice soft, Alexander said, "In the spring, we will bury them."

"I don't want to bury any more. I want to help them live!"

Alexander was quiet for a long time, then said, "We will do what is asked of us, and we will serve the living." He pulled his blanket up under his chin. "If we do not sleep, we will have no strength to help."

Yuri lay back down, folded his arms beneath his head, and stared at the ceiling. Closing his eyes, he prayed, *Make me strong, and help me do your will. And, Father, if there is a way, please free Alexander and me.*

The next morning, Yuri followed the line of workers past the pile of frozen corpses. Usually careful not to look, today his eyes were drawn to the dead. His eyes roamed over bony, grotesque bodies, and panic welled up within him. *When spring comes, we will dig a huge grave and cover them with Siberian soil.* Overwhelmed by the inhumanity, he wanted to run, to leave the horror behind. He forced his feet to keep pace with the others.

Then he saw a familiar face in the pile. The body of the pregnant woman he'd seen outside the compound had been added to the heap. Her gaunt face radiated peace.

Alexander rested his hand on Yuri's shoulder. "She no longer suffers."

Yuri's panic quieted.

"One day, we will also be free." Alexander took a breath, and his lungs made a whistling sound as he exhaled. "My time may be soon."

"No. You will live."

"I think maybe not." There was no regret in Alexander's voice as he spoke.

"You cannot die. I need you. The others need you."

"To live or die is not my decision."

"Move on! Keep your hands behind your backs! No talking!" a guard yelled.

Realizing he and Alexander had lagged behind, Yuri hurried his steps.

That day, Saodat joined Yuri on the other end of the whip-saw. Each man wore only one glove. "It is good to see you again," Yuri said and pulled the blade toward him.

"And you." A gurgling cough came from Saodat's lungs, and he struggled to breath. He dropped the saw and bent at the waist, fighting to control the hacking. Finally clearing his throat, he straightened. Perspiration dotted his face, and blood tinged the snow at his feet.

"You're sick," Yuri said.

Saodat nodded, quickly kicking snow over the blood and glancing at the guard to see if he'd noticed. "They must not know or they'll send me to the infirmary."

"I'll try harder to push the saw back toward you."

Saodat shook his head no. "I can do my share." He planted his feet and gripped the handle. "For too long, I've lived my life on the efforts of others. It is time to do my part." As if to prove his point, he said, "Ready?" and pulled hard.

As the day progressed, it became clear that Saodat would have difficulty concealing his illness. His breaths came in shorter and shorter gasps, and with each passing hour, he coughed more. Each place he worked, the snow was stained red. Despite his efforts to hold up, Yuri could feel him weakening. His face turned pasty white, and as his fever grew, he shivered with chills.

Late in the day, a guard approached Saodat. Arms folded across his chest, he studied the prisoner. Saodat kept working, not even glancing up.

The guard's expression hardened. "What is wrong with you?"

Saodat continued to pull on the saw. "I am fine," he panted. A cough rumbled in his chest, and he couldn't suppress it. Blood bubbled through his lips.

The guard stepped back. "You'll make everyone sick. You will go to the infirmary."

"I am all right," Saodat said, wiping the blood away with his gloved hand.

"You will do as you're told," he spat.

"I can work," Saodat insisted. He pointed to the trees he and Yuri had cut. "We have done all this work. We will make our quota."

The soldier leveled a loathing gaze on Saodat. Pointing at Yuri, he said, "He did your work."

"That is not true," Yuri interceded. "We did it together."

The soldier ignored Yuri's appeal and, careful to keep a safe distance between himself and Saodat, pointed his rifle at the sick man. "Go to the clearing!"

Saodat dropped the saw and shuffled several yards to the open ground.

The guard followed. "Now, you will strip," he said with a half smile.

Saodat stared at him.

"I said strip!"

Saodat didn't move.

"You will do as you're told or you'll be shot." He raised his rifle to his shoulder and aimed it at Saodat.

Saodat's face collapsed into defeat, and a veil came over his eyes. Methodically, he unbuttoned his coat, took it off, and dropped it to the ground, then removed his shirt.

"The rest," the guard snarled.

Shivering, Saodat said, "I will die." He choked back another cough.

The guard's face hardened. "Then, you will die."

Another attack of coughing forced Saodat to sit down. He wiped his bloodied hand on his pants, pulled off his boots, and unwrapped his leggings. Next, he shed two pairs of wool pants. Shakily, he pushed himself to his feet, still wearing the glove Yuri had given him.

His clothes in a pile beside him, Saodat stood before the guard, his skin peppered with goose bumps. His arms hugging his body, he stared at the ground and shook uncontrollably.

A lump had lodged in Yuri's throat. How could any man be so inhuman? He wanted to help but remained rooted where he stood and prayed for Saodat's deliverance.

The guard pointed at the gloved hand. "Take it off."

Saodat straightened and threw his shoulders back as he met the man's gaze. "It was a gift." His voice sounded surprisingly firm.

Yuri felt a bond between himself and Saodat. He hadn't fully comprehended how his sacrifice had touched his fellow prisoner. Yuri felt pride for Saodat well up. Facing death, he retained dignity. The man Yuri had once hated, he now loved.

For a long moment, guard and prisoner stared at each other. Finally, a sneer spread across the soldier's face. "Leave it, then. It will not save you." He turned his back on Saodat and walked away, making it clear the emaciated, shivering man was no one of consequence.

Saodat found Yuri's eyes. Although they weren't allowed to speak, both understood they were linked in brotherhood. Yuri nodded at him and held up his one gloved hand.

For the next three hours, Yuri and Alexander prayed, and Saodat stood.

At first, the naked prisoner shivered uncontrollably, but after a while stillness came over him. He was dying. Somehow, he stayed on his feet until the end of the work shift.

When ordered to return to camp, the prisoners filed past Saodat. Most averted their eyes.

Yuri stripped off his coat and wrapped it around the doomed man.

"You can take him to the infirmary or leave him. He will die either way," the guard said.

"We will take care of him."

The soldier studied Saodat. "If he is not better tomorrow, you will take him to the infirmary."

"Yes, we will do that," Alexander said and checked the pile of clothes. They were frozen. He took off his gloves and put them over Saodat's feet, then removed his top layer of pants and helped Saodat into them. "These will warm you," he said, taking the man's arm.

Yuri scooped up Saodat's clothing, draped the man's arm over his shoulders, and together, Yuri and Alexander half carried, half dragged Saodat back to camp.

As they entered the barracks, a guard stepped in front of the three. "This man makes it to the meal tent on his own. If you give him anything, you'll go without."

Yuri and Alexander nodded but had no intention of obeying the orders. They laid Saodat on his bunk, and while Yuri went to get his blanket, Alexander covered the shivering man, then laid beside him, trying to warm him with his own body heat. When Yuri returned, Alexander said, "You eat. Try to bring something back. I will go after you."

Yuri took his place in line, praying for a way to get food for Saodat. He held out his cup, glanced to see if any guards were looking, then whispered. "Extra for a friend?"

Glancing at Yuri, then at the guards, the attendant spooned out a normal serving, then added an extra scoop of the greasy balanda. Yuri nodded in appreciation, took his hunk of bread, and sat at a table.

After dipping his bread into the broth, he tore off a chunk with his teeth. At the end of the day, even the stale bread and brackish soup tasted good. As he ate, Yuri tried to think of a way to get some food to Saodat. Guards stood at each door, but instead of watching the prisoners, they smoked cigarettes and talked. Yuri took another bite of bread, then quickly tucked the remainder in his shirt. He glanced at the guards. Still visiting, they seemed unconcerned with the *zeks*. Nearby prisoners concentrated on their food. Swiftly, he shoved the bowl under his coat, bracing it between his arm and waist. No one noticed.

He hurried back to the barracks. When he reached Saodat's bunk, Alexander was still lying beside the man. Both seemed to be sleeping. "I got a little soup and some bread," Yuri whispered, taking the food out from under his coat. His arm ached where he'd pressed the bowl against his side.

Alexander rolled out of bed. "Good."

"I wish I could have gotten more."

"He's not going to get much down," Alexander said.

Yuri sat on the edge of the bed. "How is he?"

"Bad. Really bad. Besides his lungs, he's got frostbite on his face, hands, and feet."

"Saodat," Yuri said. "Saodat?"

The dying man blinked slowly several times before he managed to keep his eyes open. "I am alive," he whispered.

"Can you eat? I have soup and bread."

Saodat tried to push himself up. "I will eat," he croaked.

Yuri supported his shoulders and held the bowl to his lips. Saodat swallowed a few mouthfuls of broth. After that, he ate the bread. Looking intently at Yuri, he asked, "Are you an angel?"

"No," Yuri answered with a chuckle. "But I think we have some here."

Saodat lay back down, still shivering.

"I will get you another blanket," Alexander said, taking one off his bunk. He lay it over Saodat and tucked in the sides. "I need to eat." With a smile, he left.

Saodat continued to shiver, so Yuri climbed beneath the blankets and wrapped his arms around the man, forgetting it was he who had turned Yuri over to the secret police. No remnant of bitterness remained.

Gradually, Saodat's raspy breathing became more even, and he slept. His cold skin became hot, and heat radiated from him. Knowing a powerful infection raged, Yuri crawled from beneath the blankets. He doubted Saodat would live through the night. But death would be a relief only if he knew the Lord. Yuri knelt on the floor, his forearms stretched out on the rough boards in front of him. Resting his face in his hands, he prayed that somehow Saodat would know Christ.

The following morning, when Yuri rose, he immediately went to the sick man's bed, expecting to find him dead. Saodat still lived, although he labored for each breath. Yuri went to the water bucket and dipped out a cup. Returning, he sat on the bed.

Saodat's eyes fluttered open, then closed.

"Drink this," Yuri said, lifting the man's shoulders off the straw mattress. Saodat managed to open his glazed eyes. He rested his hand on Yuri's arm and took a sip of the liquid. Powerful coughing shook his body. Exhausted, he lay back, and in a weak, raspy voice he said, "You *are* an angel."

Yuri smiled. "No, I am not. But I know what you mean. Once when I was sick, I thought my sister, Tatyana, was an angel. Our mother was gone, and she took care of me. Just like an angel, Tatyana never left my side while my fever raged."

His voice barely a whisper, Saodat said, "She must be special, your Tatyana."

"She lives in America now."

"I knew a man once . . . who met a woman . . ." his eyes closed for a moment. "Her name was Tatyana. She was going to . . . America."

Yuri's pulse quickened. "When was this?"

Saodat struggled to remember. "I . . . I think he said it was in spring . . . almost two years ago."

"How did this man know her?"

"He . . . he met her on a train . . . going to Leningrad."

Yuri gripped Saodat's arm. "Did he say any more?"

"He got . . . a letter from her, and she wanted to . . . to find her brother."

"What was the brother's name?"

Saodat's eyes closed and he was quiet.

"Saodat!" Yuri shook him. "Saodat!"

Opening his eyes, he tried to focus on Yuri.

"The brother's name, what was it?"

Surprise registering in his eyes, he said, "I . . . I think it was your name. Yuri."

Yuri's head whirled. "My name?" He swallowed hard. "Who was the man who knew her?"

"His name . . ." Saodat's eyes closed again.

"Who?"

"It was . . . it was . . . Isaac, Isaac Minls."

"Where is he? Here in the camp?"

Saodat peered at Yuri. "He . . . he was a Christian like you. He wanted to help me too. A good man."

"Where is Isaac now?"

"Prison. He was in my cell."

"Do you know what happened to him?"

"No. I hated him. He was . . . there when I left. I shouldn't have hated him. He told me Jesus loved me. Maybe he does." Saodat gripped Yuri's arm. "Does Jesus love me?"

Pushing aside thoughts of Tatyana, Yuri spoke gently. "Yes. He does."

"Good." Saodat's grip relaxed, and his hand fell to the bed. "Saodat?" Yuri asked.

There was no answer. Lifeless eyes stared at the ceiling.

He was gone.

Yuri gently closed the man's eyes. "May you find peace."

He stood beside the bed for a long while, then walked to the doorway. "Isaac Minls, Isaac Minls," he repeated, imprinting the name into his memory. Gazing toward the west, he thought of his sister. "Tatyana, one day I will find you."

CHAPTER 16

THE PERCOLATOR GURGLED, and Tatyana took the coffee off the stove. She splashed the dark brew into Dimitri's cup, then filled hers. "There is a little sugar. Would you like some?"

His elbows propped on the table, Dimitri stared into his cup. "Yeah. I could use some sweetening this morning." Tatyana set the sugar bowl in front of him, and he dipped out a half teaspoon and stirred it into his coffee, then took a sip.

Tatyana sat across from him and warmed her hands on her cup. She studied her husband. A blonde curl fell onto his furrowed brow. "Try not to worry. God will provide."

He barely glanced at her. "I want to believe that."

"I know. Sometimes it is not easy." Tatyana placed her hand over his.

"Tatyana, it was hard to make it when I worked full time. Now what are we going to do? Working two days a week just isn't enough." He stood and walked to the window. Hands in his pockets, he stared outside. "I'm making less than half of what I was."

"Susie told me that the mine always cuts back in the spring when the weather is warm. There will be more work in the fall."

"And what are we supposed to do until then?"

"I heard some of the others found jobs at mills."

Dimitri turned and looked at Tatyana. "I was told they only want men with experience. I don't have any."

Tatyana joined her husband, took his hand, and leaned against him. "You will find something. You are a good worker and strong." Kissing him on the cheek, she asked, "Now, what can I make you for breakfast?"

"I'm not really hungry."

"Josephine brought us some eggs yesterday, and I have fresh bread. If you don't eat, you'll be starved by dinner."

"All right. I'll have some." Dimitri refocused his attention on Tatyana. "How is Josephine?"

Tatyana placed four slices of bread on the oven rack to toast. "She is thinking of moving into her sister's house here in Black Diamond. It would be nice if she lived closer. I like her very much." She cracked two eggs into the frying pan.

"I do too."

Tatyana flipped the toast. "Maybe we can have them here for dinner soon?"

"After I have a job," Dimitri said, emptying his cup.

Tatyana refilled it, then turned the eggs. "Maybe you will find something today." Removing the toast from the oven, she buttered the slices and set them on a dish. Turning the eggs again, she gently poked the yokes, then slid two eggs onto a plate, added two slices of toast, and set the meal in front of Dimitri.

Chapter *16*

"Aren't you going to have anything?"

"I will have toast."

Dimitri took a bite of eggs. "These are good."

"I'll tell Josephine," Tatyana said with a smile.

"I heard they might be hiring down at the Lake Wilderness mill." Dimitri dipped his toast into the yolks and took a bite.

Forcing a smile, Tatyana kissed his cheek. "That sounds good. I am certain everything will be all right."

Dimitri speared another bite of eggs and chewed. His expression bleak, he rested his hand on Tatyana's rounded belly. "How will we take care of the baby?"

Tatyana's stomach jumped beneath his palm. "Oh! I felt that!" he said startled.

"See, he is not worried," Tatyana said. "He just wants to come out and join his family."

Dimitri found his smile. "So, you're sure it's a he?"

"Maybe. It just does not sound right to call the baby an it."

"Well, 'he' it is then." Dimitri patted her stomach and took a deep breath. "I better go." He took another bite of toast and egg, gulped down the last of his coffee, and stood.

Tatyana took Dimitri's hand. "Husband, I am not worried. God will provide."

Dimitri gave her hand a quick kiss. "I hope you're right."

"I know I am."

"I'll see if I can hitch a ride out to the mill." He didn't sound optimistic. "I'm sorry for being such a grouch. I just hoped things would be better for us."

"You are doing all you can. You cannot ask any more of yourself."

He hugged Tatyana tightly. "I love you." Grabbing his jacket off the back of a chair, he pulled it on, then picked his hat up off the table and pushed it onto his head. Strands of blonde hair stuck out the sides. "Wish me luck."

Tatyana tucked the stray locks beneath his cap. "I will be thinking of you and praying."

He opened the back door, and with his hand on the knob, said, "I might be late. Don't worry." He stepped outside and pulled the door closed.

Tatyana watched through the window. Hands in his pockets, he looked at the ground as he walked toward the road. She wished it could be easier for him. "Father, please help Dimitri," she prayed.

After eating a slice of toast and drinking a cup of coffee, Tatyana took the cups and saucers to the sink. She could already feel pressure on her pelvis, and the baby wasn't due for another three months.

Running water into the sink, she gazed out the window. The grasses were growing tall and had turned vivid green. Tall stems topped with bright yellow blossoms swayed in the breeze. Other flowers grew close to the ground in clusters, daubing the fields with pastels. In Russia the earth would still be hidden beneath a blanket of white. Tatyana liked the early spring in Black Diamond.

Deciding a morning walk to the post office would be refreshing, she quickly finished the dishes and straightened the house. Mud and puddles still covered the road, so she pulled a pair of galoshes over her shoes, then slipped on a sweater and buttoned it. It stretched across her rounded abdomen, and she chuckled, unfastening all but the top button.

As she stepped out the front door, she automatically looked at the mountain. Wispy clouds encircled its white peak. Closing her eyes, she took a deep breath, enjoying the fragrance of spring grass and flowers.

In spite of her added girth, her step was light as she headed toward town. When she passed Susie's house, the windows were dark. Although pregnant, Susie still worked. Tatyana felt a momentary pang of jealousy. Neither Susie nor Carl had had their hours cut. Disgusted with her selfish attitude, Tatyana chastised herself. *You should be happy for them. They are your friends. And they have worked at the mine a long time. Of course, newcomers' hours are the ones to be cut back. That is as it should be.*

As Tatyana passed a house with a small yard, she smiled at a man pushing a grass mower. The smell of fresh-cut grass filled the air, and she breathed deeply through her nose. It smelled wonderful. "Good morning," she said.

"It's a beautiful day, isn't it?" the man said.

"Yes, it is." Tatyana spotted several tiny lavender flowers blooming in the grass along the edge of the road. She bent and picked one. The flower grew in a cluster of lavender petals with yellow stars in the center of each bloom. She held the delicate blossom to her nose. It had a subtle fragrance. Keeping the flower, she strolled on, finding others along the way until she had a small bouquet of pink, blue, lavender, and yellow.

Birds sang as they built nests and courted. Evergreen trees were dressed in variegated shades of green, their new growth hanging along the outer branches. Buds sprouted on maple, birch, and alder, promising shade for summer picnics.

Tatyana looked at her belly and rested her hand on it. When the baby came, she and Dimitri would picnic on a blanket in the shade of a maple and play with the baby, then nap in the afternoon warmth. She smiled at the lovely thought.

"Out! Get out!" someone yelled, pulling Tatyana from her reverie. The noise came from the bakery.

Dragging a young man by the scruff of the neck, Mr. Siebold, the owner, shoved him out the door. "I won't have a thief working for me!"

The lad fell right in front of Tatyana. His face red with rage, he glared at the proprietor. Tatyana stepped back.

Pushing himself to his feet, the boy yelled, "I don't need your lousy job anyway!" He bent and picked up his cap, dusted it off, and plopped it on his head. "This is the best thing that could have happened to me," he snapped and strode off, heading east toward Morganville.

Mr. Siebold watched him go, his face pinched with anger. He glanced at Tatyana. "Sorry you had to see that. I hate it when I lose my temper, but the boy had it coming. He's been stealing from me—taking bread and baked goods home with him." He brushed flour from his pant leg. "If he needed food, all he had to do was ask. I like to help when I can." With a disgusted look, he continued, "But he didn't need it. He was selling the stuff." Mr. Siebold leaned against the door frame and folded his arms across his chest. "Now I'll have to find someone to take his place. And train the person."

Tatyana's heart skipped a beat. This would be an answer to her prayers. "How many hours would a person have to work?"

"About fifteen a week."

Tatyana let her eyes wander across the street as she tried to decide the right thing to do. She looked back at the proprietor. "What kind of work is it?"

"Oh, simple things mostly. Cleaning up around the place. You know, sweeping, washing pans and utensils, and sometimes helping make breads and sweet rolls."

Dimitri will not like it if I come home with a job. I should ask him. But if I wait, the position might be gone. Tatyana decided she couldn't wait. She looked directly at Mr. Siebold. "I would like the job."

"You?" Mr. Siebold asked incredulously. "But, you . . ." He blushed. "You're in a family way."

"I am very healthy and strong."

"What about after the baby's born?"

Tatyana lifted her chin slightly. "You need someone now. The baby is not due until summer."

"Have you ever done this kind of work?"

"No, but I keep a clean house and have been told I am a good cook." She chewed on her lip, wondering if she'd been too bold.

Mr. Siebold scratched his head. "I don't know . . ."

"I need the job, sir. My husband works at the mine and his hours have been cut."

Mr. Siebold studied her. "Could you be here early tomorrow morning?"

"Yes! What time?"

"We start mixing dough at 4:00 A.M., then clean the embers out of the ovens. To make sure the bread and sweetrolls are on the shelf early, we start baking by 5:30."

"That is fine. I will be here at 4:00." Before he could change his mind, she said, "Thank you," and walked on. *Oh, dear Lord, what have I done? How will I tell Dimitri?* She knew he'd be angry with her. He'd made it clear that he believed it was his place to provide for them, especially while Tatyana was pregnant. He'd talked about how much he'd hated that his mother had to work when he was younger.

Taking long strides, she told herself, "I had no choice. It was as if God gave me this job. It is a gift." *Oh, dear, I forgot to ask Mr. Siebold how much it pays. It doesn't matter,* she decided. *Something is always better than nothing.*

By the time she'd made it to the post office, excitement had replaced her anxiety. She'd convinced herself that Dimitri would understand and it would be fun to work.

She stepped up to the window and leaned on the counter. The room smelled dusty. Mr. Boseman, the postmaster, was busy poking envelopes into small boxes and didn't notice her. She cleared her throat. He didn't respond. "Sir, could you tell me if I have any mail?"

Turning, Mr. Boseman peered at Tatyana over small round glasses. His face looked pinched. Smoothing his mustache, he said, "I don't remember any, but let me check." He peeked inside her box and took out a long envelope. "My mistake. You do have some." He studied the envelope. "New York."

Over the last several weeks, Mr. Boseman had become meddlesome, and Tatyana had to check her irritation. She held out her hand. Struggling to keep her tone pleasant, she said, "I wish you would not read my mail."

His lips became thin lines. "Being the postmaster is an important position. I consider it my responsibility to make certain everything is as it should be." He talked in a clipped staccato. By crinkling his face, he adjusted his glasses. "To be honest, your being Russian . . ." he let the sentence hang.

Inwardly, Tatyana flinched. He'd made it clear he didn't trust immigrants, especially those from Russia.

"You know how careful we have to be about Communists."

"No, I do not know," Tatyana said, snatching her letter out of his hand.

"If we don't watch out, they'll take over this country too."

Furious, she turned and left the office. After walking a little way, her anger cooled, and she slowed her pace.

* * * * *

Wanting to savor the letter, Tatyana left the envelope and wild flower bouquet on the table. She set water on to boil, measured tea into a piece of cheesecloth, tied it off, then placed it in the water. Filling a vase with tap water, she arranged the flowers and set them on the windowsill. After that, she removed her galoshes, put them in the closet, and hung her sweater on a hanger.

When her tea was ready, she poured it into a cup and sat down to enjoy it and her letter. She looked at the return address, then reread it. It was from Augusta, but the address was the same as Mr. Meyers'! Quickly, she slid her fingernail beneath the seal and tore open the envelope.

As always, Augusta wrote in Russian. She began by chatting about the family and reassuring Tatyana and Dimitri that everyone was well. The children were enjoying school, and Flora's health remained good. But, what Augusta said next sent shivers down Tatyana's spine.

"If not for little Teddy," Augusta explained, "we all would have died in our sleep. The tenement caught fire, and somehow the dog knew we were in danger. He wouldn't stop barking until he had us all up. Pavel wondered what was wrong and looked out in the hallway. It was filled with smoke. We couldn't get to the stairway, so we crawled out a window and onto the fire escape. I didn't get scared until it was all over. I guess I didn't have time to. Thanks to God, we managed to get down safely.

"We lost everything. If not for Mr. Meyers, we would have ended up in the streets. He was very kind and took us in. At first, I wondered about his motives, but the rumors about him are true. He is a changed man. He even gave Pavel a job working with his gardener."

Tatyana tried to envision the new Reynold Meyers. It wasn't easy. He'd been so difficult to work for and had so little respect for anyone of lower status. She could still feel the embarrassment of his advances. And yet, as she remembered her last encounter with him at her wedding, she'd sensed a difference in the man.

Augusta went on to tell her about how nice it was to live in his beautiful house and that she worried about the children being a nuisance, but Mr. Meyers didn't seem to mind. "Also, something everyone expected finally happened. You remember Allison, the maid from Ireland? Well, she and her young man, Johnny, were married. There's some talk about his involvement with the mob, but we're all praying it isn't true. Allison is too sweet a girl to have that kind of heartache."

Tatyana thought about the young Irish girl. She'd been a good friend. She missed her. *Father, take special care of Allison,* she prayed, then returned to the letter.

"Dear ones, we all miss you," Augusta continued. "Samuel never stops talking about how one day he will live in Black Diamond like his brother and raise cows and chickens. We're so excited about the baby, and we hope and pray you remain safe. If only there were some way for us to be there with you. You are in our thoughts every day. All our love, . . ."

The lines blurred as Tatyana's eyes filled with tears. She folded the letter and returned it to the envelope. "I miss you too," she whispered.

That evening, Dimitri came through the back door, his thumb hooked into the gill of a large salmon. Wearing a broad smile, he held it up. "Should make a couple of fine meals."

"More than that. It is so big." Tatyana took the fish. "Now we will have to invite Carl and Susie for dinner."

"They'd like that."

Tatyana wondered if Dimitri had found work but didn't ask, afraid to hear the answer. Plus, she wasn't ready to tell him about her job yet. Taking the fish and plopping it into the sink, she said, "It is beautiful. Was it hard to catch?" She ran cold water over it and began scrubbing away the scales.

"No. I was only at the river about a half an hour before I hooked it. He could fight, though. There was an old-timer on the shore telling me just how to play him."

"I already made soup, but salmon will taste wonderful with it." Tatyana cut the fish into meal-size portions. After melting butter in a frying pan, she set a chunk of meat in to cook, then wrapped the rest in paper and put it in the freezer box.

Dimitri washed up and sat at the table, a smile on his face.

Tatyana turned the fish, put a hot pad in the center of the table, and placed the pot of soup on it. Lifting the lid, she swirled the contents with a ladle, and steam smelling of meat and vegetables rose into the air.

"Mmm, smells good," Dimitri said. "I'm starved. Fishing made me hungry."

Tatyana set a plate of sliced bread beside the soup. She filled Dimitri's bowl, then hers, and sat down. "You look much happier than you did this morning. I think you should go fishing more."

"I just might do that." Dimitri bowed his head. "Thank you Lord, for all you give us. Please take good care of Tatyana and the baby. Amen." Still wearing a smile, he took a slice of bread, dipped it into his stew, and took a bite. "This is very good." He glanced at the stove. "Is the fish done? It smells good."

"Almost." Tatyana studied Dimitri. "Is there something you want to tell me? You have been grinning ever since you came in."

Dimitri leaned forward on his elbows. "I have good news. I got on at the mill at Lake Wilderness. I'll be working two days a week. It doesn't pay as much as the mine, but it will help."

"That is wonderful! What will you be doing?"

"They're going to start me on the planing crew."

"What does that mean? Is it hard?"

"No. Just backbreaking."

"Backbreaking?" Tatyana asked him, her voice laced with concern.

He grinned. "Not really. It's just a term that means it will take a lot of muscle. I'll be pulling green chain. All I have to do is take the rough lumber off the chain as it comes down from the planer." He leaned toward Tatyana. "It's work." Sitting up, he took another bite of bread. "Plus, I already have a ride with a fella who lives right here in Black Diamond."

Her stomach churning, Tatyana tried to think of the best way to tell Dimitri about her job. "The salmon should be done." She went to the stove and transferred the fish onto a plate. "Smells good," she said, setting it on the table.

Dimitri broke off a piece and stuffed it in his mouth. "Tastes good too." He took a sizable chunk and set it on his plate, then gave Tatyana a smaller portion. "Did you do anything exciting today?"

Tatyana stared at her soup. "Not really."

"Is something wrong?"

"No. I had a good day." She picked at the crust of her bread. "We got a letter from your mother." She wanted to tell him about the fire and Mr. Meyers but knew it would only be putting off the inevitability of sharing her news. She gathered her courage. "On my way to the post office, something interesting happened."

"What?"

"When I passed the bakery, Mr. Siebold was firing a boy who works there. He told me he needed someone to take his place right away."

Listening intently, Dimitri set his spoon in his bowl.

"I . . . I told him I would work for him."

"What?"

"I start tomorrow."

Dimitri sat up straight. "Tatyana, you're going to have a baby. You can't work."

"I can. I do here—cleaning house and cooking."

"But that's different."

"How is it different?"

Dimitri brushed a strand of hair off his forehead. "What will people think when they see my pregnant wife working?"

"Is that what you care about? What people think?" Tatyana's anger flared. "We need money. And there are things we have to get for the baby, and . . ."

"I have another job. You don't need to work."

"It is still not enough," Tatyana said as she poked at her fish. "Susie works. Do you think it is a bad thing?" She knew her voice sounded shrill but couldn't control it.

"She was working before." Dimitri stood, picked up his glass, and filled it with water from the tap. Turning to look at Tatyana, he said, "And I do think it's kind of strange that she's still working."

"I hoped you would be happy," Tatyana said, close to tears. "I am trying to help."

"It's just that . . ." Dimitri shrugged, unable to meet her eyes. "Oh, I don't know. I didn't want my wife to work. I want to take care of my family."

"It is only for a little while. After you go back to work full time at the mine, I can quit."

Silence wedged itself between them.

Finally, Dimitri stood and moved around the table. He knelt beside Tatyana and put his arms around her waist. "You're a good wife, Tatyana. I'm sorry for being short-tempered with you. I know you want to help. But if you work, I feel like I'm not taking good care of you and the baby."

"But you are. You do all you can." Tatyana looked directly at Dimitri. "I told Mr. Siebold I would be there tomorrow. He is depending on me." She caressed his cheek. "These are difficult times."

Dimitri took Tatyana's hands in his, turned the palms up, and pressed his lips against them. "We will try it."

CHAPTER 17

THE SUN WARMED TATYANA'S back as she folded the edge of a sheet over the clothesline. The wind caught at the white cotton, threatening to snatch it away. She quickly secured it with a wooden pin, and the bed linen flapped in the breeze.

Sighing, she closed her eyes and stretched to one side, then the other. After working at the bakery, she was weary. Something touched her face, and she opened her eyes to find her bloomers fluttering just inches away.

"Hello!" called Susie.

Tatyana turned and waved at her friend. "Good morning."

Dimitri looked up from where he worked in the garden patch and waved.

Waddling because of her advanced pregnancy, Susie made her way across the yard. She looked up at the deep blue sky. "Isn't it a beautiful day?"

Tatyana glanced up. "Yes. It is." Tatyana gave Susie a serious look. "Should you be walking so much with the baby overdue?"

"All the more reason. I'm hoping it will help start something." Pressing her hands against the small of her back, she eyed her protruding stomach. "I'm so tired of being pregnant. I want this baby out." Patting her abdomen, she continued, "There's no room left for it to grow. I can barely breathe."

Tatyana rested her hand on her own belly. "I know. I still have almost two months left, and already the baby feels crowded."

"You look tired. How is work?"

"I like it. Mr. Siebold is a nice man and is teaching me how to do some baking and use the machinery." Taking a deep breath, Tatyana admitted, "But, I am tired, and sometimes my feet get very swollen."

"I think mine are in a permanent swell," Susie said with a chuckle. She glanced at the garden patch. "You'll have your garden in soon."

"We should. Dimitri works in it every extra minute. He loves working with soil and plants. It will be very nice to have fresh vegetables this summer."

"I guess so. To me, it always seemed like a lot of effort for something I can buy."

"I like the work, and one day our children will help."

Resting her hand on Tatyana's arm, Susie said, "Sometimes it's hard to believe we're going to be mothers. It will be fun having our babies so close together. I hope they will be good friends." A gust of wind caught hold of Tatyana's bloomers, and again, they danced. Susie grinned. "I don't know about leaving those out. The men will be here soon to help build the fence. Carl told me Ben White is going to come."

"Is it wrong?" Tatyana asked.

"No, but when the men start working on the fences, you might wish they weren't there. I've actually seen guys blush when they see underwear on a clothesline. I always thought they were being silly, but that's how some men are."

"What can I do? I do not want to hang them in the house. Everything is much better when it dries outdoors."

"You could put them in a sack. I've done it before. Do you have a feed sack?"

"Uh-huh." Tatyana smiled. "I will get it, then we can sit and have a glass of ice tea."

※ ※ ※ ※ ※

After saying good-bye to Susie, Tatyana joined Dimitri.

Leaning on his hoe, he looked at his wife. "How are you feeling?"

"Good," Tatyana said. Then she bent, picked up a handful of soil, held it to her nose, and sniffed. "I love the smell of dirt." She sifted the loam through her fingers. "We will have a nice garden."

"Soil's good," Dimitri said, wiping his face with his handkerchief. He bent and picked up a rock and tossed it into the field at the back of the yard. "Not too many rocks, and the dirt isn't heavy."

"I can hardly wait to see the garden filled with vegetables. When can we plant?"

"Today. All I have to do is stake out the rows. I won't be able to finish though. Carl will be here soon to help me put up the fence." A bell jangled, and Dimitri eyed a cow lumbering past. "Without a fence, we might as well not bother having a garden. The neighborhood livestock would have it trampled in no time." Abruptly changing the subject, Dimitri took Tatyana's hand. "I brought you something," he said, leading her toward the shed.

"What is it?"

"You'll see." Dimitri's eyes sparkled with mischief.

When Tatyana stepped inside the shed, she was blinded for a moment and waited for her eyes to adjust. Gradually, the interior of the shed revealed itself. Along the nearest wall, a hoe, shovel, and pitchfork rested against aged wood. An old washtub hung above the tools, and on the opposite wall, a shelf held an assortment of boxes and cans. The room smelled musty and damp. She took a step forward.

"This is what I wanted you to see." Dimitri led her to a workbench covered with planters containing sprouting seedlings.

"What are these?" Tatyana asked.

Dimitri handed her a planter box. "Take it outside where you can see better."

With the box in her hands, Tatyana stepped outside. She blinked in the bright sunlight, then studied the small, broad-leafed plants huddled against the dirt. She looked closer. "Strawberries! These are strawberries!"

Dimitri grinned.

Tatyana gently touched a leaf. "You remembered how much I love strawberries. Thank you! They are my favorite!" Hugging him with one arm, she kissed him. "You are good to me."

"Anything for my wife," Dimitri said with mock smugness.

"Just think! We'll have a whole garden of strawberries! I can make preserves and pies!"

Dimitri laughed. "I'm glad you're excited, but it will take a while for the plants to mature. They won't produce many berries their first season, but next year there will be more."

"Is the garden ready? Can we plant them now?"

Dimitri nodded and took the box. He glanced down the street. "Well, Carl's late so why not?"

That morning was one of the best Tatyana had known since arriving in America. She and Dimitri planted the strawberries. With the aroma of rich loam, birds' songs all around, and the heat of the sun warming the earth, she hollowed out a place for each plant, then gently pressed dirt over the roots. Today, Black Diamond felt like home.

After the strawberries were in, Dimitri and Tatyana set out rows of peas and lettuce. Beside the lettuce, they put in tomato starts and ran a line for green beans.

Dirty hands resting against the small of her back, Tatyana stood beside her husband and studied their work. The sun was high in the sky and hot, but Tatyana felt good. She leaned against her husband. "It is hard to believe I have a real garden again. It has been so long." Remembering Dimitri's small roof-top garden, she quickly added, "Your garden in New York was very good, but this is much better."

Dimitri draped his arm across her shoulders. "I agree."

She dusted her hands, then looked at them and smiled. "There is dirt under my nails. My mother used to get frustrated with me for not cleaning the grime from under my nails." Leaning her head against Dimitri's shoulder, she added, "I do not think she would mind now." She took a deep breath. "I am happy, Dimitri. Really happy."

"And what about Russia?"

"I still think of it. I miss it. But not so much as before."

Dimitri squeezed her a little tighter.

"Hey, neighbor!" yelled Carl. "You ready to go to work?"

"I've been working," Dimitri called back.

Taking long strides, Carl crossed the yard. Hands on his hips, feet parted, he stood beside Dimitri and studied the garden. "It looks like you have been working."

"The day is nearly half over. I thought we were going to get to the fence first thing."

"I would have been here sooner, but Susie managed to find a bunch of chores for me to do."

"Soon, you will have more to do," Dimitri said with a grin. "Are you ready to be a father?"

"I think so, but I still get this funny feeling in the pit of my stomach when I think about it." He threw his hands up. "Hey, what choice do I have now? I pray God will help me."

"You will be a good father, I know it," Tatyana assured him.

"I hope you're right." Carl swept his hat off his head. "I saw Ben White this morning. He said he'd stop by and give us a hand."

"Good," Dimitri said. "How is the old-timer doing? I haven't seen him at work all week."

"According to him, he's great. Said he was out of town visiting his sister."

"That guy is unbelievable. He must be nearly eighty. Why is he still doing down?"

"He's seventy-five, and he'll be working the mines until his dying day or until they force him out. It's his life." Carl smoothed his hair back and replaced his cap. "So, you ready to start?"

"I got the corner posts like you told me. Should we put them in first?"

"No. We need to string the lines, then do the posts."

After the lines were done, Carl and Dimitri hauled the posts and braces from the shed and set them in the ground. Just as they were finishing, Ben arrived in a rickety pickup. The door groaned when he opened it. Bent with age, he stepped out and waved. "Good day to ya."

"Hi, Ben. Good to see you," called Dimitri.

Ben slammed the truck door and hobbled across the grass. "Seems you've got a good start here." He spat tobacco juice on the ground. "But it looks like you've got plenty of work left yet. What can I do?"

"Could you hold this post while I pound it into the ground?" Carl asked.

"I'm your man." Ben grinned and grabbed the post. "I s'pose you and Susie are pretty anxious about the baby."

"We are." Carl took a deep breath. "Waiting is hard. I just wish it would happen soon."

"It will, don't you worry," the old man said, smiling. He looked at Dimitri. "And you too. How long 'til your baby is due?"

"We've got another two months to wait."

Ben nodded. "Yep, yep," he said thoughtfully. "Lots of babies bein' born this time of year. It's always that way. It's them cold winters," he said as he chuckled.

"It's nice of you to come out and help us," Dimitri said.

Ben squinted up at Dimitri. "Well, what are neighbors for? Gotta protect each other from roamin' cows. Can't grow nothin' around here without a fence. And I'll tell you, over the years, I've stepped in more than a few cow pies. I sure wouldn't want them in my yard." Ben spit again. "Plus, I figured I ain't got much else to do. There's no work at the mine." Grinning, he revealed even, brown teeth. "What's next?"

"We've got two more corner posts to put in, and then we can begin stringing the fence. And it's not going to get done if we keep standing around talking. Hang on to that post, Ben," Carl said as he swung the sledgehammer.

Late in the afternoon, Tatyana made a pitcher of lemonade and took it out to the men. "Would you like some lemonade?"

"Sounds good," Carl said, pounding in one last nail, then setting his hammer on a post.

Ben straightened a little. "I could use a break."

Dimitri wiped sweat from his forehead and joined Tatyana. Planting a kiss on her cheek, he said, "Thank you."

Tatyana filled the glasses and handed one to each man. "I made cookies," she said as she held out a basket filled with oatmeal cookies.

"Those look mighty good." Using one hand, Ben stacked one cookie on top of the other until he had a four-tiered pile.

"I don't get sweets much. My missus passed away a couple years ago."

"You eat all you want," Tatyana said and turned to leave.

"Hey, you gonna leave us?" Ben asked. "Why don't you stay? It's not often I get to be in the company of a beautiful woman," he said grinning.

Tatyana blushed. "All right." Taking Dimitri's hand, she sat on the grass, careful to tuck her skirt under her legs. The men joined her.

"We're nearly done," Carl said, taking a long drink of lemonade. "All that's left is that section there." He pointed toward the front of the yard along the roadway.

"It will be nice not to worry about having cows in the yard. I thank you for your help," Tatyana said.

"Glad to do it." Carl took a cookie and bit into it. He chewed, then took another. "These are good. You'll have to give Susie the recipe."

"Thank you," Tatyana said.

"We owe you," Dimitri said. "We wouldn't even be putting up a fence if not for you. Thanks for the wire."

"I had some extra. No sense in leaving it laying around."

"Hello," Susie called.

Everyone turned to watch her shuffle across the yard.

Smiling, she said, "I had to see how the fence was coming along." She scanned the yard. "It looks good."

Carl stood. "I thought you were resting."

"I was, but I can only spend so much time lying down." She tossed her red hair back and looked at Tatyana. "Now you won't have to worry about the cows."

"I'll get you a chair." Carl headed toward the house, then glanced back at Tatyana. "I'll get one for you too." With a quick glance at Dimitri he added, "Since your husband forgot to." He grinned, then disappeared inside and returned with chairs for Tatyana and Susie.

Stretching her legs out in front of her, Susie leaned back in her chair. "This is wonderful. I've been craving the sun."

Dimitri refilled the glasses.

Taking a sip of Carl's drink, Susie asked, "What do you think is going to happen in Europe?"

Tatyana wiped a drip of moisture from the outside of her glass. "What do you mean?"

"Hitler and his Nazi party. The papers say he's rearming the military, and the German government is treating the Jews badly. There have been beatings and riots. In fact, one article I read said he doesn't believe Jews should even be allowed to exist."

Ben leaned back on his elbows. "What can he do? He's only one man."

"Well, he's proclaimed himself Fuhrer. From what I understand, that gives him absolute power," Carl said. "I think he can do whatever he wants."

"Do you think he could start a war?" Dimitri asked.

"Nah, the rest of Europe would stop him." Ben took another cookie.

Tatyana leaned back and kicked her feet out in front of her. "Could we talk about something else? It is too nice a day to think about war." She'd seen enough of war's aftermath. She couldn't remember a time when soldiers didn't dominate the countryside and the people. She'd always been frightened by them. She looked at Ben. "So, you still work in the mines?"

"Oh, yeah. I'm gettin' old, but I can still put in a good day's work. Sometimes my back gives me fits. Broke it back in 1920. I was ridin' the trip and didn't see a beam. Caught me just like that, and before I knew it, I was flat out." He grinned. "I'm more careful now." He drained his lemonade. "Things were different in the old days. The mines used to be real dangerous. That's not to say they're not now, but things were worse. We have better equipment now, and the company builds safer mines. I remember when the Lawson Mine went up. Why, the poles actually got blown right out of the ground and were scattered all over the place."

"I heard it was a bad one," Carl said, leaning forward and placing his arms on his knees.

"Yeah, sixteen men died. They only got up eleven of the bodies. And they were burned bad." Ben's voice sounded strained. "I was workin' that day too." He looked at the sky. "God spared my life. Don't know why, but I'm thankful for the years he's given me."

"Why do you keep working in the mines?" Tatyana asked.

Ben shrugged. "Don't know exactly. Just can't stay out of them I guess. It's in my blood. Heard a lot of men get stuck on it. Don't want to give it up. I'm seventy-four and still riding the trips down and doing my share."

"Have you seen a lot of accidents?" Dimitri asked, shoving the last of a cookie in his mouth.

"Oh, yeah, I've seen my share. Probably the worst though, was the Ravensdale explosion. That mine was a dangerous one. The owners knew it too. A lot of gas and dust."

"What happened?" Tatyana asked, fear needling her. She was afraid to hear, but something in her needed to know.

"Well, they never kept the sprinkling system up to par in that mine. Dust was a problem, and when it builds up, it's explosive. Doesn't take much. In my opinion, the company was at fault. The company knew that things needed to be kept damp." Ben's eyes turned hard and a muscle in his jaw twitched.

"Things went bad that day," he continued. "The fans that push the air around weren't workin' right. When it happened, a lot of miners had just come off shift. The body count could have been a lot higher." He tipped his glass up to his mouth, but it was empty.

"Would you like more?" Tatyana asked.

"No thanks." He pushed his cap back. "Anyway, somethin' set off all that dust. Someone probably snuck out and had a smoke. You'd think a man would have more sense. When the dust exploded, it went right on up one level, then the next, and the next, until it blew out the top. Smoke poured out of that place, black as soot. I never seen nothin' like it. And down below, the men were chokin' to death. One of the miners said it was like walking into a black wall of suffocating powder. And they had to breathe that stuff." Ben shook his head. "We lost thirty-one good men that day."

"How awful," Tatyana said, her stomach tightening into a knot. "When did it happen?"

"Oh, way back in 1915. I was a lot younger then, but it spooked me pretty bad. I nearly quit workin' the mines." He scratched his whiskers. "I'll tell ya, I never have been completely comfortable since then."

Dimitri studied Tatyana's face a moment, then stood. "We're going to lose the light soon. We better get back to that fence." He helped Tatyana to her feet.

Carl stood and helped Susie, then handed his glass to Tatyana. "Thank you for the lemonade and cookies. They were real good."

"You are welcome." Feeling sick inside over what she'd just heard, Tatyana gave Carl a feeble smile. What if there were another accident? She kept a hold of Dimitri's hand, needing to feel his strength. Their eyes met and held for a moment, but neither said a word.

That night, as she lay beside Dimitri, Tatyana stared at the ceiling. She couldn't pry Ben's stories from her mind. Images of her husband dying beneath a pile of rubble alone and deep within a mine harassed her.

Dimitri rolled over and laid his arm across her stomach. "You still awake?" he asked sleepily and nuzzled her neck. "Is everything all right? You were awful quiet tonight."

Tatyana rested her hand on his. "I am thinking about the baby."

"You have lots of time to get ready."

She ran her hand over Dimitri's arm. "What if something happens to you? What about the baby? It will have no father."

"You're spooked because of what Ben said today, aren't you?"

Tatyana didn't answer.

"I wish he'd kept his mouth shut. Those accidents happened a long time ago. The mines are safer these days." He propped himself up on one elbow. "Don't forget all the weeks and months we work and nothing bad happens. Accidents are rare." He took her hand and squeezed it. "Try not to worry."

"But accidents can still happen." She turned onto her side and looked at him. "I know we talked about this before, but I cannot make the fear go away."

Dimitri took a deep breath. "I wish I could say something that would make you feel better, but I don't know what it would be. Right now, I'm lucky to be working at all."

"Could you get more hours at the mill?"

"They don't need me full time." He caressed her hair. "Besides, this mine has a good safety record. It doesn't have the problems Ravensdale did. There's no dust to speak of, and it's damp down there." He kissed her. "All you need to think about right now is taking good care of yourself and the baby." He kissed her tenderly. "I love you," he said, then laid back.

"I love you too," Tatyana managed to say, but she continued to stare at the ceiling.

CHAPTER 18

K NEES HURTING FROM KNEELING in the dirt, Tatyana leaned back on her heels. Pressing her hands against the small of her back, she looked at the brilliant blue sky. *What a beautiful day,* she thought and dusted the dirt from her palms. It felt good to work with the plants and soil again. While growing up on the farm, she'd always enjoyed her time in the fields, the sun warming her back, and the smell of dirt and vegetables in the air.

Plucking one last weed from the row of peas, she studied the plants winding their way up the string runners. Soon, the plants would yield green pods, plump with sweet fruits and ready to harvest. Her mouth watered at the thought of creamed peas and baby potatoes. *It won't be long.*

Perspiration trailed down her forehead, and she wiped it away with the back of her hand. The baby kicked hard and, for a moment, she felt breathless.

"Tatyana," called Susie.

Tatyana glanced over her shoulder at her friend pushing a baby carriage across her yard. Susie and Carl's little girl had arrived three weeks before with wisps of red hair and a tiny nose. She looked like her mother, and Tatyana had marveled at how small and perfect she was.

Feeling cumbersome, Tatyana struggled to her feet. "Hello. It is good to see you. How are you feeling?"

"Evelyn and I are wonderful." Susie gave Tatyana a quick hug, then peered into the carriage. "Would you like to hold her?"

"Yes." Tatyana glanced at her dirty hands. "No." She held them up, palms out. "She is such a beautiful baby," Tatyana said, wishing her own child were in her arms. "How did she sleep last night?"

"Oh, about the same. We were up at midnight and then again at four. Carl's a wonder and helps all he can, but he has to get up early for work and is worthless when it comes to meals," she said laughing.

"It will get better," Tatyana reassured her. "Evelyn will grow and eat less often."

"I know." Susie touched her daughter's hand, and Evelyn grabbed hold of her finger. Susie looked at Tatyana. "How are *you* feeling?"

"Good but tired. I'll take a nap later. I saw Dr. Logan yesterday and he said the baby will not be here for a few weeks. It is hard to wait."

"I know, but you can't rush babies. They come when they're ready and not before."

Tatyana smiled. "Still, waiting is difficult, especially when I watch you with Evelyn."

CHAPTER 18

"Your garden is looking good." Susie frowned. "You're not working too hard are you? It's awfully warm today. You should be inside with your feet up."

"Working in the garden is good for me. I like it. Anyway, I am done for today. Would you like some lemonade? Dimitri enjoys it, so I make it when I can get lemons."

"That sounds good." Susie pushed the pram toward the house. "Are you going to the baseball game this afternoon?"

"Baseball? Dimitri said something about a game this morning before he left for Auburn. I have not seen a baseball game before. What is it?"

"You lived in New York and never went to a Yankees game?"

"No," Tatyana said. "But I did hear about them."

"If you've never been to a baseball game, then you have to go. Black Diamond is playing Enumclaw. The two teams have had a rivalry for years. The kids have a good time playing while the adults cheer them on. And Enumclaw has a nice field with bleachers. Carl and I are going and thought you and Dimitri could go with us."

"Dimitri should be home soon."

"Well, we plan to leave about one o'clock. You and Dimitri can ride with us if you want to go."

"That would be nice."

※ ※ ※ ※ ※

Just as Dimitri and Tatyana were finishing lunch, Carl and Susie pulled up in front of the house and honked the car horn.

"Are you sure you want to go?" Dimitri asked, eyeing Tatyana's bulging stomach. "You might be uncomfortable."

"I have a blanket we can sit on." She smiled. "I will be fine." She picked up a quilt draped over the end of the couch. "Do you know how to play this game of baseball?"

"Yes and no. When I was a boy, I went to a few games, and we kids used to play stickball on the street. It's kind of like baseball. I wasn't very good."

"Why? You are big and strong."

"I was thirteen before I ever played. The other kids had been playing since they were little."

Carl honked his horn again.

"A jug of water and a basket with sandwiches are on the kitchen table. Could you get them?" Tatyana asked.

Dimitri disappeared through the kitchen door and reemerged a moment later with the jug and basket. "I guess we're ready." He took his wife's arm and escorted her to the door.

When they reached the ball field, the stands were filled with spectators. Blankets with picnickers littered the grass, and men crowded the first-base line.

"This must be a very important game," Tatyana said as Susie helped her lay out the blanket.

"Around here, people love baseball." Susie sat and laid Evelyn in her lap. Sucking on her fist, the baby gazed at her mother.

Dimitri held Tatyana's hand as she carefully sat and folded her legs beneath her. "I feel like an overfed cow," she said, tucking her skirt under her.

"You look beautiful," Dimitri said and sat beside her.

"I always stand on the sidelines," Carl said, heading toward the playing field. "You want to join me?"

Dimitri looked at Tatyana, indecision on his face.

"Go with Carl."

"You sure?"

"Yes. Susie and I will be fine right here."

With a quick kiss, Dimitri jumped up and joined Carl along the baseline.

CHAPTER *18*

"Sometimes, they're like little boys," Susie said. "I don't think they ever really grow up."

Tatyana smiled as she watched her husband. "I am glad Dimitri came. He works hard."

The players took their positions, and after a short warm-up, the first pitch was thrown.

As Tatyana watched the game, she became confused. None of it made sense. Finally, she asked, "Tell me why the boy swings the stick at the ball, and what are the others standing on the cushions supposed to do?"

Susie laughed. "I guess it must look strange to you since you've never seen a game before. I'll try to explain it. The boy who is at bat . . ."

"At bat—what does that mean?"

"That's when someone is batting. I mean, they have the stick and try to hit the ball. Anyway, if he hits it, he runs around the bases, the cushions. If he makes it all the way around and gets back to where he started, the team gets a point."

"Why would he want to go back where he started?"

Susie stared at Tatyana, then shrugged her shoulders. "It's just the way the game is played."

"All right, but why do they throw the ball back and forth to each other when the batter is running around the bases?"

"If they touch the runner with the ball, he's out, or if they get it to the base before the runner does, he's out."

"Out? What does that mean?"

"It just means he loses his turn and can't score." Evelyn whimpered and Susie picked her up. "What is it, sweetheart?" Holding the baby against her shoulder, Susie patted her back.

"I do not understand, but I can see the children like to play." She watched a few moments longer, her attention especially drawn to the men who shouted instructions and waved their arms as children batted and ran the bases. "I think our husbands are having the most fun."

Rocking back and forth, Susie said with a smile, "I think you're right."

Even though Tatyana didn't understand all that was going on, the excitement of the other spectators was contagious. As they hooted and cheered, she found herself smiling and wanting to join in. According to Susie, the two clubs were evenly matched, even though the Black Diamond team was behind by one point.

Midway through the game, Dimitri and Carl returned to their wives.

Dimitri sat beside Tatyana. "How do you like baseball?"

"I like it. And I understand some of it." She leaned against her husband.

"Are you tired?"

"A little."

The baby moved, causing a temporary lump to appear on Tatyana's belly. "Did you see that?" Dimitri asked.

"Yes. And I felt it," Tatyana said. "This baby feels big."

Dimitri rested his hand on her stomach.

"Dimitri," Tatyana whispered. "People will see." She took his hand in hers.

"Nobody cares."

"Still, it does not seem proper."

"Just think, one day our son will be playing baseball. And we'll be here to watch him."

"And what if it's a girl?"

"She'll come with us to watch the games."

"Black Diamond has a girls' basketball team," Susie interjected. "Why not a girls' baseball team? I think girls should be able to play if they want. Isn't that right, Evelyn?"

Carl took his daughter, held her out in front of him, and carefully cradling her head, he smiled at her and said, "I don't think I want her out there playing such a rough game. She might get hurt."

CHAPTER *18*

"So, it is all right for boys to get hurt, but not girls?" Susie challenged.

"Boys are tougher." Carl smiled as he moved to avoid Susie's playful slap. He laughed. "I was only teasing. Of course she'll play if she wants." He kissed his daughter's cheek. "Even if I have to form an all-girl team just for her."

"Oh, what a beautiful baby," Josephine Simmons said, peering over Carl's shoulder.

"Josephine. It's good to see you," Dimitri said. "You're a long way from home. Are you here just for the game?"

"Oh, yes. I'm a big fan. And I don't live so far away anymore. I moved to Black Diamond a few days ago. I live with my sister, Miranda, now."

Standing several yards away, Miranda bobbed her head once and flashed a quick smile at the group, then gave Josephine an exasperated look. "Come on, sister. We must hurry."

"Hold your horses. I'll be there," Josephine said. "She invited company for dinner, so she's got to get home. I hate missing the rest of the game. It's a good one." She frowned. "I'd better get a move on."

"It is nice having you live close. I hope you will visit us," Tatyana said.

"I would like that." An unexpected gust of wind nearly swirled away Josephine's straw hat. She trapped it under her hand and said, "By the way, I have some extra chickens. When I moved in with Miranda, she already had a flock. After adding mine, we've got more than we can take care of. Would you like a few?" She looked from Tatyana to Susie.

"Thank you, but I've never liked chickens much," Susie said. "I buy eggs from a friend."

Dimitri looked at Tatyana, then back at Josephine. "We don't have any place to put them."

"They don't need anything special. A small coop will do. Just a place to lay their eggs. Actually, you could do without a coop,

229

but then you'd have to search for your eggs every day." She chuckled. "You do that, and sometimes you're bound to come across one that's a little ripe."

"Josephine," Miranda snipped.

Josephine shot her sister an annoyed look. "Let me know what you decide." With a smile, she turned and joined Miranda, and the two hurried on their way.

As Tatyana watched her go, she said, "It would be nice to have our own hens."

"I'd like that," Dimitri said. "I'll build a coop right away."

As the sun dropped toward the west, the Enumclaw team squeaked by the Black Diamond boys. The visiting team took the loss in stride, vowing to beat their rivals the next time.

It had been a pleasant afternoon, but Tatyana was exhausted and glad to be heading home. As they followed the winding road to Black Diamond, Evelyn made it clear she'd had enough excitement for one day. No matter what Susie did to quiet the infant, she cried.

Carl drove faster, his daughter's wailing obviously getting on his nerves. He stopped the car in front of Dimitri and Tatyana's house. "Sorry for all the racket," he said.

"Don't worry about it," Dimitri said, nearly shouting over the baby's shrieking as he stepped from the car and helped Tatyana out. "We had a good time. And besides, the noise is going with you."

"It'll be your turn soon," Carl quipped.

Dimitri grinned and slammed the door. Waving at their friends, Tatyana and Dimitri watched them drive away, Evelyn's cries carrying from up the street.

Dimitri took Tatyana's arm and walked down the path. "I need to get some material for that coop. I think I heard Tom say he had some extra wood he wanted to get rid of."

"Do you have to do it tonight? It is late. The sun will be down soon."

"I want to get started first thing in the morning. I won't be gone long."

"All right. I will fix dinner." Tatyana kissed Dimitri. "I had a good time today. Maybe we can go again?"

"Yeah. I had fun too. I think I'll take the shortcut through the draw," he said and loped down the hill.

❈ ❈ ❈ ❈ ❈

As Dimitri approached the creek bed, he heard a strangled bellow. "What is that?" he wondered aloud. The sun rested just above the Olympic range and cast long shadows between the trees, making it difficult to see through the dense underbrush.

The noise didn't let up, so Dimitri edged towards it, his hair prickling on the back of his neck. Edging closer, he peered around a thicket but still couldn't see anything. The noise came again, and he stopped, then took one step forward. A hulking dark shape huddled in the mud along the creek. Careful to stay hidden, he took another step. The strange bawling sound reverberated and, this time, he recognized the cry of a calf. Feeling silly over his nervousness, he straightened and walked into the clearing. The animal was in a desperate predicament. Evidently, in an effort to cross the creek, it had mired itself in mud and was now buried up to its chest. With each bawl, the calf struggled and lunged forward but only managed to embed itself more firmly. If someone didn't help, the animal would die.

As Dimitri waded into the creek, muck pulled at his boots. When he reached the animal, he grabbed it around the neck and yanked but couldn't budge it. Keeping his voice soft and gentle, he said, "You'll be all right, baby. I'll get help." The calf rolled its eyes, the white showing all around, and bawled. Saliva foamed and dripped from its mouth.

Knowing time counted, Dimitri trudged back through the muck, and when his feet found solid ground, he ran. Scrambling up the hill, he rushed into his tool shed, grabbed a rope, then raced to Carl's. Banging on the door, he shouted, "Carl! Carl! I need your help!" As he tried the knob, it was jerked out of his hand. Carl stood in the doorway. Her face troubled, Susie stood behind him.

Carl asked, "What's wrong? Is it Tatyana?"

"No." Dimitri struggled for breath. "There's a calf down at the creek stuck in the mud. It'll die if we don't get it out."

"You nearly stopped my heart over a calf?" Carl accused.

"Dimitri Broido, I could wallop you," Susie said.

"Sorry, but I need help." He held up a length of rope. "I already stopped at the shed and got this."

Pulling on his coat, Carl said to Susie, "I'll be right back."

The two hurried down the hill to the animal. When they arrived, the calf was mired up to its shoulders, and its head rested on top of the mud; it no longer struggled.

Dimitri tramped through the mire, then reached out and patted the animal's head. The pathetic calf opened its eyes and looked at Dimitri but uttered no sound. "It's still alive. Throw me the rope."

Carl quickly tied a loop and tossed the line to Dimitri.

Dimitri tightened it around the calf's neck. "I'll pull from here."

As the men pulled, the rope tightened around the calf's neck and it bawled pathetically. Still, the mud held fast.

Dimitri loosened his hold. "Wait. Let me try something." He scooped away the mud pressing against the animal's chest.

Carl waded in beside him. "I can't believe I'm doing this," he said as he joined Dimitri in his efforts. "I had plans for a quiet supper, some time with my baby girl, and then a good book."

"Life takes funny twists and turns," Dimitri said with a grin. Mud splashed his mouth, and he spluttered and spit. "I could think of better things to do myself."

Carl removed the rope and quickly fashioned a makeshift harness that he placed over the animal's nose and face.

After most of the calf's chest was exposed, the men hauled on the rope again. Saliva bubbled around the calf's mouth, and its eyes widened, but gradually the mud gave way. Soon, the shoulders, then legs were free, and the men hauled the calf onto the bank.

Sides heaving, the calf stood trembling, its nose nearly resting on the ground.

Carl studied the animal more closely. "She's probably one of Hanson's. He doesn't live far from here. We better get her moving."

"I don't know if she can walk." Dimitri pulled gently on the rope, but the calf refused to budge. Bending his knees, he placed one arm under her neck, the other under her hind end, and lifted her. "Uhh. She weighs more than she looks. Show me the way."

Carl led and Dimitri followed. Soon, his arms ached and he panted for breath. "How much further?"

Carl pointed at a small cabin across the road from Lake Fourteen. "That's his place." Smoke curled from the rooftop.

"If we weren't so close, I'd make you take a turn," Dimitri said but kept walking.

When they reached the house, Carl went to the door and knocked. A large whiskered man wearing dirty overalls came to the door. He peered into the gathering gloom. "You're a sight. What happened to you?"

Carl grinned. "We had an encounter with a calf. Have you lost one?"

"Can't say I have, can't say I haven't. I was just going out to feed." He peered beyond the porch at Dimitri, who'd set the calf on the ground. He stepped onto the porch and studied the shivering animal. "What happened?"

"We found her stuck in the mud down by the creek," Dimitri said.

Mr. Hanson grinned. "Looks like she got the best of you."

"She nearly did." Dimitri glanced down at his mud-caked clothing.

"Well, it might be one of mine. Hard to say with all the mud." Pulling the door closed, he said, "Let's have a look." Swinging his arms at his sides, Mr. Hanson walked toward the barn.

The calf allowed itself to be led on wobbly legs.

"I've had several cows come fresh recently." When he reached the barn, he hefted down a bale of hay and carried it to the crib. Separating off sections, he spread the hay out, and a small herd of cows and calves pushed their way in to feed.

Mr. Hanson counted cows and calves, then searched the paddock. "So, Merribell, where's your new heifer?" As if in answer to the question, the muddied calf bawled and pressed its nose against the wooden gate. A honey-colored cow poked her nose through the fencing and nuzzled her baby.

"Seems we have a pair," Mr. Hanson said as he undid the latch on the gate. The calf needed no urging and quickly found its mother. After a short greeting, she suckled, her tail flicking happily.

"I wonder how she got out. I'll check the fence lines in the morning." He turned to Dimitri and Carl. "Thanks very much for your help. It's not every man who'd go out of his way and muddy himself to save an animal." He scrubbed at his beard. "Tell you what. As soon as this young heifer is weaned, she's yours. That is, if you want her."

"It was Dimitri who saved her," Carl said. "He came and got me. All I did was help."

Mr. Hanson looked at Dimitri. "She's yours then."

Dimitri knew the value of the calf. "Thank you, sir, but you don't have to do that. I was glad to help."

"Nevertheless, I want you to have her. She'll make a fine mama one day and give you and your family all the milk you need plus some."

CHAPTER *18*

Dimitri took Mr. Hanson's hand and pumped it up and down. "Thank you. Thank you."

※ ※ ※ ※ ※

Exhausted, Dimitri sat on the back porch. He pulled off his muddy boots.

"Dimitri, is that you?" Tatyana asked, opening the door.

"Yes." He looked up at his wife silhouetted in the light from the kitchen. "I can't come in like this."

"Like what?" Tatyana opened the door wider, and light flooded the porch. Her mouth fell open. "What happened?"

"Carl and I saved a calf stuck in the mud down at the creek." He stood, boots in hand. "What do you want me to do with my clothes?"

"Come in. A little mud can be mopped up." She moved away from the door.

Gingerly, Dimitri stepped inside. "Because we saved the calf, Mr. Hanson gave her to us, as soon as she's weaned, that is."

"A calf?"

"It's a heifer."

"How wonderful! I never thought I would have a cow again." She smiled. "God is good to us! Now we have a garden, chickens, and a cow!"

"I have to admit, life is good," Dimitri agreed and set his boots on the floor, then unbuttoned his shirt.

Tatyana took it. "I remember how your brother said he wanted to move here. He always talked about living on a farm with cows and chickens. Now we have a farm, kind of, and I wish Samuel could be here. And your whole family."

Dimitri sat and pulled off his socks. "It would be nice, but how? They could never get together enough money to move out. And if they did, what would Papa do for a job?"

"He used to work in a bakery. I will have to quit my job soon, and Mr. Siebold will need someone. Your papa knows all about the machinery and the baking." Dimitri handed her his socks, and she dropped them and his shirt in a clothes basket. "We cannot forget that God takes good care of his children," Tatyana continued.

"I just don't have the kind of faith it takes to ignore practicality," Dimitri said shivering.

"You need a hot bath," Tatyana said. "Maybe you can rest a little and pray about your unbelief?"

Dimitri stared at her. "My unbelief? Just because I don't think like you?" He took a breath. "I believe in God. I just don't think he really pays that much attention to the little things in life. Now, if we were having a war or famine or something, that would be different." He stopped and thought a moment. "You don't have a good reason to be angry with me. There are lots of ways to believe."

"I am not angry, only disappointed," Tatyana said quietly. She didn't tell him the ache in her heart or that she longed for him to know the Lord as she did and to understand that God did care about the details of their lives. *Father, help him. He is missing so much.*

CHAPTER 19

THE MAN TRIP MADE ITS WAY deep into the mountain. Tom Olson, one of the crew bosses, sat beside Dimitri, muttering.

As Tom griped, his anger grew and so did the volume of his voice. "That lazy sod! I told him if he missed another day, I'd fire him! This is it! No more chances!" He gripped the side rim of the car. "He's fired," Tom said and looked directly at Dimitri. "How would you like to take on more work? I can give you two more days a week."

"Sure. I guess. I need the work."

"You working Tuesday and Thursday?"

"Uh-huh."

"Now you're working Monday through Thursday."

Dimitri's pulse quickened. "I want the job, but what about Matt? He's been with the company a long time."

"Matt?" Tom exploded. "Does it look like I care about Matt?" He didn't give Dimitri a chance to respond. "If he can't bother to show up, I don't owe him anything. The job is yours." With that, he folded his arms over his chest and glared straight ahead.

A smile creased Dimitri's face. He could probably stay on at the mill one day a week, and with these added hours, he and Tatyana would have plenty of money. Tatyana could quit her job right away. She'd been working three mornings a week and the extra time on her feet made her ankles and feet swell. Some days she came home limping. She never complained, but her quiet sacrifice only made Dimitri feel guilty. He should be able to provide for his family. *Tatyana should be home sewing clothes for the baby, decorating the nursery, and working the garden she loves so much. Now she will have more time for those things,* he thought with satisfaction.

After his shift ended, Dimitri washed up, quickly donned clean clothing, and hurried to the waiting train. He was the first one to board and waited impatiently for the others. He couldn't wait to tell Tatyana the news.

Carl sat beside him and set his clothing bag on the floor between his feet. "I was told about your new work schedule. Congratulations." He shook Dimitri's hand. "God answers prayers and rewards hard work."

"I'm sorry about Matt but glad to get the work. Tatyana will be relieved. It was getting harder and harder for her to put in the hours at the bakery."

"Too bad for Matt, though. He's got a whole passel of kids." Carl shook his head slowly. "It's his own fault. He should have known this would happen. He did a good job, but he's never been dependable."

By the time Dimitri made it home, he'd decided he would take Tatyana out to celebrate. He stepped in the front door and called, "Tatyana."

Walking out of the kitchen, Tatyana smiled. "Hello. Did you have a good day?"

Dimitri took three long strides and pulled her into his arms. "Yes. Very good."

Tatyana laughed. "What is it?"

Dropping his arms but hanging onto Tatyana's hands, Dimitri stepped back and said, "Do you know how beautiful you are?" Then he kissed her soundly.

"Dimitri, what has happened?"

He smiled broadly. "I've been hired on two more days a week at the mine. That's almost full time. Plus, I'll still be able to work one day at the mill. You'll be able to quit the bakery."

"How did this happen? I thought nothing would change until fall."

"You know Matt Johnson?"

"Is he the man with the Indian wife and five children?"

"That's him. Well, Matt didn't show up again today, so Tom fired him and asked me to take on two extra days."

"Why did Tom fire him?"

"It's been coming. Matt has never been good about getting to work on time or at all. And today, Tom had enough."

"Poor Matt. What will happen to him and his family?"

"I don't know. I feel bad about it, but it's not something I can change. And now life will be easier for us."

Tatyana hugged Dimitri.

He caressed her long hair. "I think we should celebrate. There's a new movie playing at the theater. I thought we could go on Friday night."

"That would be fun."

Dimitri rested his hands on Tatyana's forearms and looked straight into her eyes. "You need to tell Mr. Siebold that you can't work for him anymore. He'll understand. He's a good man."

"He is, but I will have to keep working until he finds someone to take my place."

"That shouldn't take long. There are lots of people looking for work. He'll find someone right away."

"I like my job and the people. They were teaching me more and more about baking. I will miss it."

"How can you say that? You're dead tired, trying to do that and everything else."

"I know, but still, I liked it."

Dimitri kissed the tip of Tatyana's nose. "Now you'll have more time to get ready for the baby." He rested his hand on her belly.

Tatyana cuddled close to her husband and took a contented breath. "I will like that. I have sewing to do, and maybe I could paint the nursery?"

Dimitri grinned. "I think we can afford it."

"Then, I will go tomorrow and buy the paint." Tatyana walked into the kitchen. "Are you sure you want to keep working at the mill?"

"Yeah, just one day, though. I still need time to work around here." He hung his jacket and hat on the peg next to the back door. "What smells so good?"

"Susie gave me a venison roast, and I made bread. Plus, I dug our first potatoes and picked fresh peas."

"Mmm. That sounds good. I'm starving." Dimitri slung his leg over a chair and sat down. Leaning his elbows on the table, he studied Tatyana. Smiling, he said, "You look beautiful."

Tatyana blushed. "I look fat."

❋ ❋ ❋ ❋ ❋

The next evening, Susie approached Dimitri while he worked in the garden. She glanced around. Speaking quietly, she said, "Dimitri, don't forget the baby shower Friday."

"Friday. Okay." Dimitri stopped hoeing. "Oh, I already forgot. Tatyana and I are going to the movie Friday night. How can I cancel? She'll know something's up."

Susie thought a moment. "What if you bring her over after the movie? Or even better, we can set up here after you leave and be waiting when you get home."

Dimitri grinned. "That sounds good. She'll still have a night at the movies and won't suspect a thing."

❋ ❋ ❋ ❋ ❋

It Happened One Night had been applauded as one of the best pictures of the year, so as Dimitri and Tatyana settled in their seats, Tatyana was eager for the movie to begin. Going to the theater was still a special treat. She doubted she'd ever take it for granted. Anyway, she hoped not. Glancing around the movie house, she looked for her friends but didn't see any. "That is odd. I do not see anyone I know."

"Don't worry about them," Dimitri said.

Tatyana snuggled as close to Dimitri as the seats would allow. "I heard this is a love story."

Dimitri lifted her hand to his lips. "It's meant for us, then."

Tatyana felt passion stir.

The theater turned dark, the screen brightened, and black numbers flashed through a countdown before a newsreel began. Tatyana settled back to watch, hoping for reports from her homeland. A man with a deep voice talked of unrest in Europe and Hitler's aggressive rhetoric, while clips of a tight-lipped little man standing before admiring crowds lifting their arms in salute were shown. Apprehension washed over Tatyana. The man frightened her.

The only news of home was a feature showing how Russia had flourished under Stalin's five-year plans. Scenes rolled of giant bridges, new factories, and healthy children frolicking across a lawn while a narrator reported new prosperity under Joseph Stalin's leadership.

"Do you think what they say is true?" Tatyana asked.

"They were showing clips like these even before you came here. It's propaganda."

Anger welled up in Tatyana. "How can they tell such lies?" she whispered. "Do you think people believe it?"

"I don't know. Some reports are coming out that are accurate." Dimitri squeezed her hand. "I'm sure our government knows the truth."

"Then why do they let these news clips be shown?"

"I don't know."

A Mickey Mouse cartoon followed the news, and Tatyana relaxed. She enjoyed the animated character with his squeaky voice and silly antics.

"I hope they don't show another cartoon or a Flash Gordon film," Dimitri said, squirming in his seat.

"Why? Do you want to leave? Is something wrong?"

"No. I just want to watch the movie."

Mickey Mouse faded, and the screen went black. A few moments later, the music swelled and the credits ran. "At last." Dimitri visibly relaxed in his seat. He looked at Tatyana. "Do you remember our first movie?"

"Yes. I knew nothing then. I felt like a fool."

"You *were* kind of funny. I remember how your eyes got real big when the movie started."

"Were you watching me?"

"Yes. I tried hard not to let you know."

"I was very nervous that night. I was with the rudest man I had ever met and watching something I had never seen before. I did not know what to expect."

Dimitri chuckled. "I'm glad you changed your mind about me." He rested his arm on her shoulders and squeezed affectionately.

"So am I."

The man in front of them turned around, held his finger to his lips, and shushed them.

Embarrassed, Dimitri and Tatyana apologized simultaneously, then stared silently at the screen.

As Claudette Colbert and Clark Gable verbally sparred then flirted, Tatyana thought of the early months with Dimitri. The story reminded her of how it had been between the two of them in the beginning. Both had cared for the other but kept their feelings private, and neither had been truthful with the other. She hadn't even been honest with herself. *Thank you, Lord, for watching over us and helping us when we act stupidly.*

As the story concluded with the lovers finally in each others arms, the screen turned black and Tatyana wished she could remain in the dark cocoon of make-believe. But the lights went on, forcing the moviegoers to release the fantasy.

Dimitri stood immediately. "We'd better go."

"Why are you in a hurry?"

"I'm not," he said as he took her arm, helped her up, and guided her through the crowds to the front of the theater. The sun blazed atop the rugged Olympic peaks, coloring the sky gold.

Tatyana stopped and leaned against Dimitri as people streamed past. "Can we sit here on the steps and watch the sun set?"

Dimitri hesitated. "Why?"

Puzzled and a little irritated, Tatyana stared at her husband. "We watch a romantic movie, and I ask you to watch the sunset with me, and you ask why?" She looked at her rounded belly and tears filled her eyes. "You do not see me like you used to because I am fat."

"No. That's not true."

"Then, why?"

Dimitri searched for an answer, then without saying a word, sat on the step. Taking her hand, he said, "We will watch the sunset."

Tatyana stood for a long moment and looked at her husband, wishing she could understand him; then she finally sat beside him. "Is something wrong? Aren't you feeling well? You do not seem like yourself."

"No. I'm just tired. That's all."

"Then we should go home," Tatyana said and stood.

"Are you sure?"

"Yes." Tatyana walked down the last two steps. "Are you coming? You were the one in a hurry."

Dimitri jumped past two steps to the bottom and reached for his wife's hand.

Tatyana avoided his grasp, folded her arms over her stomach, and walked toward home. Neither spoke.

When they reached the house, Dimitri hurried ahead and said loudly, "It's good to be home." He opened the door and stepped aside, allowing Tatyana to enter ahead of him.

"Surprise!" shouted a chorus of voices.

"What is this?" Tatyana asked.

"A party for you and the baby," Susie said as she hugged her friend. "When we heard Dimitri was taking you to the movies, we decided to surprise you."

"That's why I was in a hurry to get home," Dimitri explained.

"Oh, Dimitri. I am sorry. I should have known you would never push me away." She took his hand.

Blushing a little, he glanced at the room of women. "I'd better go." He bent, kissed Tatyana on the cheek, and whispered, "I did feel romantic."

Tatyana smiled. "I love you."

"Enough of that," Susie said, stepping between the couple. "We have a party to put on." She guided Dimitri toward the door.

"Have fun," Dimitri said as the door closed on him.

Tatyana was ushered to the sofa.

"You sit right here," Susie said.

★ ★ ★ ★ ★

The evening passed in a blur of games, gifts, and laughter. Tatyana had never been to a baby shower but quickly decided she liked the American custom. In Russia, friends and family often contributed needed items to an expectant mother, but never with so much flamboyance. By evening's end, she had a pile of baby supplies. The women had brought blankets, diapers, sheets, infant clothing, and other necessary items. Tatyana was overwhelmed by their generosity, knowing that for many it had required real sacrifice.

As the guests left, Tatyana thanked each one, but saying thank you seemed inadequate to express her gratitude. Her heart swelled with joy at the love shown. After everyone had gone, Tatyana and Susie sat on the sofa. "This is a very special thing you did for me."

"I wanted to do it," Susie said.

"But I did not do anything for you."

"You didn't even know about baby showers. Besides, the ladies gave me a party. Remember the invitation you received?"

"Oh, yes. I was ill and could not go. So, this is what I missed?"

"Uh-huh. But, I'll count on you next time." Susie leaned her head against the back of the couch. "It feels good to have a night away from the baby. I almost forgot what it was like." She gave Tatyana's belly a quick pat. "Your turn soon," she said as she hugged her friend. "If you need anything after the baby comes, you just ask, okay?"

"I will."

"Good. Well, I'd better get home. Carl is probably beside himself by now. He's not used to taking care of Evelyn all by himself. And I doubt Dimitri is much help."

Tatyana chuckled. "Then, you'd better go."

With Susie gone, the house seemed especially quiet. Tatyana sat and thought about the evening. It had been fun. Exhausted, she looked at the stack of gifts and knew they needed to be put away, but she didn't have the energy. Resting her hand on her stomach, she thought about the child tucked safely inside. Was it a boy or a girl?

The door creaked open and Dimitri stepped into the front room. "Is everyone gone?"

"Yes."

Eyeing the gifts, Dimitri asked, "You got all this?"

"Yes. The women were so generous." She grinned at her husband. "I cannot believe you kept this secret from me."

"Well, you know Susie. She threatened me with my life. And I still paid dearly with my wife's wrath. When we were walking home, I wondered if you would ever speak to me again."

Tatyana laughed. "I am sorry." She scanned the baby items. "We have everything we need for our baby, except a crib."

Dimitri smiled. "I was saving it for a surprise, but now is a good time. I'll be right back." Dimitri stepped outside and returned a few minutes later, carrying a brand new ivory, enamel crib. "When I saw this at the company store, I decided our baby should have it." He set it up. "I have a mattress, but it's still in the shed."

Tatyana was overwhelmed. She had so much. In such a short time, her life had changed dramatically. When her brother sent her off on the train, she couldn't have imagined the course her life would take. She crossed to Dimitri, and resting her hand on his arm, said, "Thank you. It is beautiful." She ran her hand over the smooth wood.

"I wanted to surprise you."

"You have." Tatyana hugged Dimitri. "It is perfect. Can we put it in the nursery now?"

"Sure," Dimitri said, and he carried it into the bedroom. He set it up underneath the window. "I'll get the mattress," he said as he hurried out of the room. A few minutes later, he returned and set the mattress in place.

Tatyana unfolded a sheet and put it on the mattress, then laid a bright blue and red quilt over the sheet. The two stood back and looked at the bed. Now everything was ready.

"It is a wonderful bed, Dimitri." Leaning her head against his shoulder, Tatyana said, "Just think, soon our baby will be sleeping here. We will be Mama and Papa."

CHAPTER 20

Yuri GLANCED AT THE SUN. FOR months he'd craved summer warmth. Now the flaming orb that rarely left the sky brought new torments. The earth warmed, and the frozen ground was transformed into heavy, clinging mud that sucked at boots and made every step difficult. Puddles became breeding grounds for writhing larvae. When they matured, the air came alive with swarms of biting, stinging insects.

Swatting at the pests, Yuri stumbled through the mud. Beating the air drove them away only momentarily. They quickly regrouped and resumed their attack. His welted body itched, then burned as sweat coated it like a caustic ointment.

The man in front of Yuri fell flat in the mud. The insects, seeming to sense weakened prey, swarmed him. He pushed himself to his hands and knees but couldn't rise.

Immediately a guard approached. "Get up!"

The prisoner tried to stand, but with no muscles left on his bony frame, he shuddered and fell.

Yuri reached out to help.

The guard stepped between the two. "Keep to yourself," he growled.

Yuri backed off. *Come on. Get up,* he thought, willing the man to his feet.

His hands planted on the ground in front of him, the prisoner looked at Yuri. Taking quick breaths, then giving a loud grunt, he bent his left leg and placed his foot in front of him. He rested a moment. Placing a thin arm on his leg, he pushed himself upright. Swaying, he struggled to remain standing.

Yuri steadied him. Alexander held the other arm.

"Leave him! If he cannot stand on his own, then he is worthless anyway." Glaring at Yuri and Alexander through eyes so black they looked like pieces of coal, he snarled, "Step back."

Yuri loosened his hold slightly but didn't move.

Alexander kept a tight grip on the stricken man. "He needs rest and food."

Without warning, the guard's arm shot out and his fist found Alexander's jaw. Alexander staggered back but didn't let loose of the man. He continued, "After food and rest, he will work better."

Looking like he might hit Alexander again, the guard stared at him, then in a chilling voice, he said, "There will always be more *zeks* to replace the ones who die."

Tightening his hold on the frail prisoner, Yuri pleaded, "We will fill his quota plus ours." The moment the words left his mouth, Yuri wished he could take them back. How could he be so foolish? It was impossible to complete that much work in one shift.

A glint lit the guard's eyes and a sneer emerged on his face as he folded his arms over his chest. He studied Yuri and Alexander. "Have it your way. You will do your work plus his today, and if he can't work tomorrow, you'll do it again. If you do not fulfill the quotas, you will go hungry." He turned and marched toward the front of the line. "Move!"

Still propped between Alexander and Yuri, the prisoner looked at his helpers through sunken, grieving eyes. His voice trembling, he said, "Thank you. But you have killed yourselves."

"Maybe," Yuri said and hefted the man's arm over his shoulder.

Alexander supported him from the other side. Together, the three struggled through the mud, trying to keep up with the line of workers. Gradually, they fell behind.

"I have been stupid, Alexander. I am sorry."

His eyes alight with hope, Alexander smiled. "Maybe not. Sometimes our brave words come from God. Now we must look at him and not the circumstances."

Yuri's fear retreated. "You think we can do it?"

"No. But God can."

★ ★ ★ ★ ★

That day Yuri witnessed a miracle. Word circulated about his willingness to fulfill his quota plus another man's. Careful not to be caught, but with silent resolve, other prisoners helped. As they passed through Yuri and Alexander's sections, they picked up limbs and brush and added it to their own loads. Miraculously, no one was found out.

Although Yuri saw what was happening, he had trouble believing it was true. Since his first day in the camp, he'd under-stood each man took care of himself. No one had strength left to help others. Until now, the only exception had been Alexander.

At the end of the day, all three quotas had been fulfilled. Disbelieving, the guards checked the work again and again. Finally, the soldier who'd given the extra labor approached Yuri.

Meeting his cruel gaze squarely, Yuri said nothing.

"I do not know how you did this, but you will not be rewarded for trickery." Without giving any of the three a food voucher, he turned and walked away.

Struggling against disappointment and anger, Yuri took his place in line.

Beside him, Alexander said quietly, "God will reward."

Yuri nodded and kept walking.

As the prisoners returned to camp, men fell into step beside Yuri and Alexander. Some whispered encouragement and others harangued the guards. One man said, "For my brothers, I will save a portion of bread."

God had touched lives that day, and Yuri realized how small-minded he'd been. He had thought about helping one man, but God cared about many more. For the first time since walking through the compound gate, he understood he was among comrades and knew God better because of those imprisoned with him.

"Today these prisoners did something admirable," Alexander said. "Doing good is medicine for the soul."

"I should have thought before I spoke. I put us both in jeopardy. I am sorry. But I praise God who is greater than my foolishness."

"Even when we act rashly, we can trust him. The Bible says, 'All things work together for good to those who love God, to those who are called according to His purpose.'" He grinned and patted Yuri on the back. "Today he used careless words to provide hope."

✳ ✳ ✳ ✳ ✳

CHAPTER 20

Word of Yuri and Alexander's valiant attempt to help another prisoner and the work crew's response quickly traveled through camp. Men came to Yuri and Alexander with questions. Often their queries led to talk of God and faith. Many opened their souls, confessed feeling abandoned, and wondered aloud why God had rejected them. Yuri and Alexander helped them understand that God never forsakes his children and guided them to look within and discover that they, not God, had walked away. Others came, longing for the words of Jesus. Many just needed a reason to live.

Yuri and Alexander sought God and did all they could to help. They hadn't expected to be thrown into the center of a needy storm. As they served and saw lives being transformed, they were humbled by the power of God.

Nights became a time for meetings. They gathered in the barracks, and while one man watched for guards, others listened to God's word, asked questions, and prayed. At first the men prayed for freedom, for their families, for better conditions, and for Mother Russia. Gradually they included prayers for those who oppressed them.

The Light shut out darkness.

One night, just before the usual meeting, Alexander approached Yuri. "We need to talk," he said quietly.

"What is it?" Yuri asked.

Alexander took a breath. "I don't think we should meet for a while."

Stunned, Yuri asked, "Why?"

"The guards know, and they are planning to trap us. The word is, if anyone is caught in religious gatherings, he will be executed."

"How do you know this?"

"One of the cooks overheard the officers."

Yuri's mind whirled with options. The sensible thing would be to cancel the meetings, but had God asked them to do what was sensible? He prayed for guidance. "I don't know if we should stop. No one here knows when he will breathe his last breath. And what if even one man were to meet Christ tonight?"

Alexander considered Yuri's words.

Yuri grabbed his arm. "You are the one who always told me we must trust God and refuse to look at circumstances."

Alexander nodded slowly. "Yes, but I do not think God wants us to behave foolishly."

Yuri grinned. "We have been foolish before." He took two paces, then walked back to Alexander. "And what about the disciples? What would have happened if they had done only what seemed sensible? When the men began to come here, did we really think we would not be discovered?" Tightening his grip on his friend's arm, Yuri continued, "I don't want even one man to die without Christ because I was afraid."

Alexander said nothing.

Yuri knew he was praying.

A smile softened Alexander's intense look. "All right. We will meet."

※ ※ ※ ※ ※

That night the prisoners came, and although Yuri and Alexander warned them of the danger, they remained. As always, they prayed and discussed Scripture. The guards stayed away.

The following night, as men gathered, Yuri felt uneasy. A stranger sat among the regulars, and Yuri remembered Saodat's betrayal. What if this man were part of a plot? *No. I will not think about such things. I must concentrate only on what God has asked me to do.*

Alexander told the story of the prodigal son, and the stranger listened attentively. As the story came to a close, the newcomer's eyes brimmed with tears. "And he arose," Alexander continued, "and came to his father. But when he was still a great way off, his father saw him and had compassion, and ran and fell on his neck and kissed him." He stopped speaking. Meeting the man's eyes, he asked, "What can we do for you?"

The stranger wiped away tears. "I am . . . like that son. I . . ." He took a shaky breath. "I walked away from God. I have been afraid he wouldn't take me back."

Alexander reached out and grasped the man's hand. "He has been waiting for you."

The man cried openly, and the others prayed.

Yuri gazed at the bowed heads and knew this would be their last meeting.

Moments later, the guards came. A light cut through the dimness, and dogs lunged on heavy leashes. No one panicked. When ordered to their feet, the men quietly stood and faced their persecutors.

Yuri had expected fear but felt only peace. He glanced at Alexander. The gaunt man's lips moved in silent prayer.

"We know about your heretical meetings!" the guard yelled as he stood in front of Alexander and Yuri. "And we know you're the leaders," he said, his voice like ice. He spat in Yuri's face.

Yuri wanted to wipe the spittle away but forced his hands to remain still.

"Take the others to the isolator," the guard ordered. His eyes on Yuri's, he grinned. "We have something special for you."

As the guards marched the men out of the barracks, Yuri prayed for peace, strength, and God's protection.

The guard paced in front of Alexander and Yuri, his small eyes darting from one man to the other. Abruptly, he stopped. Standing midway between them, he pulled the brim of his hat down until it nearly touched his heavy eyebrows. "You were fools to believe we wouldn't find out."

Meeting his gaze, Alexander said evenly, "We knew."

The guard wiped sweat from his upper lip. "You know talking about God is forbidden."

"We know," said Alexander in the same even voice.

The guard's lip twitched, and he balled his hands into fists. "You think things can't get worse? We have a special place for people like you." He turned on his heel. "Lock them up! They'll go with the others to Banlag."

Banlag, Yuri thought, *the extermination camp.* So, this is our fate. He glanced at Alexander, knowing that he, too, understood.

Alexander offered an encouraging smile.

Yuri returned the gesture. Death would not be the end. While in prison, the apostle Paul had contemplated death, asking himself whether it was better to live or die. To die meant to be in God's presence and to live meant continuing to serve God. Both, he had decided, were good.

"Hands behind your back! No talking!" a young guard ordered, then steered Alexander and Yuri out of the barracks.

The following morning, Yuri, Alexander, and several other prisoners trudged across open country toward the railway station where they'd first arrived nearly a year before. The forest at their backs, the plains stretched out endlessly before them. Clouds of insects hovered over sprouting grasses, chased by birds who gorged on them. The prisoners arrived at the railroad station hot, parched, and covered with fresh welts from bloodthirsty insects. The *stolypin* wagons waited.

The men were herded into a single car divided into three cells. "Halt!" the guard barked, then unlocked the first cell. Yuri and half a dozen others were shoved inside. The door was slammed shut and locked. Alexander was propelled to the next compartment, and the remaining prisoners were forced into the last cell.

Exhausted, Yuri and Alexander slid to the floor. Back to back, they rested against the bars. It felt good to sit.

"So, here we are, my friend," Alexander said. "Our final journey."

Yuri bent his legs and rested his arms on his knees.

"It has been a difficult pilgrimage, but soon we will stand before the Father."

Yuri pictured himself facing God. "I wish I had been stronger," he said. "I've done so much I'm ashamed of."

"We all have."

"Thank you, Jesus, for taking my sins," Yuri whispered, knowing that because of Christ's sacrifice, he would stand pure before God. With a contented smile, he leaned his head against the bars and closed his eyes.

Couplings clanked and engines rumbled. As they inched forward, the car creaked and groaned. The train paused, jerked, and finally moved faster over the tracks, heading east.

"How long will it take to reach Banlag?" Yuri asked Alexander.

"I don't know."

Unlike his original trip into Siberia, this car was not crowded. Less than ten men occupied each cell. Some prisoners talked; others simply stared at the walls. Yuri tried to sleep.

A prisoner sat beside him. "I hope you don't mind some company."

His eyes half open, Yuri said, "No. I don't mind." The man looked kind. "Are you going to Banlag?"

"Yes. I think that's the destination of everyone on this train."

For a long moment, neither spoke. Finally, Yuri asked, "Why are they sending you?"

The stranger smiled. "I always knew that is where I would end up. After prison, where can they send a Christian who worked for the underground?"

"I am also a Christian. And I once worked for the underground too. My name is Yuri Letinof." He shook the man's hand. "It will be good to spend time with a brother." He looked for Alexander, but he'd moved to the opposite wall and was talking with another prisoner. *No doubt sharing his faith,* Yuri thought.

The stranger's eyes brightened, and he smiled. "I'm Isaac Minls. I am very glad to meet you. I've been looking for a Yuri—"

"Isaac Minls?"

"Yes."

That's the name Saodat gave me! He looked more closely at the stranger. "Your name is Isaac Minls?" He stood up, barely able to contain his excitement.

"Is something wrong?"

"Yes! No!" Yuri paced a few steps, then turned and stared at the man. "You are looking for someone named Yuri, and I am looking for Isaac Minls! It's impossible, that's all! But with God, nothing's impossible!" He took a slow breath, pressed his palms together, and said more slowly, "A man I knew told me he'd met someone named Isaac Minls in prison. He told me that this man knew my sister, Tatyana, and where she was living."

Isaac smiled and stood. "I knew a woman named Tatyana. She had a brother named Yuri. You must be that brother!"

"Yes! I am Tatyana's brother!"

A guard banged on the cell bars. "Quiet!"

Isaac closed his eyes and tipped his chin up. "Thank you, Father! I knew you had a reason."

"A reason for what? What are you saying?"

"Many months ago, before I was arrested, I received a letter from Tatyana. She told me she had been trying to contact her family and had heard from no one. She asked if I could help find her brother, Yuri . . ."

"Yes! Yes! That's me!"

Alexander now stood on the other side of the bars. He smiled. "God is not done with you yet."

"I have something for you." Isaac sat down and took off his boot. "When I was arrested, the police didn't find this. I never understood why. I kept it." He took a dirty, wrinkled envelope

from the toe of his boot. "When I found out I was being transferred, I stuffed it in here for safekeeping." Holding out the
envelope, he said, "I think this is yours."

Unable to believe what was happening, Yuri took the letter.
Hands shaking, he unfolded the paper. As he read about Tatyana's
extraordinary life in New York, tears blurred his vision. She
talked about working for a man named Reynold Meyers and
how she'd found good friends named Broido, who were also
from Russia. She shared her longing for home and her wish to
find her family, especially her brother, Yuri, who had not written since she left Russia. Pressing the letter against his chest, Yuri
sobbed.

Alexander reached through the bars and placed his hand on
Yuri's shoulder.

Wiping away tears, Yuri looked at Alexander. "It's from
Tatyana."

With tears in his eyes, Alexander managed to say, "We serve
an awesome God."

Yuri reread the letter. "Can I keep it?" he asked Isaac.

"It belongs to you."

Yuri tucked the letter into his shirt pocket. "How did you
know her?"

Isaac told Yuri how he'd met Tatyana on the train to
Leningrad and that she'd stayed at his home. "I told her I worked
with the underground. That is why she wrote me, hoping I
could find you."

His voice wistful, Yuri said, "She sounds well and happy." He
sniffed and wiped his nose on his sleeve. "If only I could see her
again."

Sorrow came over Isaac's face. "Yes, many wait for loved
ones. But we do not know what God might do."

"It would take a miracle."

"I have known him to do miracles before," Alexander said.

Yuri slid down the bars and sat with his knees bent close to his chest. "One day. One day we will be reunited."

Isaac nodded and smiled sadly. "Me and my Lenka too, one day." He blinked back tears. "She is my wife. I have a son too. His name is Joseph, and he's nearly twelve now. He's a fine boy." He sat beside Yuri. "We also have a baby girl. Madezhda is a joy to her mother and me, as is our adopted daughter, Galina. Your sister met her on the train. A beautiful child." Picking up a piece of straw from the floor, he twirled it between his fingers. "It was a very sad thing. The police arrested Galina's mother. She watches for her mama, hoping one day she will return."

Rounding a tight bend, the train swayed oddly, then jerked hard to the right. As the car left the tracks, Yuri grabbed the bars. Screeching and grinding filled the air. The car hit something and rolled. Yuri tightened his grip as his legs swung wildly away from his body. The sounds of grating metal and breaking glass exploded around him. Screams and curses echoed through the car. All of the sudden, the bar broke loose in Yuri's hand, and still gripping it, he tumbled to the back of the car. He hit hard on his shoulder, then rolled into a ball and covered his head with his arms as debris flew. Something struck him in the head, and a sharp pain stabbed him. After that, everything went black.

Yuri had no idea how long he'd been unconscious. When he opened his eyes, everything looked all askew. Was he looking at the floor or the ceiling? He couldn't tell for sure and decided it didn't matter. All that mattered was getting out. The car lay still and quiet; the only sounds were the moans and whimpers of the injured.

"Yuri! Yuri!" called Alexander in a hushed voice.

"I . . . I am here," Yuri said weakly, pushing himself up on one arm. His head pounded, and he pressed his hands against both sides of his skull. He could feel something trickle down his head and onto his neck. He looked at his bloodied hands.

CHAPTER 20

"There you are!" Alexander said, stepping over a broken window frame. Glass crunched under his boots. "Are you all right? When I couldn't find you, I thought you might be dead."

"Yes. I think I'm all right. What happened?"

"The train ran off the tracks." He glanced around the car. "We've been freed."

"What about the guards?" Yuri tried to stand, but his head spun and he sank back down.

"They're everywhere, but for now, they're busy surviving. We have to go!" Alexander yelled as he grabbed Yuri's arm. "There is little time." He pulled at Yuri. "Come on."

Closing his eyes against the spinning, Yuri pushed himself up, then taking a step to follow Alexander, remembered Isaac. "Wait! What about Isaac?" His eyes searched the wreckage. "Isaac!" There was no answer.

He spotted him pinned beneath a portion of the car, his legs and pelvis crushed. Knowing he must be dead, Yuri crawled over debris to reach him. Isaac stared skyward, his eyes unseeing. Kneeling beside him, Yuri laid his hand on the man's forehead. "Thank you, Comrade."

CHAPTER 21

ALEXANDER GRABBED YURI'S arm. "We must go now!"

With one last look at Isaac, Yuri followed Alexander. Climbing over bodies, torn metal, and broken glass, they made their way to a hole torn in the side of the car. Careful not to catch arms or legs on the jagged walls, they jumped to the ground. Outside it looked like a bomb had exploded. Broken windows, metal bars, clothing, and bodies were strewn over a field. Some cars were piled on others. The one they had just climbed from lay on its side.

"What do you think happened?" Yuri asked.

Alexander shrugged. "Maybe we were going too fast when we came around the curve, or something might be wrong with the tracks."

Steam hissed from an overturned engine. Two guards jumped out of a nearby car, and Alexander and Yuri ducked behind a jumble of planking. The soldiers looked dazed. Someone cried out for help, and another screamed his agony.

One guard headed toward Yuri and Alexander, but he had no rifle.

"We need to get out of here now," Alexander whispered.

Yuri scanned the surroundings. There was nothing but endless, empty prairie. "Where?"

"West. We'll head west," Alexander said, looking intently at Yuri. "God has released us."

"We're not free yet. What about the guards?" Yuri watched as an unarmed guard searched through debris. "They're not going to let us just walk away." Scenes of fleeing prisoners and guards shooting them down filled Yuri's mind. "They'll shoot us."

"We'll wait until they're distracted and then go. And look at them. They're in a daze."

"Hey, I need help here," one guard called, pulling on what looked like a portion of a car.

Another guard joined the first, and the two worked to free a third who was pinned beneath the rubble.

"If they see us and shoot, we're no worse off. We were going to be shot anyway," Alexander said with a half grin.

"You're right." Yuri studied the soldier. "We'll wait until they're all out of sight or preoccupied, then go. There's only a handful of them."

Two soldiers climbed into a car, and another moved out of their vision, leaving only the two who were busy freeing a fellow guard. Yuri said, "Go!"

Crouching, they ran from the train, dodging debris and casualties. Another prisoner, three cars down, did the same.

"Halt!" someone shouted, but Yuri didn't look back. His heart hammered, and his stick-thin legs strained to carry him to freedom. He heard a shot and a cry, but he kept his eyes straight ahead. Alexander ran at his side. Two more shots were fired, but none came near the two fleeing comrades. The gunfire grew faint and finally stopped.

Only when Yuri felt certain they'd put enough distance between themselves and the deadly rifles, did he look back. No one followed. Gasping for air, he dropped to the ground, rolled onto his back, and stared at the clear blue sky.

Alexander lay beside him, keeping a careful eye on the train. Still, there was no pursuit. "They must have seen us. I guess we're not worth their trouble." Smoke and flames engulfed one engine. People who looked like stick figures from this distance stood and watched the fire.

Two guards checked bodies. One looked like he was poking something, then fired. A prisoner fled the wreckage, and Yuri and Alexander silently urged him on. He managed to put several meters between himself and the train before a rifle shot brought him down.

Alexander laid back down and stared at the sky, a single tear making a rivulet down his face.

Yuri watched the train. "Maybe we should have done something to help."

"There was nothing we could do," Alexander said as he rolled onto his stomach. "God provided a way for us. We were supposed to take it."

"Maybe it is not meant for us to die in prison," Yuri said, studying the flat plains. "But what is our future? Where do we go?" He slapped a mosquito feasting on his arm. A red splotch was all that remained, and he casually wiped it away.

Alexander studied the train. More of it burned. "We just have to start walking, and God will direct us. And we need to begin now." He stood up, and staying in a crouch, headed away from the train. Yuri followed.

As the sun rose high into the sky, it baked the earth and the men and gave life to biting flies and mosquitoes. Puddles of stagnant water were their only drinking source, and thirst tortured them. They drank only enough to wet their lips and tongues.

Finally, with the sun low in the sky, Yuri sprawled out on his belly beside a puddle. "I have to drink," he said, gulping down handfuls of water. After that, he sat up in the grass and moss and studied the brilliant colors in the sky as the sun began to sink below the horizon. "I will probably pay for drinking all that," he said wryly. "But I would rather live with a cramping stomach than not live at all."

Alexander squatted beside the same puddle and drank several handfuls. He sat with his legs bent and rested his arms on his knees. Breaking a twig off a short bush, he twirled it between his fingers. A cooling breeze rustled the grass. Alexander closed his eyes, and with passion, said, "We are free!" He looked at Yuri. "God set us free!"

"We are not free. We're only out of prison. In Russia, no man is free."

Alexander broke the dried stem in half. "I am free. There is freedom. Because God is with me and I am with him. Death or life, I am free."

"Yes. You are right. It is still a mystery to me that God knows us so well and yet entrusts us with so much." A cloud of mosquitoes settled over the men. Yuri pulled his shirt over his mouth but could still feel their prickly bites through his shirt sleeves and the exposed part of his face.

Alexander covered his entire face with his shirt. "It will be dark soon, and they will go to their beds for a while. Then we will sleep too." He laid on his side and tucked his hands beneath his head. "We must sleep while we can. The sun will not be down long."

Yuri laid down, his stomach aching from hunger. "Even *balanda* and hard bread would taste good."

"Mmm," Alexander replied.

Yuri shivered. Without the sun, the ground turned cold. "Do you think they will look for us?"

"No. It will take time to identify the bodies and bury them. We will be far from here before they discover we're missing. They may not even know we're gone. If the train burns, they won't be able to identify bodies."

Yuri closed his eyes and could see Isaac's face. He'd liked the man. His wife and children would never know what happened to him. Yuri remembered Tatyana's letter and pressed his hand against his pocket to make sure it was still there. He heard the reassuring crackle of paper and wished it were light enough to read it again. The return address was faded but readable. *Maybe one day, I will go to America and find her,* he thought as sleep settled over him.

※ ※ ※ ※ ※

The next day Yuri and Alexander continued west. As Yuri had predicted, their stomachs cramped and gushed from the stale water they drank. Even so, their hunger intensified, and they picked stalks of grass and flowers and ate them. But the plants only added to their intestinal troubles.

Birds flitted over the grasses and flowers, and Yuri tried to catch one. He stripped several threads from his shirt, braided them, and made a small snare. Setting it out, he lay flat on the ground, remaining very still. Holding one end of the string, he willed a bird to step into the noose. One did, but either it was too quick or Yuri was too slow, because by the time Yuri pulled on his end, the bird had flown off, and he and Alexander went hungry.

The morning of the third day, they came to a river.

"Do you know what river this is?" Yuri asked.

"No. There are many in Siberia. But I do know people live on rivers. If we follow it, we will find a village."

"Which way should we go?"

"The river flows west. We will follow it downstream."

For hours they walked the banks, feeling stronger because of the river's presence. It would help them live, satisfying their need for water and hope. It turned northward, and the men stopped to rest and think. They slept for a time, and when they woke, prepared to move on. But which route was the right one?

"If we need to go west, we will have to cross the river and leave it," Yuri said. "There will be fewer pools to drink from. Maybe we should stay with it."

"We'll keep moving and cross when the water turns shallow, then we will decide."

They walked until late in the day when the river changed. It grew quieter, and rocks on the bottom became visible.

"This is it," Alexander said.

"I do not swim well," Yuri said as he waded in. The icy water washed into his boots and over his calves. It made his feet ache, and he hurried his steps.

"Wait for me," Alexander called. "I will go first."

"I cannot wait. It's like ice."

The water rose to his thighs and then his waist. Shivering, Yuri held his arms up out of the torrent. "The current is swift," he called to Alexander. As he stepped forward and his foot found no place to rest, he plunged into the icy water. It closed over his head as the current grabbed him. When he came up, he paddled hard, but his strokes were weak and the river dragged him down. He struggled to the surface and gulped at the air but took in a mouthful of water instead. Coughing and choking, he churned the water with his arms and legs but made no progress. *Lord, this cannot be how you meant for me to die.*

He felt a tug on his collar.

"I've got you!" Alexander called, gripping Yuri's shirt. Fighting the current and breathing hard, he hauled his friend toward shore. "Help me, Yuri! Kick!"

His legs feeling as lifeless as sticks, Yuri tried to kick. Gradually the shore came close, and he felt solid river bottom beneath his feet. When they reached the shallows, he stood, frigid water dripping from his clothes. Shivering uncontrollably, Yuri stumbled toward shore.

Scrambling up the bank, he fell into the grass, his chest heaving as he gulped for air. Alexander dropped beside him. Exhausted, the two huddled along the bank and waited for the sun to warm them.

As the cold relinquished its hold, they slept.

When Yuri woke, his hunger was strong. It drove him back to the river in search of something, anything to eat. He walked the rocky shore turning over stones. It didn't take long before he found a snail clinging to the underside of a rock. His hands shaking, he plucked it off, cracked the shell, removed the mussel, and popped it into his mouth. Chewing, he looked under other rocks, found more, and put them in his pocket.

"What are you doing?" Alexander asked.

"Ah, you're awake." Yuri smiled and held up a snail. "Dinner."

Alexander joined Yuri in the search.

Pockets bulging, the men climbed onto the bank and sat down. One by one, they emptied the shells and ate the meat inside.

Yuri looked at Alexander. "Thank you for saving me. I would have drowned."

"Before I was arrested, I was a champion swimmer," Alexander said with a grin. "We never know what abilities and talents we will need for our life. It always astounds me how God prepares us for our futures."

Cracking his last snail and eating it, Yuri looked out across the open fields. "Do you think it is much further to a village?"

"Who can say?"

Yuri walked to the bank. Crouching beside the water, he scooped handfuls of water and drank. "I never liked snails. I was hoping I wouldn't have to resort to eating them." His eyes scanned the open expanse lying to the west. "Alexander, what if there are no villages out there and no water? Maybe we should stay with the river. It changed course before; it might again."

Alexander was quiet for a long moment. "I agree. I've been considering our choices and think we should follow the river a few more days. Maybe it will change course."

They walked two more days, and the countryside changed little. Open, moss-covered ground stretched out in all directions. Tiny white flowers hid among rock crevices covered with lichen, and small birds flitted nervously from place to place seeking insects. An occasional hawk screeched overhead as it sought a meal of mouse or rabbit. Yuri watched in vain, hoping the bird would strike close by so he could steal its catch.

The afternoon of the sixth day, a smaller stream branched off the main river and flowed west. Alexander and Yuri followed the new route. Snails, insects, grass, and flowers were all they found to eat. In all his months of imprisonment, Yuri had never known such horrible, relentless hunger. He thought about food and searched for food. When a grouse flew out in front of him, he lunged for it, but the bird easily escaped. Yuri chased after it, frustrated by the sound of its wings batting the air. Winded, he finally sat and watched as the bird settled in the grass several yards away. "There must be a way to catch one."

Alexander sat beside Yuri.

"I am growing weaker, Alexander. I do not know how much further I can walk. I need food."

"I know. For now, we will rest."

"Sleep won't fill my belly. The pain is so endless and intense." Yuri pulled up a tuft of grass and chewed on it. "As we've been walking, I've been thinking about the accident." He watched a butterfly land on a nearby flower and wondered if it might be good to eat. "Do you believe God caused it?"

Alexander closed his eyes for a moment and took a deep breath. "I do not think God caused it, but he allowed it and spared our lives. He has a plan for us."

Yuri gazed across the wilderness. "What kind of plan? Look at where we are. And we're starving."

"Only he knows, but I am certain he will complete it," he said as he studied the billowy white clouds gathering on the horizon. "We need to pray and ask God to show us."

Closing his eyes and bowing his head, he said, "Father, you are a great and mighty God. You are the God who created the universe, the God who knows the very number of hairs on our heads." He paused. "The enemy has done all he can to destroy and deceive us, but you have protected us. We praise you and thank you. Now, we know you see us here in the wilderness, and we understand and believe that we're never out of your sight, and we ask that you show us the way. Renew our hope and our strength. Our lives are in your hands. We long to be worthy of your calling and pray our lives will glorify you and you only. We know your goodness and your wisdom, and we trust you. Father, if it is your will to call us home to heaven, we will join you gladly, and if we are to remain here and serve you, we will do so with joy. Thank you for loving us. Amen."

Yuri's heart echoed Alexander's prayer. He felt God's presence, and with renewed energy, stood and looked out over the land. In it, he saw the beauty of God's creation and no longer felt alone.

Once more, the men set out, refreshed. Gradually the soggy earth was replaced by solid ground, and the going became easier. Yuri kept his eyes on the horizon, searching for God's deliverance. With each step, he thought of everyone in his family and prayed for them. He knew his parents were dead but lifted them up to the Lord anyway. He thought of Tatyana and asked God to hold her close and to let her know he lived. He prayed for Lev and Olga, all his cousins, and his aunt Irina. Remembering his life in Moscow, he asked God to protect Daniel and Tanya and their underground ministry, hoping they had escaped detection. Elena's beautiful face haunted him. Her dark, proud eyes, so filled with hurt, pierced his heart. He longed to see her again and knew if the day ever arrived, he would tell her of his love. He would hold her close and reassure her he would never leave again. *Father, if it is possible, make it so.*

"Yuri!" Alexander cried. "Look there!"

Pulled from his dreams, Yuri looked to the place Alexander pointed. A wisp of gray stained the sky. "What do you think it is?"

"Smoke? From a house maybe?"

Without another word, they headed toward the distant vapor, their steps more vigorous. As they came closer, they could see a cottage silhouetted against the empty plains. Drooping fences enclosed barren fields. There were no crops, no livestock.

"The soldiers have been here," Yuri said.

They looked for any indication that people lived there. Except for the smoke rising from the chimney, it looked abandoned.

The sound of clucking chickens filled Yuri's mind with thoughts of eggs and meat. Silently, the two approached a small hen house. Using it as a shield between themselves and the cottage, they sat with their backs against one wall of the rickety structure.

"I wonder what the owners would think if they saw us?" Alexander asked, giving Yuri, then himself, a quick perusal. "We look bad."

"Could we just take a few eggs and leave?"

Alexander didn't answer.

"Would it be wrong to take just a few?"

Solemnly, Alexander said, "They are probably hungry too. It would be wrong."

"What should we do? If they find us, they might shoot us or tell the NKVD." Yuri leaned forward and looked at the house. "And what will we tell them about us?"

"We can say nothing less than the truth."

"But what if they turn us in?"

"Do we trust God or not?" Alexander asked.

Yuri leaned against the cool wood. "Yes." He shook his head slowly back and forth. "I will always struggle with my faith."

A door slammed, and a young girl of about six strolled toward the chicken house, a basket swinging from her wrist. Her dress was tattered but clean, and her dark brown hair was combed neatly and tied at the nape of her neck with a piece of string.

As she stepped into the hen house, she said, "Good morning, ladies. Do you have eggs for me?"

The hens squawked, clucked, and beat their wings.

A few minutes later, the child stepped outside, leaving the door open. The chickens hurried into the yard, pecking at the ground. A large black and gold rooster ran from the nearby field and took charge of his flock. Strutting confidently, he and the hens pecked their way to the pasture, busily searching for bugs.

"There went our eggs," Yuri whispered.

Alexander gave him an exasperated look.

Suddenly the little girl spotted something and ran into the tall grass beyond the chicken house. Yuri and Alexander flattened themselves against the wall and held completely still. If the child turned around, she would see them.

She plucked a pale blue flower, then turned and looked directly at Yuri and Alexander. Her eyes wide, she stared at them.

"We will not hurt you," Alexander said kindly.

The youngster continued to stare. Finally, she asked, "Where did you come from?"

Yuri pointed northeast. "From the forest."

"But, there is nothing there."

Moving very slowly, Yuri stood. "Our train crashed."

The little girl eyed him suspiciously. "Who are you?"

Alexander approached her. "My name is Alexander and this is Yuri. What is your name?"

"I am Musya."

Holding out his hand, he said, "It is good to meet you."

Tentatively, Musya took his hand and shook it.

Yuri stared at the eggs. "Do you have any food?"

"Mama is baking today," Musya said as she turned and began to skip back to the house. Midway, she stopped and looked at the strangers. "Please, come."

Yuri and Alexander looked at each other, then followed at a distance. Calling, *"Mamochka,"* Musya disappeared inside.

A moment later, a woman opened the door. She peered at Yuri and Alexander, then cautiously stepped onto the porch. "Yes? What is it you need?"

"We have been traveling and are hungry," Alexander explained. "We will do no harm but only wish for something to eat."

The woman considered them, her eyes compassionate. "You are from the prison camp?"

Alexander didn't hesitate. "Yes. Our train crashed."

The woman looked out into the yard and beyond. "Are there any others?"

"No. Only us," Yuri said.

"We have very little." She hesitated. "But there is enough. I am making *draniki*. You are welcome to have some."

"Thank you," Alexander said as he and Yuri stepped toward the door. The woman held up her hand. "Just a moment." She disappeared inside, then returned with bread. Giving them each a piece, she said, "I will finish cooking and you will bathe."

Yuri and Alexander said a hurried thank you and shoved the bread into their mouths.

The woman stared, then pointing toward the barn, said, "Go there. I will bring you hot water and clothing." She stepped back and closed the door.

Resting his arm across Yuri's shoulders, Alexander said, "See, God supplies." He smiled. "A bath. It has been so long."

The barn smelled of hay and manure. Yuri dropped into a deep cushion of straw and stared at the barn peak. Cobwebs littered the beams, and he could see pieces of sky through holes, but for the moment, it felt like home. Alexander lay beside him. Exhausted, they fell asleep.

The peasant woman's voice cut through Yuri's dreams. "Up. I brought you something to eat and your bath is ready. Get up!"

Yuri forced himself awake and pushed himself upright. The smell of something wonderful penetrated his senses. He pushed himself to his feet.

The woman and the little girl stood just inside the doorway. They each held a plate with steam rising off it. An older boy handed Yuri a bundle of clothes.

"Here. You eat, then bathe," the woman said, setting the plates on a bale of hay.

Yuri and Alexander stared at the food.

"It isn't much. Just some eggs, a little goat cheese, draniki, and bread." She pointed at a large wooden tub. "The bath is there. Holding her daughter's hand, the woman turned and took a step outside. The boy hesitated and stared at the strangers. "Stephan, they do not want you staring at them," the woman said. The boy blushed and hustled out.

"Thank you," Yuri called after her, then took a fork and scooped up a bite of egg. He held it under his nose a moment, eyes closed, and smelled. "Praise you, Lord," he said, then placed the bite in his mouth. He chewed slowly, relishing the hearty food. It felt warm as it went down. He quickly followed it with another bite.

Alexander piled eggs on top of a slice of bread. "I used to dream of eggs." He took a bite, then broke off a chunk of cheese and popped it into his mouth. His cheeks bulging, he grinned as he chewed.

Yuri sat beside the hay bale and took a slice of bread. It was soft and warm. As he bit into it, he could almost feel his mother's presence as he remembered the days when he'd follow her around the kitchen, hoping for the first slice of hot bread out of the oven.

Too soon, his plate was empty, but Yuri's stomach was finally filled. He crossed to the tub of hot water, dipped his hand in, and swirled the water.

Alexander joined him. Just as Yuri had done, he ran his hand through the water. "A bath," he said almost reverently. "Such a blessing." He looked at his friend. "You go first."

"No. It should be you."

"I am still sleepy. I will nap a little more." Before Yuri could object, Alexander returned to the hay and lay down.

"All right," Yuri said, stripping off his tattered clothing. He put his foot in the water. It felt warm and soothing. Climbing all the way in, he sat down and moved his hands through the water, swirling it around him. It felt like a soothing balm. He closed his eyes and scooped it into his hands and drizzled it down his chest. "This is what heaven must feel like." He grabbed a bar of soap off the bottom of the tub and rubbed it into a lather all over his body. As he washed his emaciated legs, he stopped and studied the limbs. They reminded him of a skeleton. For a moment, he thought they couldn't possibly belong to him. And how had they carried him so far?

Gratitude welled up. God had brought him and Alexander an impossible distance. When there seemed to be no hope, God had provided a way. Yuri lowered himself deeper into the water. Resting his head against the edge of the tub, he wondered what lay ahead.

CHAPTER 22

TATYANA CLOSED THE MAGAZINE and fanned herself with it. Sweat trickled down the back of her neck, and she mopped it with her handkerchief. Longing for a break from the oppressive heat, she glanced out the window.

The nurse looked at her from behind her desk. "Hope it cools down soon. Seems every July we get a hot spell, but I don't remember one this bad."

"It is very hot." Using the arm of the chair to balance herself, Tatyana stood and walked to the open door, hoping for a breeze. The air was still. Her arms folded over her belly, she leaned against the frame and watched as two boys whizzed by on bicycles. Without slowing down, they swerved around a little girl carrying a puppy in her arms. The child looked startled for a moment, then soothed the puppy. She glanced at Tatyana and smiled before walking on.

Tatyana smiled back and watched until the girl was out of sight. Returning to her seat, she said, "Children are the only ones out in this heat." The baby moved, putting pressure on Tatyana's diaphragm and making it difficult to breathe. *Oh, Lord, please let this child be born soon,* she thought.

"The doctor will see you now."

Tatyana struggled to her feet. "I do not think I can stand to wait much longer. The baby is getting so big."

Smiling sympathetically, the nurse said, "At this point, all babies seem huge." She escorted Tatyana to an examination room, weighed her, and took her blood pressure and temperature. Writing in her file, she said, "Everything seems perfectly normal." After replacing the thermometer in a bottle of rubbing alcohol, she left the room.

Tatyana tried to get comfortable on the straight-backed chair, but it wasn't possible. "Oh, how I wish you were here," she told the baby. She looked over her stomach at her swollen feet.

A soft rap came at the door, and Dr. Logan peeked in. "Good afternoon," he said and stepped inside. He picked up her file, scanned it, and set it aside. "I was hoping I wouldn't see you back here unless it was to deliver that baby."

Tatyana gave him an exasperated look. "Me too."

"Don't worry, it will happen soon."

"I am getting so fat. And my feet, look at them." She lifted them off the floor for him to see.

Dr. Logan grinned. "I know you're uncomfortable, but at this stage of pregnancy and in this kind of heat, it's common." He sat in a chair opposite her. "Do you have any other complaints?"

Tatyana thought. "No, not exactly."

"What is 'not exactly?'"

"It is aching here." She placed her hand on the lower part of her abdomen.

The doctor smiled. "That's to be expected. The baby is sitting very low." He patted the examining table. "Climb up here and we'll find out just how the baby is doing."

After the examination, Dr. Logan said, "Just as I thought. He's in the birth canal and can be born any time. I seriously doubt you'll make it another week." He shrugged. "Of course, that's what I thought last week." His expression turned professional. "As I told you before, when your pains begin and are regular, I want you to come in to the clinic."

"What if it is at night?"

"My apartment is in the back so I can be reached any time, day or night."

Tatyana had meant to ask the doctor about not having her baby at the clinic, but everyone she'd asked had advised against it. Until now, she hadn't had the courage to talk to him, but knew she couldn't wait any longer. Taking a deep breath, she said, "Doctor Logan, in Russia, women have their babies at home in their own beds."

He waited for her to continue.

Tatyana glanced at the floor. "I do not want to have my baby here."

The doctor raised one eyebrow. "Where do you want to have it?"

"At home."

He thought a moment. "It's a little unorthodox, and to be perfectly frank, I don't feel good about it. I would rather you had the baby here. We'll make sure you're comfortable."

"Please, Dr. Logan, all my people have brought their children into the world surrounded by family and friends. Children should begin life at home with people who love them, not strangers."

Frowning, the doctor looked at her chart, then at Tatyana. "You have never had a child and can't understand what it's like. It can be very difficult, and the pain is intense. Here at the clinic, I have medicines that will help."

"I know about pain, and I am not worried about that." She met his eyes. "Please, this is what I want."

The doctor thought a moment. "I suppose it would do no harm. You're healthy and strong. But," he quickly added, "if there is any kind of emergency, we will have to bring you in to the clinic. You won't have a choice."

"Of course."

Dr. Logan relaxed. Resting his hand on her shoulder, he said, "You send Dimitri to get me when it's time."

🐞 🐞 🐞 🐞 🐞

The next morning Tatyana felt exhausted, as if she hadn't slept. She yawned as she filled Dimitri's cup with coffee.

"It's going to be hot again. I can feel it," Dimitri said.

"I wish it would turn cool and rain."

Slipping his arms around his wife's waist, he pulled her against him and rested his head against her stomach. "I'm sorry this weather is so hard on you. Carl said it won't last long. It will be cooler soon."

Tatyana tousled Dimitri's hair and he released her. "I hope Carl is right." Returning the coffee pot to the stove and sitting down, she sipped her coffee. The toast and eggs on her plate looked unappealing.

Dimitri cut into his eggs. "You were asleep when I came in last night. Sorry I was so late. We had to work over."

"I tried to wait up, but I was too tired."

"You need the sleep. Soon you'll have a baby to take care of."

"I woke up, but you were asleep." Picking up her toast, she nibbled the crust. "Will you be late tonight?"

"Don't know." He soaked up egg yoke with the edge of his toast and took a bite. "What did the doctor say?"

"He thinks the baby will be born very soon." She leaned back in her chair. "I am so uncomfortable, and today is the worst."

Dimitri set his cup down and leaned forward on his elbows. "Do you think you're going to have it today?"

"I do not know. I have never had a baby before."

"Maybe I should stay home."

"No. You need to work. If something happens, I will send for you. The doctor told me first babies take a long time getting born so you will not have to hurry home." Tatyana drank her coffee, keeping her eyes on Dimitri. "Dr. Logan said I can have the baby here."

Dimitri was about to take a bite of egg but set his fork down. "Here? At home?"

"Yes."

"You're sure he thinks it's all right?"

"Uh-huh. He said I am healthy and strong and it is fine."

Using his fork, Dimitri pushed his eggs from one side of his plate to the other. He looked at Tatyana. "Do you think that's wise? Shouldn't you go to the clinic where there are people who can help?"

"Dimitri, we talked about this. I thought you understood." Tatyana placed her forearms on the table and leaned forward. "I told you, the women in my family always have their babies at home. Most Russian women do. I am Russian, and I will have mine here." She met his gaze.

"I'm not saying you can't. I'm just worried about what we'll do if something goes wrong."

"Nothing will go wrong. Having babies is natural, and Dr. Logan will be here."

"I just don't feel good about it. Sometimes things happen." Dimitri took his plate to the sink and ran water over it. "Are you sure the doctor thinks it's safe?"

"Yes."

"When you told me you wanted to have the baby at home, I didn't think he would do it." Dimitri returned to the table, bent, and kissed Tatyana's cheek. "If it's what you want, it's all right with me."

Tatyana smiled. "Thank you."

Dimitri took his lunch from the ice box. "I'd better get moving or the train will leave without me. You rest today. I'll see you tonight."

"Good-bye," Tatyana said.

The house was quiet without Dimitri. Tatyana sat at the table and finished her coffee but couldn't bring herself to eat the eggs. She tossed the leftovers off the back porch, and the chickens quickly gobbled them up. Returning to the sink, she ran hot water and soap over the dishes. As the sun rose over the mountains, the fields looked golden and dry. Tatyana sighed and decided it would be best to clean house before it got too warm.

After finishing the dishes, she scrubbed the icebox and the stove and cleaned the kitchen windows. After that, she went to the baby's room and gave it a thorough cleaning. When she finished, she stood in the doorway and imagined what it would be like to have a baby to care for. A soft breeze ruffled the blue cotton curtains she'd made, and the newly painted dresser glistened white in the early morning light.

Her feet thumped against the hardwood floor as she crossed to the chest. Opening the top drawer, she lifted out a tiny white gown. It smelled like soap and summer air. She tried to imagine her newborn in it.

The baby moved, and she rested her hand on her stomach. "You have been quiet this morning," she said as her stomach muscles tightened and a dull ache settled across her abdomen.

She wondered if it might be a labor pain and understood the enormity of how much her life was about to change. Her eyes filled with tears as she realized how God had blessed her. "Thank you," she said softly.

✹ ✹ ✹ ✹ ✹

"How is Tatyana feeling?" Carl asked as he climbed out of the man trip.

"All right, I guess. She looked tired this morning. Doctor says any time, though."

"Don't look so worried. Babies are born every day."

"I know, but this morning Tatyana told me she's planning to have the baby at home. The doctor said he'd come to the house."

"Is that safe?"

"I guess so, or the doctor wouldn't do it would he?"

"Well, Doc Logan is a good man. I don't believe he'd put Tatyana or the baby in danger." Carl brightened. "Hey, you might get to see him born. At the hospital, fathers aren't allowed anywhere near the mothers."

Dimitri picked up his shovel and rested it on his shoulder. "I don't know if I want to see. I mean, isn't it kind of private? Just for women?"

"Yeah, but I wish I had seen Evelyn born. When Susie got to the hospital, they took her away and made me sit in the waiting room. I wanted to be with her."

"Why did you go to the hospital instead of the clinic?"

"Oh, Susie's mother insisted she have the baby at a 'real' hospital." He set his lunch pail against the wall. "Anyway, at the Renton hospital they don't let men in, and wives are left alone with the nurses and doctor."

A heavy thump shook the mine. Dimitri's heart jumped. *Settle down,* he told himself.

Carl looked a little uneasy and was quiet.

"Is something wrong?"

At first, Carl didn't answer. "I was just listening." He pulled his hat down tighter. "We're fine." He headed back to the workings.

Dimitri followed. "I heard they've been having problems with the bottom squeezing up."

"Yeah, some, but I don't expect any real trouble."

Dimitri stuck his shovel into a pile of coal. "Do you think Tatyana will have the baby today?"

"How should I know?" Carl laughed.

"I guess I'm getting a little crazy waiting. Plus, I've never been a father. How do I know if I'll be any good?"

"No one does. You just love your kid the best you can and pray," Carl said.

"Yeah, I know, but what if something happens to me? Who will take care of Tatyana and the baby?"

"I know how you feel," Carl said soberly. "Right after Evelyn was born, I had some of the same thoughts. Sometimes, I still worry. I figure it's part of being a husband and father. But if we'll remember God is taking care of us and our families, we'll be fine." He swept off his hat and wiped the sweat from his forehead. "There's no way around the fact that working in a mine is dangerous, but we've got to deal with it. And so do our families." Brushing his hair back, he replaced his hat. "Sometimes when something smells strange or doesn't sound just right, I get spooked." He looked directly at Dimitri. "I have to remind myself to trust God."

Dimitri didn't know how to respond. Although he'd grown up watching his parents' faith, and now Tatyana's and Carl's, he still didn't understand how they could believe so strongly in a God they couldn't see.

※ ※ ※ ※ ※

Susie knocked on the door and stepped inside. Tatyana was on her hands and knees scrubbing the front room floor. "What are you doing?" Susie demanded.

Tatyana sat back on her heels and looked at her friend. "I did not hear you." Hair fell into her eyes, and she swept it back.

"Don't you know better than to work so hard when you're this close to having a baby?" Susie held out her hand to help Tatyana up.

Tatyana dropped her mop in the bucket and took Susie's hand. She groaned as she stood. "I am tired, but the house needed to be cleaned." She wiped her hands on her apron. "And maybe this will hurry the baby." Again, the pain and muscle cramping came. Tatyana breathed slowly until it passed, then smiled. "I am having pains."

"Then you sit down and rest." Susie ushered Tatyana to the sofa. "Labor is hard work. You don't need to be exhausted before you begin."

Tatyana studied the floor. With a satisfied smile, she said, "I was finished anyway." She looked at Susie. "I am thirsty," she said and started to rise.

"I'll get you a glass of water," Susie said and hurried to the kitchen.

"Where is Evelyn?"

"She's asleep in her crib. I thought I'd just take a minute to check on you. It's a good thing too." Glass in hand, Susie walked to the sofa and handed Tatyana the water. She wrung out the mop and carried it and the bucket to the back porch. When she returned, she asked, "Do you really think you're in labor?"

"Maybe. I am having pains about every fifteen minutes."

"They're regular then?"

"Yes. And they are getting stronger."

"Maybe it's time to go to the clinic?"

"The doctor said he would come here when it was time."

"I know you wanted to have the baby at home, but you're not really going to, are you? Babies should be born in a sterile hospital with nurses and doctors."

"No. That is not the right way. My baby will not be born among strangers."

Susie slowly shook her head back and forth. "I don't know, Tatyana. I think you're taking a risk."

Tatyana stood up and a pain knifed through her, doubling her over. "Ohh."

"You need to sit down," Susie said, then helped Tatyana back onto the couch.

Allowing her head to rest against the sofa, Tatyana closed her eyes and breathed slowly. When the contraction ended, she said, "That one was stronger." She smiled. "I think the baby will be born today."

"You stay put," Susie said and went to the door. "I'll send someone for the doctor and Dimitri." Gripping the door handle, she asked, "Are you sure you'll be all right?"

"Yes. Everything is good. Very good."

CHAPTER 23

THROUGHOUT THE MORNING, Dimitri's thoughts were with Tatyana. Was she having the baby? Did she need him? No, she'd promised to send for him if her time came. He did his best to concentrate on work but couldn't pry her from his mind. He wanted to go home. More than once he decided to leave, but each time the memory of Tom's anger over Mike missing work convinced him to stay. He couldn't risk losing this job.

When they stopped for lunch, the rest of the crew walked down the tunnel toward the gangway. But after the morning break, Dimitri put his lunch and water at the workings, so he sat down and opened his pail.

"My stuff is down in the gangway. I'll be right back," Carl said.

Dimitri started to get up. "I can go down with you."

"No. Stay put." Carl strolled down the tunnel. He returned a few moments later, lunch pail in hand. Sitting beside Dimitri, he said, "John's been griping all day. I don't think I can stand another minute with him." He opened his pail. "Ah, ginger cookies." He unwrapped the cookies and bit into one. "Since Susie's been home, she's baking. I love it."

Dimitri took a bite of sandwich. "Mmm, roast beef."

Carl picked up his sandwich. "Peanut butter and honey again," he groaned. "Changing to one income hasn't been easy. Susie's been cutting back."

"Here, you can have part of mine." Dimitri handed him the other half of his own.

They heard the rumble of cars, then someone called from the gangway, "Dimitri Broido?"

"Up here. I'm up here." Dimitri stood, wondering if Tatyana had sent for him.

A man walked up the tunnel. "Dimitri?"

"That's me." He swallowed his mouthful of sandwich.

"You're needed at home. Your wife is having a baby." He grinned. "Congratulations," he said and extended his hand.

Grasping the man's hand, Dimitri felt joy well up. "Is she all right?"

"As far as I know."

"So, it's time!" Carl stood up and called to the men down in the gangway. "Hey, did you hear that? Dimitri's about to be a father!"

His voice echoed through the tunnel but was drowned out by a menacing rumble. The ground shook, and a booming-like thunder filled the workings as a deluge of rock and coal hailed down around the men. Dimitri dove toward the back of the workings. Something hit his shoulder, tearing into his flesh, but he felt no pain, only terror. He heard a scream and watched the man who'd just brought the good news disappear in the avalanche of dirt and coal.

As quickly as it began, it was over. Choking dust filled the air, and Dimitri could hear the last rocks spill into the dark cavern. Deep, tomblike silence settled over the blackness. Trying to quiet his breathing, Dimitri held still, fearing any movement might bring down more of the roof.

He needed a light. Slowly reaching up, he felt for his hat. It was gone. He searched the ground around him, but his fingers found only broken rock and coal. Feeling like a blinded rat, he strained to see, and his chest burned as he choked on coal dust. He grabbed a handkerchief from his pocket and held it over his mouth.

Panic filled him. "Is anyone there?" he called. There was no reply. Where was Carl? *Stay calm. Hysteria won't help,* he told himself. Careful to take shallow breaths, he called, "Carl? Carl?" There was no response. Fear roiled through him again, and he struggled to control his terror. "God, help me." He tried to relax his tight muscles and called again. Still, no answer.

Careful to keep the handkerchief over his mouth, he pushed himself onto his knees. His shoulder ached and he clamped one hand over it, feeling a sticky wetness. *Something must have hit me,* he thought as he crawled across the cluttered floor, heading in the direction he thought the tunnel should be. He hadn't gone more than ten feet when he came to a pile of rock. He dug at it, but more broke free. Throwing his arms over his head, he hunched down and waited for the rain of stones to stop. *I'm trapped!*

He crawled back the way he'd come. Leaning against the wall, he stared into a black void and tried not to think about the hundreds of feet of earth above him. Bending his legs, he pulled them close to his chest and laid his arms on his knees. He was scared. "God, don't leave me here alone to die. Tatyana and the baby need me." He thought of the baby who might even now be coming into the world. "Please, Lord, don't take my life the day my child is born. You can't." His words sounded dull in the tiny room.

As he sat there, anger replaced his fear. "I'm not going to die. Think, Dimitri. There must be a way out." But he knew he could do nothing, so he leaned against the wall and listened. Were men already searching? What if no one knew he was trapped? "Don't be stupid. They know we're here. They'll come for us." *Us. What had happened to Carl?*

"Carl?" he called again. "Carl, are you there?" He waited and closed his eyes. "Please let him be alive."

A whisper of noise came from his left. Was it a groan? He listened carefully. When he heard nothing more, he called, "Carl! Carl! Is that you?" He crawled toward the place he'd heard the noise. "Carl?"

"Here. I'm here," came a weak reply.

Dimitri clambered over the littered floor, barely noticing as his knee came down on a sharp stone. "I'm coming," he said, searching the floor with his hands. He reached the cave-in. "Where are you? Keep talking to me."

"Here."

The voice came from his right. *I missed him,* Dimitri thought.

Keeping the pile of debris on his left, he felt his way. His hand touched a face he thought was Carl's, but it felt cold and lifeless. His fingers found the man's throat and felt for a pulse. There was none.

"Oh, dear God! No! He can't be dead!"

"Who? Who is dead?" Carl asked.

Dimitri realized the dead man must be the messenger. "Thank God! Carl, I thought it was you. Keep talking; I'll find you."

"I'm here. Not far from the cave-in. I jumped out of the way when it came down."

On hands and knees, Dimitri continued forward until his hand landed on Carl's leg.

"Ahh!" Carl cried.

As if he'd been burned, Dimitri retracted his hand. "I'm sorry." He crawled alongside Carl.

"I think my leg's broken. It hurts bad."

Dimitri felt in the darkness until he found his friend's shoulders. Keeping his hand on Carl, he said, "I thought you were dead. I called, but you didn't answer."

"I must have been knocked out. My head's pounding."

"I'm sorry you didn't get out."

"They'll find us. It probably wasn't a big cave-in, just a small section of tunnel."

A volley of rocks fell, and the men braced themselves for the worst. It was only a small collapse and quickly ceased, but the air filled with dust again.

Coughing, Carl said, "They'd better find us soon."

"Maybe we should wait beside the wall. At least we'll have something to lean against."

Carl tried to rise. "Ohh. Oh, my leg. I can't move."

"I'll pull you." Dimitri hooked his arms under Carl's, and digging his feet into the ground, pushed with his legs and slowly dragged Carl across the floor.

Sucking in his breath, Carl couldn't suppress a groan.

Dimitri stopped. "Do you want to rest here?"

"No. Keep going."

Dimitri carefully pulled Carl the rest of the way. Panting, both men leaned against the wall.

"This feels like a small space," Carl said. "I wish we had some light so we could see. I lost my hat."

"Me too. Maybe I can find it." Dimitri crawled away, searching the ground with his hands. He crisscrossed the small room several times before his fingers closed over a hat. "I found one!" He picked it up, plugged it into his battery, and pressed the switch. Blackness was transformed into a hazy, dusty room.

He smiled at Carl. "It works." Holding the light in front of him, he turned around slowly, illuminating the small chamber. A queasy feeling settled in his stomach. With no fresh air supply, the oxygen wouldn't last long.

"We need a rescue team soon," Carl said.

Dimitri continued his perusal, hesitating when the light found the dead man. Only his shoulders and head were free. Rock had buried the rest of his body.

Abruptly, he turned away and walked back to Carl. His friend didn't look good. Just below the knee, his torn pants were blood-stained and so was the ground under his leg. "You're bleeding pretty bad. How are you feeling?"

"Bum."

Taking his knife out of its sheath, Dimitri gently cut the pant away from Carl's leg, exposing a gash with a protruding bone.

Carl winced.

"It doesn't look good. We've got to stop the bleeding. I'll have to bind the leg, but to do that, it'll have to be straightened."

Carl nodded slowly. "All right. Do what you have to." He closed his eyes, braced his hands on the ground on either side of him, pressed his back against the wall, and took a deep breath.

"I need you to bend your other leg."

Carl did what Dimitri asked him to do.

"I'm sorry," Dimitri said as he gripped his friend's ankle and placed his foot against the knee of his good leg.

Sweat beaded up on Carl's forehead, and he squeezed his eyes shut. Through clenched teeth, he said, "Do it. Get it over with."

With a quick jerk, Dimitri pulled.

Carl screamed.

Dimitri carefully lowered the adjusted leg and quickly ripped two strips off his undershirt and wrapped them tightly around the wound. Pressing his hand against the laceration, he waited for the bleeding to slow. "It's better," he said and sat back. Carl's skin looked pasty, and Dimitri wondered how much blood he'd lost. "Are you doing all right, buddy?"

"I've had better days," he said with a half grin.

Dimitri studied the cave. "Do you think there is air coming in?"

"Doubt it. Where would it come from? Things look pretty well sealed up."

"Maybe I can dig through," Dimitri said, taking his knife out again. "Tatyana gave this to me at Christmas." He studied the gift. "I don't think she had this in mind when she bought it. I hope she and the baby are all right."

"I'm sure she's in good hands," Carl mumbled, his eyes nearly closed.

Dimitri looked at the pile of rock. "This was a stupid idea. It will do nothing." He returned the knife to its case and sat beside Carl.

Carl forced a smile. "It's a good thing the rescue crew has bigger digging tools than that." He gazed around the room. "Until they come, we'd better keep our activity down to conserve oxygen."

"I've heard of cave-ins where they never found the men. Do you think we'll die?"

"They know we're here, and they'll do everything they can," Carl said.

"If part of the gangway caved in, there might not be anyone alive out there."

Carl set his jaw and looked straight at Dimitri. "They'll find us," he said with resolve. Wiping away sweat dribbling down his forehead and into his eyes, he dug his good foot into the earth and pushed himself more upright. Grimacing, he sucked in air through clenched teeth.

Dimitri stood and paced.

"Sit down and be still. We need to conserve air."

Dimitri studied the rock pile and began tearing away chunks of coal and earth.

"Stop. You might bring the rest down on us," Carl warned as more rock and dust fell.

"I've got a wife and baby who need me. I have to do something."

"We have to wait. Just wait."

"And what if no one comes? Should we just sit here and calmly die?"

Meeting Dimitri's gaze, Carl said in a calm voice, "We will do what we can to live."

Dimitri sat back down. "I'm not ready to die. I have a life." He kicked at a chunk of coal. "What will Tatyana and the baby do without me?"

"You have no control over any of this," Carl said, placing his hand on Dimitri's arm.

Dimitri looked at Carl. "How can you be so calm?"

"What good would it do to rage and fight against circumstances I can't change?" He took a shallow breath. "Trust God, Dimitri. He hasn't forsaken us. We're still alive."

Dimitri stared at the ground, then said quietly, "He's never been real to me. Not like he is to you and Susie and Tatyana." He looked at Carl. "Over the years, I've heard it all. I just never really understood. I went to church and read my Bible. And prayed, when I remembered to, but all of that has never been anything more than a set of duties."

Carl's eyes looked sad. "That's not what it's about. Going to church and reading your Bible are good things, but if you don't have a relationship with the Lord, they mean nothing. Dimitri, two thousand years ago when Jesus hung on a cross and died, he looked down through the centuries and said, 'I know Dimitri Broido. I love him, and he's going to need me. I'll be there for him.'" Carl paused. "He's done his part. You need to know him."

Carl's words shocked Dimitri. He'd never heard it explained quite that way before. For a long moment, he was silent, then quietly said, "I'll think on it."

❈ ❈ ❈ ❈ ❈

As Dr. Logan walked out of the bedroom, Tatyana settled back against her pillows. She heard him tell Susie and Josephine, "She's doing fine, but it will probably be several more hours. First babies take their time."

Joy welled up at the realization that soon she'd hold her child. *Come home soon, Dimitri,* she thought and closed her eyes.

Someone pounded on the front door, then a voice said, "Doctor Logan, we need you at the mine! There's been an accident!"

Tatyana's heart quickened and she sat up.

"What's wrong? What happened?" Susie asked.

"There was a cave-in. Some men are trapped. I don't know how bad it is. I was just told to find the doc."

Tatyana started to shake and climbed out of bed. Walking into the front room, she wondered, *Is this why Dimitri hasn't come home?* Gripping the door frame, she asked, "Do you know who is trapped?" Her voice sounded foreign to her ears.

The stranger looked at her. "I don't know anything except what I already told you."

Crying, Susie joined Tatyana and the two women held each other.

Josephine looked at the doctor. "I'll stay with Tatyana. We'll be fine here. Susie, you need to go."

"Can I ride with you, doctor?" Susie asked.

"Sure." He pulled on his jacket and picked up his bag. Looking at Josephine, he said, "When the pains get bad, take her to the hospital. I'll be back as soon as I can." Taking Tatyana's hands, he said, "You do as Josephine says."

Tatyana gripped his hands. "Please, if it is Dimitri, help him."

"I'll do everything I can, but you have a job too. And I want you to go to the hospital."

Tatyana shook her head no. "I will wait for you . . . and my husband. I will wait here."

"I don't have time to argue." He looked at Josephine. "See if you can talk some sense into her."

"I doubt I can," Josephine said, joining Tatyana and placing an arm around her shoulders.

Susie picked up Evelyn and cradled her against her shoulder. "What am I going to do about the baby? I can't take her with me. It could be hours."

"My sister's home," Josephine said. "And her place is right on the way. She'll be happy to watch her for you." Calmly, she added, "We'll be praying. Don't forget, God is in our midst. We're never alone and neither are our loved ones."

Susie went to Tatyana and hugged her. "I wanted to be here with you."

Tears flowing freely, Tatyana said, "You must go. I must stay."

Susie nodded and kissed her friend's cheek, then followed the doctor out the door.

CHAPTER 24

"WE BETTER GET YOU BACK TO bed," Josephine said, wrapping her arm around Tatyana's waist.

"No. I want to sit for a while." Choking back tears, Tatyana leaned heavily on her friend and allowed herself to be escorted to the rocking chair. "What if Dimitri is trapped? What if he's hurt or . . . ?"

"Shh, now. We'll have to let the Lord be in charge of Dimitri. You need to think about this baby. I'll make you a cup of tea."

A contraction knifed itself through Tatyana's abdomen. Clutching the arm of the chair, she clenched her teeth as pain and thoughts of Dimitri washed over her. *Please, please, let him be all right. Don't take him from me,* she prayed.

Finally, the contraction eased and she took a slow, deep breath.

Josephine returned with the tea. Handing it to her, she said, "I put in a little sugar. I hope that's all right."

"Yes. Thank you," Tatyana said, taking the cup. "I hope Dimitri and Carl aren't trapped." As Josephine turned to leave, Tatyana caught the old woman's hand. "Do you think they are? What will I do if Dimitri is dead?"

Her voice gentle, Josephine said, "I don't believe he's dead. You can't give up hope."

"Josephine, I'm afraid. I don't think I can live without him. It seems he has always been part of my life. From our first meeting, he was kind to me. For a long time, I didn't know I loved him and then . . ." A sob escaped her lips. "Now I can't bear the thought of living without him."

Josephine took the cup of tea and set it aside, then pulled Tatyana into her arms. She held her while the young woman sobbed against her shoulder. Smoothing Tatyana's hair, Josephine said, "I know it's not easy, but you must trust God. He loves you. No matter what happens, you won't be alone." She held Tatyana away from her and smiled. "I bet you that right this moment, Dimitri is waiting for a ride so he can come home and see his wife and new baby. He's probably more worried about you than you are about him."

Her hand shaking, Tatyana wiped the wetness from her cheeks. "Do you think so?"

Josephine stood up and handed her a handkerchief. "I do."

Blowing her nose, Tatyana said, "I pray you are right." She gazed out the window. "I have this feeling he needs me."

Josephine handed the cup back to Tatyana. "You finish your tea, then I'll help you back to bed. You need to rest while you can."

Tatyana drank the tea, then went to bed as ordered. Her contractions became stronger and more frequent, giving her little time for rest. Staring at the ceiling, she counted the cracks in the blistered paint. She tried to imagine Dimitri standing at the mine, waiting for a ride, but an image of him trapped in darkness pressed in. Closing her eyes, she prayed, *Father, please watch over him.* Tears leaked from the corners of her eyes. Dimitri wasn't waiting for a ride. She knew he was trapped. The terrifying truth threatened to overwhelm her. Opening her eyes, she said loudly, "Dimitri, I love you. Come home to me."

Another contraction began to build, and she braced herself against it. Pain surged, and she gripped the headboard and clenched her teeth. Wrapped in a cloud of pain, she didn't know Josephine had joined her.

"There now," the kindly woman said as she placed a cool cloth on Tatyana's forehead.

As the pain peaked, Tatyana felt as if she were being wrenched in two. A scream tore from her throat, but it sounded far away. Finally, the agony ended.

"Take deep breaths, honey. Relax, and it will hurt less."

Tatyana held Josephine's hand against her cheek. "Thank you for staying with me."

"I'm glad I can be here. Now, why don't you sit up a little so I can fluff your pillows."

Tatyana sat up. "Do you know a lot about having babies? I did not think you had children," she said, leaning back.

"No. I have none of my own, but I've been at the bedside of many who did. Labor is a hard thing, but at the end God gives you a miracle." She sat in a chair beside the bed. "It's kind of like our lives. Sometimes, hard times block our path and we want to run from the pain, but there is beauty even in hardship if we look for it. Some gifts come in unusual packages. It's God who brings goodness from adversity."

Tatyana looked straight at her friend. "Do you really think Dimitri is alive?"

Josephine squeezed her hand. "Yes. I do. He's a strong man, and he's not alone. God is with him." She gazed out the window at the dusk settling over the outside world. "I'm sure we'll hear something soon." Gently, she brushed Tatyana's hair off her face. Her voice serious, she said, "I do think you should go to the hospital, though. I have my truck and can drive you."

Tatyana set her jaw. "No. I will be here when Dimitri gets home. And the doctor said he would come back."

"He also said you should go to the hospital when the pains got bad. He didn't know how long he'd be gone."

"He'll be back. I know it." Tatyana spoke fearlessly, but inwardly she quaked. "The women in my family have their babies at home." Her mother's loving face flashed through her mind. The warm, green eyes crinkled at the corners as she smiled, and Tatyana felt her assurance.

Josephine rubbed Tatyana's arm. "I guess you'll do what you think is best."

Tatyana studied the woman's face. Etched with fine lines, it was kind, and her eyes sparkled with life. "I am glad you are here."

"Me too."

※ ※ ※ ※ ※

Dimitri studied Carl. It didn't look like he was breathing. He laid his hand on his friend's chest. It still rose and fell.

Carl opened his eyes. "I'm still here."

"I know. I was just . . ."

"You were checking to see if I was still alive." He took a shallow breath. "I don't give up easily. I figure God had a purpose in putting me on this earth, and I'm going to stay as long as I can." He glanced around the cavern. "I've always felt at home down here, even from my first day. I was pretty young and scared until I got on the man trip and went to work. My nerves settled right down. Being here felt right."

CHAPTER 24

Dimitri slowly shook his head back and forth. "All I can think about right now is the mountain of earth above us. If we lose the lights, it will be black as ink."

Carl grinned. "I hate to remind you, but the lights will probably outlast the oxygen."

"Thanks for making me feel better." He swept grimy hair off his forehead. "I'd just like to be up top and breathing fresh air."

Carl reached out and rested his hand on his friend's arm. "You will."

"You don't know that."

He thought a moment. "I believe it. God is with us."

Carl's words made Dimitri feel calmer. "I hope you're right. But, I can't get the picture of my bones remaining here through eternity out of my mind." He took a deep breath. "Carl, are you afraid of dying?"

"I don't like the idea much, but it comes to each of us eventually. God promises I'll be with him. And I like that."

"I've never really been afraid of death, but I didn't plan to die this way. When I was a boy in Russia, I wanted to be a soldier, and I believed that one day I would be. I also believed that as a man I'd die a brave death in battle against our enemies. I would tell my mother, and she'd give me a sad smile and ask, 'Do you think that is what God wants for you?'" He sat back. "I always said, 'Yes, of course.'"

Leaning against the wall, Dimitri thought of his family. News of his death would wound them deeply.

Carl changed position and groaned. "My leg hurts like fire." For a moment, he closed his eyes and leaned his head against the wall. "I wonder if you're a father yet."

"A father," Dimitri whispered.

✷ ✷ ✷ ✷ ✷

Tatyana's labor continued into the night. Between contractions, her mind whirled with questions about her husband. She should have heard from him.

Josephine nodded off in the chair next to the bed and nearly toppled over. Embarrassed, she looked at Tatyana. "Oh, I'm sorry, dear."

"No. Do not apologize. You are kind to stay with me."

"Remember, I've done this before, but I'm older now. I recall when my mama was having my little brother. We lived on a ranch in Montana then."

"A ranch?"

"Oh, it wasn't nothin' special, just a lot of open ground. We had a couple horses, some cattle, and grew vegetables. My daddy worked real hard just to put food on the table. Anyway, Mama was laboring, and Daddy went for the doctor. A storm had descended on the valley and Daddy didn't come back."

"How old were you?"

Josephine thought a moment. "Oh, I must have been about twelve. That's right, because a few days before we'd celebrated Miranda's thirteenth birthday." She smiled. "Our parents always made a big deal out of birthdays. Anyway, we were real scared. Mama's labor was getting bad, and us girls didn't know what to do. We'd seen critters born, but never a baby. Miranda panicked and was about as much help as a two-legged chair. She always was a bit high strung," Josephine chuckled.

Tatyana smiled. She relaxed a little, thankful for the story.

Josephine folded her arms over her chest and leaned forward. "It was up to me. Together, me and Mama delivered a baby boy that night. Daddy didn't make it back until the next day." A serene look settled over her face. "After that, Mama and I were closer than ever before." She looked at Tatyana. "When you share something so amazing it changes you."

"Where is your brother now?"

Josephine ran her hand over her chin. "He's in heaven. Died of scarlet fever when he was four." She cleared her throat. "He was a fun-loving boy. After he was gone, the place seemed real quiet."

"I'm sorry."

"Oh, death is part of life. We have to accept it."

Another contraction washed over Tatyana. Gripping the bed frame, she closed her eyes. "Ohhh, Josephine, it hurts so much! I can't do this!"

"You can do it. Try to relax and breathe slow." She rubbed Tatyana's arm and hummed softly.

When the contraction passed, Josephine gave Tatyana a glass of water, and she took a drink. "Thank you." Tatyana didn't want to think about the next contraction. She said, "Tell me about living on a ranch. Is it like a farm?"

"I suppose. Like I said, we ran some cattle and sheep. That's all, besides growing our vegetables. There was always a lot of work to be done."

"I have not been to Montana. What is it like?"

"It's big. Wide open plains and huge mountains all around and forests. There's a lot wildlife. I never did like the grizzlies, though. They'd get at the sheep and even take down a cow now and then."

It had only been a few minutes, but another contraction gripped Tatyana. She pressed her foot against the mattress. "Here comes another one."

Josephine took her hand.

Pain swept over her in an agonizing wave, and she squeezed her eyes closed and groaned.

"You holler if you want."

When the pain finally relented, Tatyana relaxed her hold on Josephine's hand. "I do not think this baby will ever get here. I am so tired."

"Take a deep breath and try to rest a little, honey."

"Do you think it will take much longer?" Tatyana stared at the door, longing to see Dimitri standing there.

"I'm sure it will be soon."

Tatyana felt a momentary flush of panic. "Do you really think so?"

"Yes. As far as a person can know about these things."

Tatyana closed her eyes. "Good."

✹ ✹ ✹ ✹ ✹

Three intense contractions came one on top of the other, and Tatyana was suddenly scared. "I should be at the hospital. I was wrong to stay here. Is it too late to go?"

Josephine chuckled. "I'm afraid so. You don't want to have this baby in my truck do you?"

Tatyana shook her head as pain knifed through her. This time she felt an urge to push. "It hurts! Josephine! Please, help me!" Panting, she said, "I . . . I have to push!"

"Bend your legs for me, honey. I'll have to take a look." Josephine gently pulled the blankets back.

Tatyana did her best to do as she was told, but the pain had taken over and was all she knew. The real world seemed far away somewhere beyond her torment.

"I can see the baby's head! It's almost here!"

The contraction eased, and Tatyana took a deep breath and stared at the ceiling. "I don't think I can do this."

With a chuckle, Josephine said, "You don't have any choice."

"Here it comes again," Tatyana gripped the bars of her headboard. "Ohhh!"

"Keep pushing!"

The agony seemed to go on and on but finally released Tatyana, and she panted and waited for the next onslaught. "How much more?"

"Probably only a couple more pushes. You're almost there." Josephine wiped perspiration from her face.

Spent and weak, Tatyana said, "I do not think I can push any more."

"Sure you can. You're strong. And just think, soon you'll be able to hold your baby in your arms."

Tatyana braced herself as another contraction built. Clenching her teeth, she bore down and tried to expel the child.

"Tatyana."

Through a fog, Tatyana thought she heard her name. She glanced toward the door. A man covered in black coal dust stood there. "Dimitri?" she asked, wondering if the image was an illusion.

Taking two long strides, he reached her bedside. "I'm here," he said, leaning over the bed and kissing her cheek. "I love you. I love you."

"Oh, Dimitri!" Tatyana gasped. "You're alive!" Gently she touched his face. "I was so afraid."

"Me too, for a while. Carl and I were trapped, but the men dug us out."

Tatyana gripped her husband's hand as another contraction began to build.

"It looks like I got here just in time," Dr. Logan said, drying his hands on a towel as he walked into the room.

Josephine stepped aside. "I'm glad to see you. This baby is ready."

"I can see that. All right," he said calmly. "This should do it. Give me one great big push." He glanced at Dimitri. "Hold up her shoulders. It will make it easier for her to deliver."

Dimitri did as he was told and cradled Tatyana against him.

Through excruciating pain, Tatyana pushed.

"It's almost here. Keep pushing," Dr. Logan coached.

"I can see it!" Dimitri cried.

"The head is out!" Dr. Logan said, quickly clearing the child's mouth.

The baby let out a squall.

"What a glorious sound!" Josephine's eyes brimmed.

"All right, one last push."

Exhausted, Tatyana gathered all her strength, and her child entered the world, crying its outrage.

"It's a boy," Dr. Logan announced.

"A son!" Dimitri cried and held Tatyana close. He kissed her cheek, then her forehead. "We have a son!" He caressed her cheek.

The doctor cut the cord, quickly bundled the baby in a blanket, and handed him to his mother. Tatyana cradled the pudgy child against her chest. Immediately, he tried to suckle.

"Why, he's already hungry," Josephine said.

Tatyana turned her face up to Dimitri. "He's here."

Tears made pale trails down Dimitri's cheeks. "Thank you."

"He's a big one." Dr. Logan said as he patted Tatyana's arm. "You did good."

"She was wonderful," Josephine said as she looked at Dimitri. "It's good to see you." She hugged him.

"I'm getting you dirty," Dimitri said, stepping back.

"I'm not worried about a little dirt. I'm just so glad to see you safe and sound."

Dimitri sat on the edge of the bed and caressed the baby's blonde, downy hair. "Can I hold him?"

Tatyana held the baby out to her husband.

"Make sure to hold his head up," Josephine said.

Awkwardly, Dimitri cradled him. He gazed down at his son. "I thought our rescue was a miracle, but he's the real miracle."

"Oh, Dimitri, I was so scared. I thought I would never see you again."

The baby gripped his father's finger. "God saved my life. And Carl's."

Josephine's eyes filled with fresh tears, and she wiped them with her apron. Clearing her throat, she said, "I'll get us all a cup of tea." She hurried out of the room.

"What should we name him?" Tatyana asked. "We did not decide."

Dimitri stroked his son's tiny hands. "What about Yuri? It's a good name."

Tears flowed and wet Tatyana's cheeks. "My brother would be honored." She reached out and caressed the baby's cheek. "I wish he could know his uncle."

"He will. You will tell him."